The Fame Game

BOOKS BY LAUREN CONRAD

L.A. Candy

Sweet Little Lies
AN L.A. CANDY NOVEL

Sugar and Spice
AN L.A. CANDY NOVEL

LAUREN CONRAD
Style

LAUREN CONRAD

The Fame Game

HARPER

An Imprint of HarperCollins*Publishers*

The Fame Game
Copyright © 2012 by Lauren Conrad
All rights reserved. Printed in the United States of America.
No part of this book may be used or reproduced in any manner whatsoever without written permission except in the case of brief quotations embodied in critical articles and reviews. For information address HarperCollins Children's Books, a division of HarperCollins Publishers, 10 East 53rd Street, New York, NY 10022.
www.epicreads.com

Library of Congress Cataloging-in-Publication Data is available.
ISBN 978-0-06-207328-0 (trade bdg.)
ISBN 978-0-06-209271-7 (int. ed.)

Typography by Andrea Vandergrift
12 13 14 15 16 CG/RRDH 10 9 8 7 6 5 4 3 2 1

First Edition

To Adam DiVello, who plucked me from obscurity and gave me a career I never could have imagined. Thank you for every opportunity you gave me and for gifting me with the best video diary anyone could ever want.

Dear Madison,

You must hear this all the time, but I'm your biggest fan. I've watched every episode of Madison's Makeovers ten times. I didn't think you'd ever convince Tanya to cut that hair and get her teeth done, but you did—and she looked amazing! And you were so right about that girl from Idaho: Nobody looks good in a knee-length jean skirt and athletic shoes, especially not someone with cankles—ha ha.

You were my fave on L.A. Candy. I mean, you are who you are and you proved that! Especially when your past came out. Jane sort of became the star of the show, but it should've been you. Girls like Jane get everything handed to them, and how is that fair?

Have you talked to Sophia? Obvs she's your little sister and you love her, but can I just say how ungrateful she was? She was so wrong to out you the way she did. I know you love your fans and you would have told us everything when you were ready.

It is so amazing what you've done for yourself. You didn't have anything growing up, and now you have it all!! You had a dream and you went for it. Seeing someone like you, who made everything happen through hard work and courage and just rocking every opportunity that you got, makes me feel like it might be possible for me. You know? You really have been an inspiration to me. So thank you and I love you. Seriously, you are my idol!

My best friend, Emma, said she heard that you're going to star in a new show for PopTV. Is it true? I hope so!!! Please write me back and please send an autographed picture!

Love you!!!!!
Xoxoxo Becca B.

Dear Becca,

Thanks so much for your letter. Without you and my millions of other fans, I wouldn't enjoy my amazing life. And thank you for watching Madison's Makeovers! *I really feel like I am giving back with each makeover I do. Every girl deserves a little beauty, don't you think?*

No one expects their sister to betray them (especially not on national TV), but Sophie was in a very dark place. I am just so lucky that I was able to pay for her rehab and that she and I have each other. Thank you for loving me through all the pain and for understanding why I kept my past a secret.

As for a new show, I'm not supposed to say anything, but since you are one of my biggest fans . . . Yes, there is a new show in the works, and yes, of course, I am the star.

I hope you like the photo I've included. I think it's one of my best. And don't forget to follow me on Twitter @MissMadParker.

Love,
Madison

PS: Don't ever give up on your dreams, and don't ever expect anything to be handed to you. I know I didn't—and look at me now!

1

A STEP FORWARD

Madison Parker had made Trevor Lord come to *her* this time. If he wanted her for his new show as badly as he said he did, what was a little Sunset Boulevard traffic between friends? Anyway, he'd just added another sleek new sports car to his collection—he might as well put it to use.

"*The Fame Game* needs you, Madison." Trevor leaned forward in his chair, his eyes intent on her perfectly made-up face. "PopTV wants another hit show. And you and I know how to make that happen." His voice was low, almost conspiratorial.

Madison took a sip of her coconut water. She'd already told her agent, Nick, she was going to say yes—the network had met her financial demands (only slightly begrudgingly), and a new TV show meant more magazine coverage and better endorsement deals—but she wanted to make Trevor work for it. He didn't know that *Madison's Makeovers* wasn't getting picked up for a second season—no one did yet—and she wasn't about to tell him. After all, the ratings had been totally decent by PopTV standards. Why else would Trevor Lord, the executive producer of *L.A. Candy*, and his cohort (aka minion) Dana be here at Soho House (which Madison had picked for its proximity to her apartment and its to-die-for seared-ahi salad, and because she liked to exercise her membership privileges as much as possible) to lure her away from it? Besides, this way she could have her publicist leak a story from "a source close to her" saying that Madison, not the network, had decided to end *Madison's Makeovers* so she could film *The Fame Game*.

Trevor ignored the hovering waiter, who was trying to decide whether or not to refill the producer's coffee cup. "*Madison's Makeovers* is a great show, but it's not about you. Aren't you tired of telling people to get a haircut and lose twenty pounds? I mean, *Self* magazine tells them to do that every month." Trevor finally glanced up at the waiter, but only to shoo him away. "Your talents are being wasted, Madison," he said.

Madison raised a carefully plucked eyebrow. "Wow, Trev, you really know how to charm a girl."

He offered the barest hint of a smile. "You know what I mean."

Madison turned to Dana, who was, as usual, emanating super-stress vibes. Bluish bags sat below her eyes and her hair looked drier than a pile of autumn leaves. Talk about someone who could use a Madison makeover! She was such a contrast to Trevor, who always appeared effortlessly poised and polished, as if someone had taken a buffer cloth to him. Dana didn't smile at her, and Madison swiveled back toward Trevor. "I don't think I do know what you mean," she said. "Why don't you spell it out for me?" This was the best part of the process. Being wooed. And if anyone knew how to make a girl feel like the most spectacular thing that ever walked this planet it was Trevor. Unfortunately he could take it away just as quickly. So Madison was going to draw this moment out. Savor it.

"You crave drama. You love to be the center of attention. You want all eyes on you, Madison Parker." He sat back and folded his arms across his broad chest.

Madison sniffed, unimpressed. Trevor couldn't come up with anything better than stating the obvious and then acting as if he'd made some brilliant discovery? He thought he was so slick!

Admittedly, during the filming of *L.A. Candy*, Madison had needed Trevor. He was the one who had the power: He chose the story lines; he decided who got the most airtime. But now? Trevor needed *her*. Madison knew from Nick that without her, PopTV wouldn't green-light *The Fame Game*.

Madison gazed off toward the far side of the restaurant, as if contemplating the view (the Pacific Design Center, the primary-colored structures standing out amid the surrounding white buildings and green trees), and then snapped her blue eyes back to Trevor. "I'm the star?"

"Always," Trevor said with a smile. "Your fans want to see you."

Madison couldn't suppress a small return smile. Of *course* her fans wanted to see her. For two seasons of *L.A. Candy*, Madison had shared her life, her ambitions, and even her painful, once-secret past with them. At first Madison had been furious—like, almost homicidally so—at her sister for revealing the trailer-park roots that she'd worked so hard to hide. But once the tabloid storm blew over, she realized that her hardscrabble past had only made her more popular. More relatable. She hadn't exactly forgiven Sophie (or *Sophia*, as she now insisted on being called), but she no longer wanted to cut off her air supply at first glance.

"It'll be similar to *L.A. Candy*," Trevor went on. "You and some other girls."

He said this as if it hardly mattered, but immediately Madison stiffened. "What other girls?" she said coolly.

She understood that this was how these shows worked— the producers got together a group of supposed friends, or a crazy, dysfunctional family, or a bunch of outrageous coworkers at a quirky salon/construction site/tattoo parlor—but she had no interest in sharing the spotlight. She'd done that in *L.A. Candy*. She'd put in her time, and now it was time for Madison Parker to take center stage. It was her turn to shine.

Trevor shrugged noncommittally. "PopTV likes the format of four girls on the verge of making it."

"Oh, Trev," Madison sighed, as if speaking to a child who couldn't possibly understand. "I've already made it.

I'm no longer on the verge."

Trevor and Dana shared a look Madison couldn't decipher, and she felt an unpleasant jolt of anxiety. Maybe they did know about *Madison's Makeovers* after all. Although she hated to admit it, Madison knew that Trevor was right: She hadn't made it, not yet. Every time she took a step forward, something was there to knock her right back. How was she supposed to know that that innocent-seeming girl from Walnut Creek was allergic to Botox? (But not at all allergic to lawsuits? And that if someone sued the show, they were suing Madison's production company, too?) And how was she supposed to know that the trainer the show had hired was married? He never wore a ring, and he certainly didn't mention his wife when he was hooking up with Madison in an airplane bathroom. The network had managed to keep these things quiet so far, but various uptight executives had apparently decided that they couldn't afford for the show to go on.

"Oh, you're on the verge all right," Trevor said. "The verge of hitting the next level."

Nice save, Madison thought. "And the other three girls?" she asked. "Who are they?"

"Gaby." Trevor touched his pointer fingers together, ticking off a list. "Plus two others, obviously. We're still working on casting them."

Madison nodded. Gaby made sense. She was far from the brightest candle on the cake (and that was putting it nicely), but she was good for a laugh at least. She was the

7

only other person left standing from *L.A. Candy,* after Scarlett split for Columbia and Jane metamorphosed back into the boring girl next door that Madison had always known she was. So, okay, Madison and Gaby would be reunited on the small screen. Fine. But Madison didn't believe for one millisecond that Trevor was still searching for the girls who'd play the other two parts.

"Give me a hint about the other two, at least," she tried.

Trevor looked at Dana, who tapped her long fingers anxiously on the table. "We're not sure yet, but we want someone in the music industry. And we need someone who is trying to be an actress," he said. "I mean, this is L.A., after all. Every waitress has a demo reel and a head shot."

Madison stifled a laugh. An Adele wannabe and some misguided silver-screen striver! The musician, whatever. But the actress? Madison would like to meet the poor girl who thought that a reality show was a ticket to future starring roles. Unless you were already established, a reality show was *death* to an acting career. That was Hollywood 101. Sure, you gained notoriety, but you spent your entire career battling the stigma of being a "reality star." No serious producer would have you in his movie unless it was a one-line cameo during which you mocked your small-screen self. Sad.

Madison toyed with a lock of her perfectly platinum hair. "You know, Trevor, I'm not sure about this. I shared the spotlight on *L.A. Candy* and—"

Trevor didn't even hold up a hand to stop her. He just interrupted with, "How about another thirty grand per episode? Will that ease your worries? But we'll need your answer by the end of today. Or we'll have to look for someone else. And I'm sure we won't have any trouble finding someone who wants the job."

Madison took a deep breath and willed her facial expression to remain neutral. (Thanks to years of Botox injections this wasn't much of a challenge.) Suddenly they were talking *money*—like, *real* money. And Madison always needed money, because looking as good as she did didn't come cheap. She could already imagine the expression on her agent's face when she told him. Nick would be so proud of her.

"PopTV will send over the revised offer to your agent," Trevor said, as if reading her mind. He was an expert at staying one step ahead of his girls and hitting them with an unforeseen twist—both on the show and off.

"And I'm the star," Madison said firmly.

Trevor smiled. "You can't make a star, Madison," he said smoothly. "You can only show her off to the world."

Madison laughed. Another thing about Trevor? He always knew just what bullshit thing to say. She loved that about him.

"And no one makes more than me?"

Trevor laughed. "After you, do you really think the network can afford it?"

She took another sip of her coconut water and then, ever so slowly, extended her hand. "Then I think," she said, the corners of her mouth pulling up into a brilliant, ten-thousand-dollar smile, "we may have a deal."

2

A GOOD SIGN

Kate Hayes tore off her Coffee Bean & Tea Leaf apron and pulled her strawberry-blond hair from its elastic as she raced to her car. This was her final interview for the new Trevor Lord show and she didn't want to be late. She'd met with Dana twice already, and apparently she'd done well, because Trevor's assistant had called that morning, telling Kate to come at two. *And make sure to bring your guitar,* she'd said, her voice syrupy but firm.

When Dana first approached her at the Coffee Bean, Kate didn't know what to think. She'd noticed the tall, tired-looking woman staring at her from behind the food case long after she'd paid for her sugar-free Soy Vanilla Blended. Blank-faced, Kate had gone about grinding beans and pulling shots, pretending that nothing was unusual about having a stranger ogle her like she was some misplaced exotic animal. Finally, when Kate was beginning to feel slightly freaked out by the attention, Dana had introduced herself. She was a TV producer, she said, and she wondered if Kate was the girl who'd done that YouTube cover of "Girls Just Want to Have Fun."

"Who *hasn't* done a cover of 'Girls Just Want to Have Fun'?" Kate had asked, still not trusting that Dana was the real deal. "It's like the number-one karaoke song ever."

Dana had run her fingers through her frazzled hair and sighed. No, she'd said, she meant the one that took Cyndi Lauper's 1980s party anthem and transformed it into a slow, quiet, nearly heartbreaking look at class anxiety and a young girl's longing for independence. "That was *you*, wasn't it?" Dana asked, narrowing her brown eyes.

Kate was taken aback. It was one thing to be recognized in her hometown of Columbus, Ohio, but in L.A.? Sure, her YouTube video had gone viral, ever since Courtney Love had tweeted something barely comprehensible about it (*whos this brillient chica I found bymistake loveher!*), the girls over at HelloGiggles.com had made her a pick of the day, and *Rolling Stone* had done a small profile of her on its website. Kate still had no idea how all that had happened, but it had made her, briefly, just a little bit famous.

But hey, this was Los Angeles, land of a thousand people who were just a little bit famous. It was a sea of *Where do I know you from?* faces where nearly everyone had had a brief encounter with celebrity only to have it taken away just as swiftly.

Dana had asked her to come in for a screen test, and Kate had surprised herself by agreeing. But as she sat in a small, sparely decorated room with Dana and a single camera, Kate had to fight the urge to downplay the video, which she'd made on a lark last year with her ex-boyfriend. She'd had no idea Ethan was going to upload it to the web, and they'd gotten into a huge fight once she found out he had. But then people started commenting on the video, liking it and sharing it and reposting it. Everyone had agreed that her voice was incredible, unusual. *Like Lucinda Williams meets Joni Mitchell, watched over by the ghost of Nina Simone,* someone wrote. (And it hadn't hurt that as she'd strummed the last chords of the song, Ethan's Bernese mountain dog had flat-out *howled,* as if he couldn't bear to live in a world in which Kate Hayes was no longer singing. That got all the dog lovers on her team faster than you could say Purina Brand Puppy Chow.)

The problem with the video was that it wasn't *her* music, which Kate had been writing obsessively ever since she was eleven years old and started teaching herself to play her dad's old guitar. It was someone else's. Which meant that the video was, in a way, just a glorified version of karaoke.

But it was enough to make you pack up your things and move to L.A., Kate reminded herself. *It was enough to make you think you might be able to make it.*

Yes, she could admit it: She'd thought her video would be the beginning of something. But ever since she'd arrived in L.A. it had seemed like more of a dead end.

Speaking of dead ends, Kate was now stuck in traffic.

Again. Even though she'd been in the city for a year, she still hadn't figured out how to get anywhere on time. She checked the clock—she had twenty minutes to get to Trevor Lord's office, which was probably thirty minutes away at this rate. She glanced next at the little brass chime that hung from her rearview mirror, something her mother called "the bell of safe travel." Marlene Hayes said it would protect against accidents on the crowded L.A. freeways. But as Kate sat in the exhaust cloud of a Cadillac Escalade, stopped at yet another red light, she wished her mother had given her a bell of speedy travel. *That* she could have used.

She figured she might as well multitask and felt around for an eyeliner in the bottom of her purse. Obviously she hoped Trevor would appreciate her talent, but it couldn't hurt to put on some makeup. As she finished smudging the black kohl a touch, her phone buzzed beside her on the passenger seat. She picked up. "I'm late," she said into the mouthpiece, not even caring to whom she was talking.

"Well, that's certainly a surprise," said the cheerful voice on the other end of the line.

"Oh, hey, Jess," Kate said. Jessica was her sister, older by fifteen months and taller by five inches. She was calling from Durham, North Carolina, where she played center on the Duke women's basketball team. "What's up?"

"Just calling to check in on my favorite chanteuse. That's French for singer, you know."

Kate snorted. "Just because I didn't go straight to

14

college doesn't mean I'm an idiot."

"I know, I'm just kidding. How are you?"

Kate thought about this for a moment before answering. She hardly talked to her sister these days (Jess was so busy with classes and basketball practice), and Kate didn't want to sound like a bummer. On the other hand, they were best friends and blood relations, and there was no reason to lie. "Well, I'm stuck in traffic. I'm late for an interview. There are termites in my apartment building. And I went to an open mic last night and couldn't even get on stage."

"Oh, Katie," Jessica said, her tone sympathetic.

"Yeah, I know. I drove all the way to Glendale for some singer-songwriter thing, and then fifteen minutes before I was supposed to get on stage my hands started to tingle and my stomach, like, grew a bowling ball inside of it. I took two tequila shots at the bar, but it only made me feel worse. So I turned around and drove home."

Kate sighed as she finished her story. Not for the first time, she pondered the irony of a person with major stage fright hoping to make it in the entertainment business. No doubt her sister was thinking the same thing, but Jess was too nice to state the obvious. She would never, for example, bring up Kate's sophomore year in high school, when she waited for ten hours to audition for *American Idol* and made it past the pre-screening round, only to panic and bomb on stage. (*You might want to reconsider your career aspirations*, Simon Cowell had said, not unkindly.)

"You're in excellent company," Jess soothed. "Think about Cat Power. She was so crippled by stage fright, she could only sing in utter darkness. But then she got over it."

Ahead of Kate, the Escalade started inching forward. She gingerly tapped the gas pedal. "So you think there's hope for me? Or am I just being crazy?" she asked wistfully.

"Of course there's hope," Jess said. "Like my coach says, you just need to keep dribbling."

An image of herself holding a guitar in one hand and trying to dribble a basketball with the other popped into Kate's head. She gave a little laugh as she clutched the phone tighter in her hand. (She really needed to get a headset; one of these days some cop was going to bust her.) "The thing is, I'm sort of stalled," she admitted. "I mean, I've been here since graduation. That's over a *year*, which means I've got another year to make something happen before Mom comes out here, ties me up, drags me back to Columbus, and forces me into college."

"But you're *trying*," Jess said. "You made more awesome videos. And didn't you write, like, ten songs in the last few months?"

"Yes, but no one hears them," Kate wailed. "I just sing and play for myself!"

Thinking about this made Kate want to pull over to the side of the road and curl up in the backseat of her hand-me-down Saab. The thing was, she'd lied to Dana about what she'd been doing to further her music career. *Oh sure*, she'd told her, *I do open mics all the time!* And Dana had nodded, looking pleased; an open mic was pretty much a talent show, and who didn't love a talent show? It'd be like a mini acoustic *American Idol*. No fancy lights, no celebrity judges, just some would-be musicians with their instruments and their songs. America would love it!

But of course Kate's real attempts at furthering her music career consisted of playing her guitar, scribbling down lyrics and chord progressions, and recording bits of songs on her old-school four-track. And that didn't seem like it would make for exciting TV.

"Well, you're just going to have to get out there more," Jess said matter-of-factly. "Like I said, *keep dribbling*. What about that show you emailed me about?"

"That's the interview I'm late for," Kate admitted. She craned her neck out the window, trying to see past the Escalade. Was there construction? An accident? "I don't know why people insist on driving SUVs in L.A. It isn't exactly known for its rough terrain," she huffed.

"Stay focused," Jess said. "Tell me about this show."

"It's about four girls trying to make it in Los Angeles," Kate said. "It's by the people who did that show *L.A. Candy*," she added, slightly embarrassed. (But also kind of thrilled.)

Jess hooted. "Shut up! You didn't tell me that."

"Hey, you loved that show as much as I did," Kate laughed. "So don't pretend like you didn't."

"Guilty as charged," Jess said. "I always had a soft spot for Scarlett."

"Yeah, me too." Kate had loved Jane Roberts, of course, but Scarlett Harp was her favorite. Scarlett was smart, sassy, and down-to-earth, and she didn't care about hair or makeup or fame. Or so it had seemed, anyway. But in an interview after she left the show, Scarlett had complained that the producers had edited her life into something that it wasn't. *The real me got left somewhere on the cutting room floor,* she'd said.

That line had stuck with Kate, especially after her first meeting with Dana, in which the seemingly perpetually stressed-out woman had grilled her about her dating life ("um, a little slow these days since I'm holding down two jobs—you know, to afford my rock 'n' roll lifestyle"— that got a smile out of Dana at least), her exercise routine ("I wouldn't call it a routine, exactly"), her family ("single mom, normal, nice, and almost two thousand miles away"—she hadn't felt like bringing up her father, who had died when she was ten, but figured she might have to eventually if she made it onto the show), and a hundred other things. If the PopTV people offered her the part, would she be able to be herself in front of a camera? And if by some miracle she could, would they edit that real self into something different? It was a worrisome thought.

"But being on a TV show—that's totally amazing," Jess went on. "I mean, you could be a star!"

"Yeah, right," Kate said, applying a little lip gloss touch-up in her rearview mirror. "Let's not set our hopes too high."

"Well, at the very least you'll get paid well," Jess pointed out.

Kate's ears pricked up at this. "Paid well?"

Jess laughed. "Yes, dummy. What, you think it's like some kind of extended open mic, where you do it for free?"

"Oh, uh, no, of course not," Kate stammered. The truth was she hadn't even considered the fact that she might get paid. Weren't there millions of girls across the U.S. who'd give *anything* to be on a PopTV show? Trevor Lord could sell his spots to the highest bidder if he wanted to.

Suddenly she felt even more grateful that Dana had stumbled into her branch of the Coffee Bean & Tea Leaf. What if she actually nailed the audition? Money meant being able to quit at least one of her two jobs. Money meant being able to afford an eight-track digital recorder or a new MacBook with a functioning version of Garage-Band—or, even better, time in an actual studio. Money meant her mom couldn't drag her back to Columbus.

"You're such a nerd," Jess said affectionately.

"I know," Kate said. "Believe me, I know."

Ahead of her, the Escalade began to pick up speed, and Kate was able to shift into second gear for the first time in ten minutes.

"You're going to do great," Jess assured her.

Kate felt her heart flutter lightly in her chest. If she

could just keep moving, she'd be only five minutes late to meet Trevor Lord. She had made up her mind: Forget stage fright. She was going to rock this interview.

"I should go, Jess," she said. "Love you. Call you later."

As Kate sailed through the intersection, she glanced up and saw Madison Parker, probably thirty feet tall, smiling down at her from a giant billboard. It was an ad for *Madison's Makeovers*. *Beauty's a bitch* read the tagline.

Kate smiled in return. Madison hovered over the corner of Venice and Sepulveda like some guardian angel of reality TV.

Surely that was a good sign.

3

EYES WIDE OPEN

Carmen Curtis rushed around her bedroom, madly searching for her new brown leather ankle boots. Shoe boxes and shopping bags were littered across her floor, testament to an outrageous (even by Carmen's standards) shopping extravaganza that had taken place earlier that day. Three nine-hundred-dollar sweaters dangled off the edge of her bed, and a ridiculously expensive silk dress lay, already crumpled, in a corner. Even though the amount of free clothing and accessories that were sent to her mother could fill a room in their very large, but not obscene, house, the two always spent a day demolishing Barneys before Cassandra left on tour. Cassandra would soon be leaving for ten sold-out concerts in Japan and Australia, so they had practically emptied the place out.

Plus, they were celebrating Carmen's news: She was going to be on *The Fame Game*, Trevor Lord's newest reality series. Filming began in two weeks, and now Carm had a pile of cute things to wear.

She had been worried that her mom might not want her working in "reality" TV (after all, there was nothing *real* about it), especially since the whole family had been the subject of a documentary about Cassandra's comeback tour nearly a decade earlier. Cassandra had had extremely mixed feelings about *Cassandra's Back*, but she said that *The Fame Game* sounded cute. She also agreed with their publicist, Sam, who argued that it was the perfect thing to help Carmen out of the shoplifting mess she'd gotten herself into a few months earlier.

Carmen tossed a new lacy La Perla bra on top of her dresser and flung a pretty little Lanvin handbag onto the chaise longue. *Where were those damn ankle boots?*

For the record, she hadn't actually shoplifted anything. But it had been a crazy time in her life, full of ups and downs. Ups: She'd just graduated high school and was free from the tyranny of textbooks. Her role in an indie movie about estranged sisters who go on a road trip to find their mom, which she'd filmed the summer before her senior year, was getting great reviews. (She only wished the critics didn't sound so shocked, as if they'd assumed she got the part only because of who her parents were. Which, okay, hadn't hurt—her dad was a producer on the film, after all—but the director wouldn't have cast her if she couldn't act.) But there were downs, too: She'd deferred her acceptance to Sarah Lawrence because she wasn't convinced college was for her, and her dad wasn't thrilled about it. She'd broken up with her boyfriend of six months when she saw pictures of him on D-lish.com getting a lap dance. (Somehow "liar" and "cheater" had not been included in his photo caption when the jerk made it into *People*'s Most Beautiful issue; even worse, he'd managed to spin it so that Carmen was perceived as "needy" and he was oppressed in the relationship.) And she'd taken the blame for shoplifting a Phillip Lim top because her friend Fawn was still on probation from her last failed attempt at a five-finger discount, and she was afraid the judge wouldn't be so lenient this time. Naturally the tabloids ran with it.

That particular incident had pissed off her dad even more—at first because he'd thought she'd done it (thanks for the vote of confidence, Dad!), and then because she'd taken the blame for someone he'd never really liked that much in the first place. Ever since Carmen had started hanging out with Fawn after they'd met at an acting workshop, her dad had grumbled about how he wished she'd find friends her own age. (Fawn was only two years older—no biggie.) But all of this meant that Philip Curtis was not exactly keen on his daughter's judgment as of late, which was going to make it somewhat difficult to persuade him that a role on *The Fame Game* would not exploit her, goad her into getting breast implants, or otherwise ruin her life.

She had to make him understand that she knew exactly what she was getting into. She'd grown up in L.A.—around actors, writers, singers, directors, producers—and she knew how the game was played; now she wanted to officially get into it. She'd spent the past few years dabbling, taking acting classes and working hard, yeah, but dabbling nonetheless. She'd never committed to auditioning, hadn't much cared about her "image," and had been content to coast along as mini-Cassandra. Now she was ready to take what could so easily be hers.

But convincing Philip Curtis of anything that he didn't think up himself—well, that could be a challenge. As he was fond of saying, *I didn't get to be the founder and president of Rock It! Records by doing what people told me to do or thinking what people wanted me to think.*

Yeah, yeah, yeah, Carmen thought. Anyway, the point was, she was trying *not* to do what people told her to do. Her dad wanted her to go to college? Well, she had a better idea. She adored him, she really did, but she could do without his stubbornness sometimes. Whenever she tried to turn it around and tell him that she agreed wholeheartedly with his "think for yourself" philosophy, that it was *exactly* what she was trying to do, he refused to engage. He'd just look at her calmly and then wander away, as if the conversation had been a competition and he had already won it. The only person he could never pull that with was Cassandra.

"Carm," her mother called from downstairs. "Drew is here. And dinner's almost ready."

"Coming," Carmen called back. Too bad: She was going to have to eat dinner sans her fantastic new ankle boots.

Just as it was a tradition for Carmen and her mom to

shop before Cassandra went on tour, it was a longstanding tradition for her family to have a big meal at home on Friday nights. Drew Scott being invited was now tradition, too. He was her best friend, and he'd been at the table at least every other week since Carmen was in tenth grade and he was in eleventh. Drew's mom, an entertainment lawyer, and his dad, a dermatologist to the stars, had been in the midst of an ugly divorce back then, and Drew liked to avoid them as much as possible. Even now that peace (aka total avoidance) reigned between his parents and he lived on campus at UCLA during the school year, Drew still showed up at the Curtis family's dinner table. Often he'd even wear an Oxford over his tattooed arms and his hair nicely combed.

Carmen slipped on her pink custom-made Chopard watch—her graduation present from her parents when she finished at Archer—and ran downstairs to the living room, where her dad had cornered Drew to chat him up about some band he'd just signed. (Drew was studying composing and music production at UCLA, so he liked talking shop.) Just as Carmen headed toward them, her mom floated into the room. Seriously, Cassandra Curtis never did anything as pedestrian as *walk*. Even in jeans and a plain white sweater, she looked amazing, her dark hair in perfect waves and her light olive skin perfectly dewy, as if she'd stepped off the cover of *Vogue*—which, incidentally, she had actually been on three times and counting.

"The salmon is ready, everyone," Cassandra said. Her

voice was smooth and sultry, even when she was talking about dinner. "Carm, hon, you look fabulous—I love those L'Wren Scott skinnies on you." She leaned closer to her daughter and whispered, smilingly, "Just don't tell your father how much they cost." Philip Curtis didn't actually care what they spent on clothes, but it was a running joke at their house: How many pairs of shoes and jeans could two women possibly own? Then, at a normal volume, her mom mused, "What I wouldn't give to be able to get away with white jeans."

Carmen rolled her eyes. "Yeah, Mom, you're huge. Better skip dinner. It's lemon juice and cayenne pepper for you tonight."

Drew detached himself from Carmen's dad and walked over to plant a kiss on her cheek. "Curtis," he said.

"Scott," Carmen returned, then punched him gently on the arm.

"No hitting before dinner," Drew said, laughing.

"That's right," Cassandra said. "We save violence for dessert."

In the huge, French-blue dining room, Philip took his usual spot at the head of the table and Cassandra sat at hers on the other end. Carmen and Drew sat across from each other, a gigantic spray of hot-pink lilies between them. Philip cleared his throat and lifted his wineglass. "A toast to my amazing wife and daughter. May they remain forever beautiful and never grow tired of me."

Carmen giggled—it was the same thing he said every

Friday night. She raised her glass of Perrier. "And to Philip Alan Curtis, beloved husband and father. May he one day manage to come up with a new toast."

As they ate, they bantered lightly about music (what exactly *was* the difference between speed metal and grind-core?) and sports (were the Lakers going to take the championship this year?). But Carmen, uncharacteristically, said little. She was waiting for the right moment to talk to her dad again about *The Fame Game*. The last time she'd brought it up, the conversation hadn't gone well, and back then it was only a possibility. Now it was a done deal. Her mother had made her promise to tell him at dinner.

What her dad didn't seem to fully comprehend for some reason was that Carmen's life had *always* been in the spotlight. Heck, she'd been on the cover of *Us Weekly* when she was in utero (*Crooner Cassandra's Baby Bump!*), and her toddler outfits had been the subject of gallons of tabloid ink (*Baby CC: The World's Littlest Fashionista?*). The way Carmen saw it, the PopTV show was an opportunity to step into the limelight on her own terms. The cameras would film her because she *wanted* them to, not because they were manned by guys from TMZ who were itching to catch her stumbling drunkenly out of a nightclub or flashing her thong, or lack thereof, as she exited a car. Her entire life had been narrated by the media and she had had so little say. This was a chance for her to show people who she really was.

Trevor Lord's reality series would prove to the world

that Carmen wasn't just another celebuspawn. She was a real person with real feelings, and she was an *actress*—and she'd have been an actress no matter who her parents were.

Carmen cleared her throat. It probably wasn't the right moment, but maybe there was no such thing as a right moment for a conversation like this. She took a careful sip of her water. "So, remember that thing I told you about, Daddy?" she asked. "The opportunity my agent got approached with?"

Drew stifled a laugh, and Carmen kicked him under the table. Drew thought that Carmen was "above" reality TV and that "opportunity" was a euphemism for "bad idea." She'd never been able to get him to watch *L.A. Candy*, so maybe it was understandable that he didn't see the appeal of *The Fame Game*. Still, he'd come around to the idea eventually, though he knew her dad wouldn't be on board.

"Tell me it wasn't another *Playboy* request," Philip half hollered. "I'll kill Hef with my bare hands if they ask you to be naked in that magazine one more time."

Carmen flushed. "Ick!" she said. "No, the offer from PopTV."

"You mean PopTV *Films*," Philip said.

Carmen's stomach fluttered. Had he really forgotten the conversation they had had about it just last week? Or was he trying to pretend that it hadn't happened? "No, Daddy," she said. "PopTV. You know, Trevor Lord's new show?"

Philip's brows furrowed gently. "Trevor Lord? Why does that name sound familiar?" he asked.

"He produced *L.A. Candy*," Carmen told him. (For the second time.)

"The reality show?" He said "reality show" as if they were dirty words. Kind of like Drew had when she'd first told him.

Carmen glanced through the spray of lilies at Drew. His green eyes were full of sympathy already. He just wanted what was best for her. (And sometimes Carmen couldn't help but wonder if he simply wanted *her*. There had been a few moments in the last month or so—some extra-long hugs, a bit of hand holding, and one awkward, sweet kiss . . . But now wasn't the time to think about that.) She smiled at Drew and looked back at her father.

Before Carm could respond to him, though, Philip's cell phone buzzed and he slipped it from his pocket. He glanced at the screen and looked apologetically at Cassandra. "I have to take this."

"The music business is twenty-four/seven." Cassandra rolled her eyes toward the ceiling and smiled.

"Well," Carmen said when her dad had left the room, "so far so good."

"You think?" her mother replied.

"I was being sarcastic."

"Give him a chance," Cassandra said gently. "Believe it or not, he does trust you."

Drew reached out and moved the flowers to the antique

credenza behind him. "There," he said, "now I can see the future star of *The Fame Game*."

"Seriously, you guys," Carmen said. "You have to help me out on this one. Be, like, supportive." *Help me show the world I'm not Little CC anymore*, she thought but didn't say.

In a moment, Philip returned to the table. As he tucked his phone back into his pocket, Cassandra shot him a pointed look.

Philip smiled at his only daughter. "Carm? You were saying something about PopTV?"

Carmen took a deep breath and began. Again. "Trevor Lord is doing a show about people trying to make it in Hollywood. He said he needed a talented actress, and that I was his first and only choice. He said the network probably wouldn't even pick up the show unless I agreed to do it." She'd felt a rush of pride when her new manager (her dad made her get a manager after she got cast in *The Long and Winding Road*) told her that part. She knew it probably wasn't true; she'd seen her father stretch the truth before, hadn't she? That's just how it went in Hollywood. You told people what they needed to hear so they'd do what you wanted them to do. "Daddy, I said I'd take the part and I really want you to be happy for me."

"But why on earth do you want to do a reality show?" Philip looked genuinely perplexed. He exchanged another unreadable glance with Cassandra. "Those girls have no values. No talent! You're not like them. You're an actress."

"I told you," she said, feeling herself getting upset, "it's not like that." She hated when her father used his *I'm disappointed in you* tone. "It's about people trying to become successful doing what they love. It's a good opportunity." Carmen twisted her watch around her wrist.

"For what? To go to clubs and get in fistfights?"

"That's *Jersey Shore*," Drew clarified helpfully. "This will be more like catfights—open-handed combat, drinks thrown. . . . It's completely different."

Carmen kicked him again. "Not helping!" She turned to her dad. "There aren't going to be any fistfights *or* catfights. It's going to be about the business and how hard it is to make it—in my case, even when your parents are, y'know, you guys."

"Famous," Drew added, as if that were necessary. Carmen contemplated kicking him again but decided against it. It didn't seem to make a difference.

"Are 'us guys' going to have to be on this show?" her dad asked. "A Very Special Meet the Curtises episode?" He was joking, but Carmen could tell he wasn't into the idea at all.

"If they need that, they can just splice in scenes from the brilliant, amazing *Cassandra's Back* documentary," her mom offered teasingly. (Every time she mentioned the title, she shrugged and turned her head over one shoulder, mimicking what she had decided was the hilarious poster for it, what with its nod to the title's double entendre.)

Philip took a sip of wine and sighed. "Carm, I'm not going to forbid you to do what you want. I just want you to be sure you know what you're getting yourself into. Eyes wide open, right?"

Carmen nodded. "Eyes wide open."

Her dad looked at her—*really* looked at her—and Carmen, who could usually tell when her dad was about to soften, couldn't read his expression. "Okay," he said finally. "Well, I guess that's settled then."

Carmen let out a breath she didn't even realize she was holding. She faced forward again and found Drew staring at her, his eyes . . . wide open.

"Shut up," she said, and kicked him once more.

"Ouch! You were supposed to save the violence for dessert, remember?"

Cassandra laughed. "Next time," she said, "on a Very Special Episode of Meet the Curtises: Violent dinners. Savage Salmon. Brutal Broccoli. And—"

"Killer Cake!" Philip yelled. He grinned boyishly. "Chocolate, perhaps?"

"We're not having cake, Tubs," Cassandra said fondly, using the nickname he loved and hated in equal measure. After all, Philip Curtis wasn't at all fat; he just had a little . . . girth.

"Nice try, Mr. Curtis," Drew said.

"Sadistic Sorbet?" he asked hopefully.

And then everyone cracked up. Carmen breathed a sigh of relief—the worst was over now. But she really, *really* hoped that Trevor Lord wouldn't angle for a Curtis family episode. They were just way too weird.

4

HARDLY STAR TREATMENT

Flashes—dozens of them—exploded in bursts of brilliant light, and Madison heard her name called out over and over. "Miss Parker!" "Madison, over here!" "Mad, honey, blow me a kiss!"

Madison paused midway on the red carpet, absorbing the attention being showered upon her. She never got tired of this moment: when every eye and (much more importantly) every camera was focused on her. She offered a small, knowing smile to the bank of photographers to her left, but she made sure to avoid glancing at the PopTV camera that followed her every move. That was the one camera she had to pretend not to see.

The last two weeks had been a whirlwind. Trevor wanted to start filming immediately—clearly Madison's fans were clamoring for her return!—and so the minute the ink was dry on her contract, four beefy moving guys had showed up at her Beverly Hills doorstep, packed up her three hundred dresses and her two hundred pairs of shoes, and hauled them over to a sleek new apartment in Park Towers. There was a balcony, a chef's kitchen, and three large bedrooms: one for Madison; one for her new roommate, Gaby; and one for all the PopTV equipment.

"Who are you wearing?" someone called out, but Madison didn't answer. She liked to seem a little bit aloof at first. *Keep 'em guessing*, she thought.

Up ahead, a giant gold banner welcomed everyone to the second annual Togs for Tots benefit. Togs for Tots was a charity that provided new (*not* "gently used"—gross!) clothes to foster children, group-home residents, and homeless kids all over L.A. County. Madison didn't particularly care about the charity itself, of course, but the evening was sponsored in part by Elie Saab, one of Madison's favorite designers, and rumor had it that Anna Wintour of *Vogue* would be in attendance.

She took another few steps, then gave her best over-the-shoulder smirk. Shutters clicked furiously. The paparazzi that lined red carpets were always a step up from the ones who roamed the streets. A little more polished and respectful, although there was always an aggressive few screaming over the others from behind the velvet rope barrier. But Madison knew that she needed them all, just as much as they needed her. It was a symbiotic relationship (with escalating benefits): The more famous she got, the more they would want to take her picture; the more pictures they took and published of her, the more famous she'd be . . . and onward and upward to, as

Trevor put it, the "next level."

She held her head high, pivoted her toe in her Louboutins, and smiled her picture-perfect smile.

"Madison!"

"Over here!"

"This way!"

"Beautiful, Madison!"

She locked eyes with each individual lens. Every camera contained the potential for a "Who wore it best?" (she did, always), a post on glamour.com (*Madison stuns in red!*), or a spot on tomorrow's *Fashion Police* (being praised, not critiqued of course). Madison hadn't quite made it out of the weeklies yet (though *Life & Style*, to its credit, loved her like no other), but Sasha, her publicist, swore she'd land a cover of a monthly once *The Fame Game* started airing. Madison was already planning her *Glamour* cover look. She was thinking a sort of Marlene Dietrich pose, or perhaps a Marilyn Monroe homage. . . .

She had to hand it to Trevor. He was filming *The Fame Game* and getting advance press for his "mysterious new project" at the same time. Already the buzz was building; she could feel it. No doubt some blogger had just uploaded a shot of her to his website (*Madison Parker steps out for kids!*) and mentioned the PopTV cameras capturing her every move. By tomorrow, the word would be all over town that Madison and the PopTV cameras were spotted again. Spin-off!

It was so much different from the last time around. Madison was nobody when she started filming *L.A. Candy*.

Correction: She was *somebody*, all right, just not a somebody that the world knew about yet. If people noticed back then that the cameras were filming, the question on their minds was more of the *Who the hell is that?* variety. Now everyone was wondering what the new show was about, what it was called, and who else was on it. (Madison was still in the dark about that part.) Back when *L.A. Candy* had exploded and she (and Gaby and Scarlett and that annoying little Goody Two-shoes, Jane) had gotten famous, Trevor had struggled to make them seem like the regular girls they were still supposed to be. How many times had he had to reshoot because a paparazzo wandered into frame? He hated to count. But this time around, the paparazzi and the tabloids and the blogs (and the monthlies!) would play a crucial part in the show.

Madison offered a little coronation wave to a knot of starstruck fans.

"Luke!" she heard a girl cry, and Madison turned to see Luke Kelly, looking gorgeous but underdressed in a faded button-down and jeans, striding up the red carpet with that girl from that stupid show about a family who lives in a Winnebago.

"Doctor Rose," someone else yelled, and Luke flashed a megawatt smile. He played Sebastian Rose, a young resident on *Boston General,* and while he wasn't a lead, rumor had it he was on the short list to play the main character in *The End of Love*, a dystopian Romeo and Juliet story based on a bestselling young-adult novel.

Madison watched him and the girl, whatever her name was. They were holding hands, but Madison could see how loosely their fingers interlocked. And this told Madison, who was something of an expert in body language, that these two were either a) only pretending to be a couple, or b) five minutes away from breaking up. Which meant that Luke was, or would be, available. She gave him another once-over. He could use a shave, too, she thought, in addition to a new outfit. But he had those green eyes and that strong, broad chest, not to mention that Australian accent. Yes, she thought, she should ask Sasha to hook up a date with "Dr. Rose." Maybe they could head to the next level together.

But it was time to turn her attention back to posing. She cocked a hip and flashed a little bit more thigh through the slit in her dress. She stayed like this for a good ten seconds, then turned for another pose. Then she saw Gaby Garcia, smiling and heading up the red carpet.

"Gaby, blow us a kiss!" one of the photographers shouted.

Gaby obliged, though Madison had told her a hundred times that no one looked good in that pose. Just then she spotted Madison.

"Mad!" Gaby rushed up to her breathlessly, as if they hadn't seen each other for months, when in fact they had eaten breakfast together.

"Hey, Gaby." Madison put her arm around Gaby's shoulders (*Madison and pal Gaby hit the red carpet!*) and was surprised by its boniness. She took a step back and surveyed her roommate. What was she wearing? For one thing, she had donned an Elie Saab dress that she clearly hadn't taken the time to tailor. And for another, she'd picked the one dress in the collection that looked like it came from the Goodwill sale rack. It was supposed to be an homage to 1970s Halston or something, but the rust color made Gaby look positively yellow, and the plunging back highlighted each protruding vertebrae. Madison had to force herself to smile. "Good to see you, sweetie," she said. Gaby's best feature was her cute little body—if she kept dieting, what would she have going for her at all?

Madison forced herself to put her arm back on Gaby's shoulders. "Smile," she said.

They posed for the cameras, keeping their faces mannequin-still. If they needed to talk, they'd do it only through the corners of their mouths so as not to disrupt their perfect, doll-like smiles.

"You look amazing," Gaby said through her teeth.

"Thanks, hon," Madison said. Of course she looked amazing. It was her job to look amazing, and she worked hard at it. She began her red-carpet regimen days beforehand—more cardio, a mini-cleanse, an oxygen facial, an airbrush tan, minimized water intake (dehydration could subtract several pounds)—and today, between hair, makeup, and wardrobe, she'd already devoted eight hours to this event.

Another small crowd of dedicated fans had gathered

behind the barricade at the end of the red carpet.

"We love you, Madison!" a girl with pink hair screamed.

Madison's smile grew wider. She hoped the photographers were capturing the total adoration her fans had for her—and her own reciprocating affection, of course. (*Madison kisses fan's new baby!*) With Gaby in tow, she glided over to the pink-haired girl. The PopTV camera followed. Time for a quick autograph and photo op! But just as Madison raised the pen, she saw the photographers swing their cameras back toward the far end of the carpet. She froze. There wasn't a bigger celebrity on the carpet. What were they—

"Is that—?" Gaby whispered, her eyes wide.

Madison maintained her smile as she tried to see who was causing this unwelcome disruption.

The pink-haired girl let out a piercing shriek. "Oh my God, it's Carmen Curtis!" she cried, mere inches from Madison's ear. The poster of Madison that she'd been clutching fell to the ground and was immediately replaced by a poster of Carmen's *Nylon* magazine cover. How did that switcheroo happen so fast?

"Wow," Gaby sighed, looking positively starstruck. "She's so pretty."

Madison clenched her fists in anger, though her face maintained its photo-ready placidity. Carmen Curtis: What had *she* ever done for the world? Her mother was the biggest singer since Madonna, and her father was the

Quincy Jones of rap. Which meant that Carmen had that vaguely ethnic look that had no doubt helped her mother out, since her vocal range certainly hadn't, and she had been spoon-fed money and fame from the moment she was born. She hadn't had to work for a thing her whole life.

"I love her dress," Gaby whispered.

Madison ignored her as she inspected Carmen. She'd obviously spent hours on her red-carpet look, too. She wore a cream bandage dress that hit just above her knee, and she was wearing a pair of YSL pumps that Madison would give a kidney for, but they were sold out everywhere. She smiled and waved like everyone she met was a potential friend. And *that*, Madison knew from experience, was a load of crap. They'd been introduced once at a party for the opening of sbe's latest restaurant, and, okay, Madison hadn't exactly oozed friendliness herself, but Carmen had simply shaken her hand, smiled briefly, and then vanished into the crowd.

"She's a little big-boned, don't you think?" Madison asked coolly. Then she turned away and began to walk toward the entrance to the event. Carmen had stolen her moment. It was a total injustice. The girl had accomplished practically nothing in her eighteen years of life besides bit parts on *Law & Order* and some indie-movie role her daddy bought her.

Madison took one final glance over her shoulder before entering the building. She'd give Carmen one thing: The girl had excellent cleavage. But then again, this was Hollywood, and anyone with a credit card could get that.

"My feet hurt," Gaby said plaintively, shifting her weight from one leg to another. "I don't know why ballet flats aren't considered red-carpet worthy."

Madison rolled her eyes. "Because you want *height*, Gab," she said. "Every inch subtracts five pounds."

"Really?" Gaby said. "How?"

But Madison didn't have the energy to explain it to her. She was scanning the crowd, waiting for an event publicist to show them to their seats. She saw a couple of young stars from the latest HBO series and the members of The Royal We, Philip Curtis's newest musical discovery, but so far it wasn't exactly an A-list event. More like a B, Madison thought, or even a B minus. That was disappointing.

When, after another few moments, no publicist materialized, Madison grabbed Gaby's hand. "Come on," she said. "We'll just find our own seats." She was annoyed; this was hardly the star treatment she'd grown accustomed to.

They threaded their way through the crowd, moving toward the front row of folding chairs. At least they had front-row seats to the show, Madison thought. Maybe they'd be next to Anna Wintour.

But as they arrived at their designated spots, Madison was surprised—no, make that *shocked*—to see that they were taken.

By Carmen Curtis and some blonde with a botched nose job.

"Gaby," she hissed, "go get the event coordinator!"

Gaby looked down at her ticket and then back toward their seats with a puzzled expression on her face. "I thought we were in the front row. Hey, isn't that Carm—?"

"Gaby!" Madison whispered fiercely, while trying to maintain a smile. "Just go get the event coordinator!'

Gaby, like the good little doormat she was, did as she was told, and moments later the frazzled event coordinator appeared, a headset nestled in her updo and a clipboard clutched in her hand.

"Is there a problem?" Her tone was sharp.

Madison bristled but kept her voice low. She didn't need the PopTV cameras, not to mention every person in the room, noting that Carmen had the nerve to steal her seat. "Yes, there is," she said. "Those *girls*"—she nodded toward Carmen and her one-person entourage— "are in our seats." Madison tilted her ticket toward the woman.

The event coordinator didn't even look at it. "I've got two seats in the fifth row. We'll move you there."

Madison had to keep her mouth from falling open. The *fifth row*? "Excuse me?"

"I can place you in the fifth—"

"You mean the *back* row," Madison said icily. "I don't think you understand. I need you to ask those girls to move. Those are our seats. They were assigned to us.

PopTV guaranteed us front row, and that is the only reason we are here."

"I'm sorry, your name again?" the woman asked as she flipped through the pages on her clipboard.

Really? This glorified secretary didn't know who she was? "Madison Parker," she said through her teeth. A fire lit inside her.

The woman circled a name on her list and looked up. "Okay, Miss Parker, sorry for any confusion, but this isn't a PopTV event, and those seats belong to Miss Curtis and her friend. The show is starting in three minutes. Do you want the seats in row five or not?"

Madison didn't answer. Did she want the seats in row five? What she *wanted* was to take off her Louboutin and stab this woman in the eye with it. Everyone knew that where you were seated at a fashion show was in direct correlation to your celebrity status. Front row: star. Back row: nobody.

"We'll take them." Gaby grabbed the two new tickets from the coordinator's hand and tried to pull Madison toward the back row. "Madison, come on. Let's just go to our seats."

Madison's eyes sent daggers toward Carmen and her homely little friend. "They aren't *our* seats," she said, jerking her arm away.

The lights began to dim, but Madison stayed frozen. She watched as Luke Kelly made his way over to the place she should have been. A giant grin broke over Carmen's face as she leapt up to hug him.

And that was when Madison saw the telltale bulge at the back of Carmen's dress. A *mike*. She turned quickly toward the far end of the row. Sure enough, there was the new Dana (who'd gotten promoted, apparently) and a PopTV camera, focused not on Madison but on Carmen.

Madison took a deep breath as the information sank in. So it wasn't going to be some sad nobody doomed for obscurity; Carmen Curtis was going to be the aspiring actress on *The Fame Game*. Trevor had landed himself a piece of Hollywood royalty—and she already had a film under her belt. Bully for him.

He was probably pretty happy with himself right about now, Madison thought. Well, she'd have to do what she could to change that.

5

YOUR ROCK 'N' ROLL SIDE

Kate tossed a pile of sweaters into a cardboard box and then collapsed onto the leopard-spotted beanbag chair she'd had since junior high. She'd been packing for five hours now and her enthusiasm for the job was seriously fading.

"More coffee?" Natalie asked from the doorway.

Kate smiled up at her roommate. "Do I look like I need it?"

"You look like you need to be peeled out of that chair with a spatula," Natalie said, coming into the room and sitting down on Kate's bare bed.

"Yeah, well. There's one in the kitchen, should it come to that." She laid her head back on the faded chair and closed her eyes.

"Be more excited," Natalie scolded her. "You're moving to some fancy place in West Hollywood! You're going to be on TV! It's like my hippie grandma used to say: 'Today is the first day of the rest of your life.'"

"I *am* excited," Kate said. "I'm just resting."

But the truth was, she had begun to feel more apprehensive than anything else. She was leaving her only friend in L.A. and the shabby but totally comfortable apartment that they shared (with thanks to Craigslist for both) and heading off into unknown territory—to be followed around by TV cameras 24/7. Had she really signed up for this? Was she ready for it in the *slightest*?

She felt in her pocket for the BlackBerry that Dana had given her. "Keep it on you at all times," Dana had said sternly. "Keep it charged, and keep it on." She'd made it sound like the world would end if Kate weren't at her beck and call. "Maybe you should just get me a radio collar," Kate had joked. "You know, like a polar bear or something?" But Dana hadn't found that funny.

"What I don't get is why you have to move," Natalie said. "I mean, if it's reality TV, shouldn't they film you where you actually live? As opposed to setting you up in this new place and pretending it's where you'd live?"

"Yeah, and pretending like I could afford it." Kate smiled. "But think about it: Do you want someone filming you while you burn your toast in the morning?"

Natalie wrinkled up her little nose, looking horrified. "No!"

"Well, that's part of why I can't live here."

Natalie nodded, her dyed-black bangs falling into her eyes. "Right. Plus what else would they film me doing, studying for my textiles exams?" Natalie was in her second year at the Fashion Institute of Design & Merchandising,

aka FIDM. Every piece of furniture in the place was uphol-
stered with some amazing fabric she'd designed herself.

"Dude. Ratings fail." Kate laughed.

"So are they going to film you at the Coffee Bean?"

"No, I only have to work one job now since this is
pretty much my new second job, and they 'suggested' I
quit that one," Kate told her. "They want me working,
but apparently they don't want to highlight my amazing
coffee talents."

Natalie looked skeptical. "Coffee talents?"

"Yeah, you know, handing it to someone without
spilling it; being able to foam a latte while making small
talk with the regulars."

"Color me impressed," Natalie said. "Talking—while
foaming! I don't know why you want to be a famous musician when clearly your true calling is as a super-barista."
She giggled. Kate threw a T-shirt at her, which Natalie
then tossed into the moving box. "Look: packed! See how
helpful I am?"

"I couldn't do it without you," Kate said drily.

"But seriously—what's it going to be like? Aren't you
going to be nervous? I mean, you have to wear a microphone all the time, right? And everywhere you look there's
going to be a camera. . . ."

"Hush," Kate said, rousing herself from her beanbag
to survey the room. The walls were bare now, and the
closet was empty except for a tangle of wire hangers on
the floor. The warm breeze fluttered the gauzy curtains

she'd bought with her first Coffee Bean paycheck. They had tiny blue guitars and music notes on them.

"Mark said they were going to film you at open mics and stuff," Natalie went on. Mark Sayers was an old friend of Natalie's; Kate had gone on a semi-date with him once and found him charming but a little too goofy for her taste. "I guess that means you're finally going to have to get up on stage."

"I guess so," Kate said. There was no doubt about it: She was going to have to get a lot braver, quickly. "Are you sitting on the packing tape?"

Natalie felt around on the bed and then held up the dispenser. "Voilà," she said. "Have you met your costars?"

Kate shook her head. "Not yet. They've got an apartment in the same building, though, so I guess I'll meet them soon enough."

"That Madison Parker seems like a real Welcome Wagon type," Natalie scoffed. "Bet she'll greet you with a plate of brownies or maybe a Jell-O mold." Then her tone changed to curiosity. "Do you think you guys will end up being friends?"

"Weren't you going to make me some more coffee?" Kate asked, nudging her roommate with her foot. She didn't want to answer any more questions.

The truth of the matter was, the person she really wanted to talk to was Ethan. Even though they'd broken up over a year ago, they still kept in touch. Unlike Kate, who considered her Samsung to be an extension of her body (after all, practically everyone she knew and loved was thousands of miles away), Ethan wasn't really a phone person. But he was good with email. He liked to forward her really bad YouTube videos, like the one of the eight-year-old boy trying to channel Barry White, or the one with the high school girls absolutely murdering a Kings of Leon cover. "See?" he'd write after hearing about her latest episode of stage fright. "At least you're not like these idiots."

Days ago, she'd sent him a note about Dana approaching her, but strangely, she hadn't heard from him. She told herself that he was probably taking extra shifts at the hardware store before the school year started. She glanced over at her phone and thought about calling him. It was three hours later in Ohio—almost dinnertime. She wondered if she could catch him on the way to his favorite diner, the greasy spoon across the street from the OSU campus. Kate jumped as the phone began to buzz and vibrate on her nightstand.

Speak of the devil: It was Ethan Connor himself. Maybe this, too, was a sign, she thought. A good one.

"Hey, you," she said, suddenly feeling better. "What's up?"

"Not much, Little Miss Hollywood," Ethan said, and she could hear the smile in his voice.

"Oh, please," Kate said, flushing.

"Seriously—what's this thing you might do? A reality TV show? That's crazy, Kate!"

"Not *might* do," she corrected. "*Am* doing. It's called *The Fame Game*."

"Weeeellll, holy shit, child," he said, faking a Midwestern country drawl. "Little Kate Hayes done growed up to be a big television star."

She laughed. "Maybe. I mean, who knows if it'll work out. I haven't filmed anything yet. Maybe they'll decide I'm too boring and they'll fire me and hire some other singer."

"Hey, don't start putting yourself down," Ethan said. "Remember? Confidence is the name of the game."

Kate laughed again. Between Ethan and her sister, the sports metaphors just kept on coming. She tucked the phone against her shoulder as she gazed out her window, which overlooked the parking lot of a twenty-four-hour Walgreens. (At least she wouldn't miss the view from here.) She gave Ethan the lowdown on the show, everything from her costars to her own hopes to record an album on PopTV's dime. Then she sighed. "I mean, it's so great. But it's all pretty overwhelming, you know? One second you're grinding coffee beans, and next you're signing a contract to be on national television."

"Oh, you're going to be fine," Ethan assured her. "You're just going to have to work to stand out."

"What do you mean?" Kate asked, watching a homeless guy trying to steal a shopping cart from the parking lot.

"Well, your costars sound like pretty glitzy ladies," Ethan said. "They're used to the spotlight. They're not going to want to share it."

"Well, I'm sure—"

"Maybe you should start playing up your rock 'n' roll side," Ethan went on. "Get some tattoos. Consider a facial piercing or two. Maybe you could dye your hair black, with, like, a pink stripe or something."

Kate rubbed her temples. "Um—I think they sort of liked—"

"And be prepared to wear super-tight pants. And slutty shoes—"

"Ethan!" Kate exclaimed. "You're kind of freaking me out."

Then came Ethan's deep, familiar laugh. It reminded her of high school: of football games and study hall and cafeteria food and everything else, good and bad, she'd left behind.

"Oh, Kat," he said, using his old pet name for her. "I'm just trying to help. I mean, out of all the singer-songwriters in Los Angeles, they picked you. You don't want to disappoint them."

"Uh, no, no, you're right," she stammered, tamping down the familiar feeling that Ethan's help sometimes seemed like an insult. "Of course."

Natalie tapped her on the shoulder and held out a mug of steaming coffee. She took it gratefully. "Well, I should go. I have to finish packing."

"Don't forget about me when you're super-rich and famous," Ethan joked.

"I won't," she assured him.

And she wouldn't. But as she hung up the phone, she couldn't help but admit that talking to Ethan had not been the reassuring experience she'd hoped it would be. In fact, it had been the opposite.

"Everything okay?" Natalie asked. "Did I put enough milk in it?"

Kate smiled at her soon-to-be-former roommate. "It's perfect," she said, taking a grateful sip. "Maybe you should take over my old job at Coffee Bean."

"Oh, I'm way too surly for customer service," Natalie said, flopping back down on the bed. "I only wait on people I like." She stuck her bare feet up on the yellow wall. "What's your new life going to be like? I wonder," she said thoughtfully. "Will I be able to tell by watching you on TV? Or is that going to be just some trick—some PopTV version of reality?"

Kate shrugged. "I honestly have no idea," she said. "All I know is that I'm due at Park Towers in two hours and I am totally screwed. Look at this mess."

Natalie popped up, and her eyes took in the piles of clothes and bedding still scattered around the room. "I'll help," she said. "For real this time."

"Thanks," Kate said, wishing she had more of Natalie's practicality and levelheadedness, not to mention her uncanny ability to fit fifty songbooks into a box that looked as if it should hold about five.

Fueled by caffeine and Natalie's assistance, Kate finished packing without having a nervous breakdown. With half an hour to spare, she loaded Lucinda, her guitar (named after one of her idols, Lucinda Williams), into the back of her trusty Saab and slammed the door. She gave one last glance at the yellowing stucco walls of her apartment building and one last wave to Natalie, who was leaning out the window blowing kisses. And then she got into the car and slowly drove away, watching the Selva Vista Apartments, which she'd called home for a year, fade in her rearview mirror.

6

MAKING NICE

"So this is the place, huh?" Drew asked, pausing outside Grant's Guitar Shop in Santa Monica. He looked skeptically at the flapping awning and the weird mid-century rock work on the building's front. "Doesn't seem that impressive."

Carmen rolled her eyes. "I can't believe you've lived in L.A. your whole life, you pretend to play guitar, and you've never been to Grant's." She brushed past him and entered the small front room, which was packed, floor to ceiling, with stringed instruments: guitars, of course, but also mandolins, violins, banjos, and ukuleles. "You intern at Rock It! Records, for God's sake. Hasn't my dad made you come here for, like, research or something?"

"Nope," Drew said, brushing over the slight about his guitar playing—he was the first to admit that he taught himself to play because girls liked guys with guitars—and seemingly unembarrassed by his ignorance. He shrugged. "He sent me to Largo last week, though."

"Well, Grant's is pretty famous. All kinds of amazing people have played here," she said, making her way toward the back room where the shows took place.

Drew touched a hot-pink Gibson that hung from the wall as he followed her. "This early?" he asked.

Carmen smiled. She had to admit: 6 p.m. was not exactly party hour. But Laurel Matthews, who was a talent producer on *The Fame Game* (basically a production assistant, but somewhat better paid), had told her that this was where and when Trevor wanted to film—so here she was, miked and made-up and ready to be on TV.

Though *actually*, come to think of it, Trevor had wanted to film Carmen leaving her house in the Palisades first. Philip Curtis, however, had quickly refused. "If I wanted cameras in my face I'd live in Malibu," he said. "Absolutely no PopTV crew on my property."

Carmen had been surprised by his vehemence, but she wasn't about to pick a fight with him. And as it turned out, she didn't have to, because Drew's dad said they could film at his Brentwood mansion. It was weird, though, driving over to his house—a place she practically never went—so she could act like she spent every Sunday night palling around with Drew and his dad, Dr. Botox.

Carmen was lucky (and a little surprised) that Drew had agreed to be on the show. After she'd officially accepted her role on *The Fame Game*, Dana had sat her down and run through a laundry list of questions about her life, her family, and her friends. One of the most important queries: Which of Carmen's nearest and dearest was ready to be on-camera? Dana was obviously hoping that Carmen's parents would be up for it; the Curtises would add a major dose of glamour (and legitimacy) to the show, even if they *were* middle-aged. "Uh, let me work on them," Carmen had said, and while Dana tried to hide her disappointment so had Carmen. She had wanted to believe that Trevor had picked her because she was a rising star in her own right—he had assured her that was the case—but this exchange had made it harder to believe.

When Dana finished her questions, she folded her arms across her chest and asked Carmen if she would like to know who her fellow castmates were. *Duh,* thought Carmen, but because she was a nice person instead responded, "Yes, please." And when Dana told her, she'd nodded and kept her face friendly and open, even though she was thinking less than charitable thoughts. *Madison Parker: backstabber, fame whore. Gaby Garcia: sidekick, punch line. Kate Hayes: . . . who?* Well, it didn't matter, Carmen told herself; she'd make nice with all of them. She was highly skilled at the kind of friendliness that easily passed for actual warmth. It was just one of those things she'd learned being in the spotlight.

Carmen had been on her way out the door when Dana called her back. "Wait—your friend Drew—he works at Rock It!?" And when Carmen nodded, Dana's dark eyes lit up and she looked happier than Carmen had ever seen her look. "Perfect," she'd whispered, picking up the phone.

And that was how Drew and Carmen had ended up at tonight's open mic, because—according to the story line—Drew had "heard some insanely talented girl plays here." They'd even filmed a scene of Drew and Carmen watching the girl's YouTube video. (Three different times, actually, because Drew's dad kept wandering into the shot with a large glass of scotch in his hand.) And Carmen understood her mission: She was supposed to befriend the strawberry-blond-haired girl with the powerful voice and the unfortunate sense of style.

Carmen looked around the room at Grant's, which was less than half full, and wondered where Laurel was. She and Laurel had gone to the same high school, and though they weren't really friends back then (Laurel was three classes ahead), she'd always thought the older girl seemed cool. Not seeing any familiar faces except the sound guy who'd given her the mike pack earlier and the camera guy next to him, Carmen reached for Drew's arm and gave it a little squeeze. She was feeling uncharacteristically nervous. It had only taken her about ten minutes of filming to realize that it was one thing to recite memorized lines in front of a camera and another thing to try to be yourself. She wondered, briefly, if being a trained actress was going to make reality TV *harder* for her.

Her BlackBerry buzzed in her purse, and she reached in to fish it out. A text from Laurel:

YOU ARE SITTING IN FRONT. COME DOWN NOW.

She turned to Drew and smiled. "We're on," she said. She took a deep breath and then a little louder, for the camera, said, "Let's go sit up front."

As they walked toward the stage, Carmen noticed how the other audience members were also being directed to sit in the closest rows. *Clever Laurel*, she thought, front-loading so that when the PopTV cameras did reverse-angle shots of the audience, it would look like Kate had a full house.

"Do you think she'll be any good in person?" Drew asked.

Carmen shrugged. "Don't know," she said. "I hope so."

The host took the stage to a hearty round of applause and offered up a passable cover of a Foo Fighters song before turning the stage over to a skinny guy with a Van Dyke beard and a battered twelve-string.

Carmen scanned the room for Kate and spotted her in the corner, nearly hidden behind a standing bass. Carmen would have recognized Kate even without the PopTV cameras that flanked her, their red lights blinking, because she was wearing practically the same too-big blouse and faded jeans she'd worn in her YouTube video. Kate's hands were gripping each other and she looked almost green with fright.

Carmen nudged Drew. "There she is," she whispered.

Drew craned his neck to see. "She's kind of cute," he whispered back and gave Carmen a wolfish grin.

"Pig," Carmen returned.

As Van Dyke left the stage to polite applause and Kate took his place, Carmen had the opportunity to inspect her soon-to-be-friend (or, rather, soon-to-be-"friend") more closely. Her strawberry-blond hair fell in soft, unstyled waves past her shoulders. She wore little visible makeup, but she had long lashes and naturally red, full lips. She had a great figure, too, which for some reason she seemed intent on hiding beneath layers of sloppy clothes.

Kate sat on the stool and leaned into the microphone. "Thanks for coming," she whispered.

Carmen could see her long fingers trembling as they found their places on the neck of her guitar. She watched Kate take a deep breath and steel herself. The girl strummed a few chords, cursed softly, and stopped. She looked up at the audience through a lock of hair. "Sorry," she whispered. "Starting over."

This time, Kate's fingers seemed to go where they were supposed to. She began to play, and after a few moments Carmen recognized the opening to "Girls Just Want to Have Fun." Of course PopTV had asked Kate to perform her "hit."

I come home in the morning light, Kate sang.

Her voice was low and breathy and haunting. It sounded like she was confessing something unbearably private. Beside her, Carmen could feel Drew tense.

"What?" she whispered.

"She's amazing," he whispered back.

Carmen felt the tiniest twinge of jealousy, like the sudden prick of a needle. When had Drew ever thought *she* was amazing? But she quickly brushed this thought aside and focused on the music. The room was utterly silent, as if everyone in it was holding their breath. Kate's voice washed over them all.

When Kate strummed the final chords, Carmen clapped as loud as she could. The girl was really, really good, but she obviously needed a lot of encouragement. She still looked ill.

Kate leaned forward again and spoke, this time a little louder than a whisper. "And now for something I wrote." The PopTV camera zoomed in for a close-up.

The song was in a minor key, so it sounded eerie and sad, even though the lyrics were about sunshine and summertime. Carmen found herself nodding her head in time to the beat. *Yes*, she thought, *this is really good*.

She knew music because she'd grown up surrounded by song. (Sometimes literally: Once, when she was seven and sick with the chicken pox, the members of No Doubt had gathered around her bedside to sing her a get-well tune.) People called her dad "the hitmaker" because of his legendary ability to produce platinum albums, but as Philip Curtis always said, he didn't make the hits so much as recognize them. Carmen couldn't carry a tune in a bucket, but she had inherited his ear for talent. Carmen was the one who'd insisted her dad go check out Aja all those years ago. And then he'd signed her and made her a star. It was too bad Carmen didn't want to work at Rock It! Records; she would have made a brilliant A&R exec.

"Encore," Drew shouted when Kate's song was over. "Encore!"

But the open mic had rules: two songs, seven minutes, and you were done. So they had to sit through the rest of the show (five more musicians, and not one of them with half of Kate's talent) until they could make their way to the corner of the room where Kate was perched on a folding chair, biting her fingernails.

Carmen felt the eyes of the camera on her and Drew as she approached. Now was the moment that she would meet her castmate; she'd better hit her lines, whatever they would be.

"Hey," she said, smiling. *Wow, super-original*, she thought.

Kate looked up, the tip of her index finger still in her mouth. "Hi."

Carmen thought about sticking out her hand for Kate to shake but then decided against it. "I'm Carmen," she said, "and this is Drew." She pointed to her best friend, who grinned and said, "Dude, you were amazing."

Kate immediately flushed and looked down at her feet. "Thanks. I wish I wouldn't have screwed up so badly when I started, though."

There was something so innocent about her that Carmen felt immediately protective. Her own nervousness disappeared. "You know what?" she said. "Something like that only makes the audience root harder for you. I know one guy who pretends to mess up at least one song every show. He says his fans like it because he seems more human that way."

This appeared to cheer Kate up a little. "Really?" she said. "So there's hope for me?"

"Of course," Carmen said.

Kate smiled and nudged her guitar case with her foot. "You hear that, Lucinda? Carmen Curtis—*the* Carmen Curtis!—said I'm not completely hopeless."

Carmen was a little surprised. She didn't think Kate was supposed to know who she was. Weren't they supposed to find out all about each other as the cameras rolled? As they became "friends"? It was already so confusing trying to distinguish between real truth and TV truth.

"I saw you in *The Long and Winding Road*," Kate went on. "You were fantastic. When you and your sister didn't have enough money at that gas station and you had to, like, basically beg for a fill-up? I actually cried!" She giggled. "I know, I'm lame."

Now it was Carmen's turn to blush. "Thanks," she said. "But this is *your* time to bask in the glow of success. Let's talk some more about how great you were."

"Yeah," Drew piped up. "Your bridge on that second song was totally inspired."

But Kate, laughing, waved away their compliments. "Stop, you're embarrassing me. Let's talk about where you can get a burger around here. I was so nervous I couldn't eat all day, and now I'm starving."

Carmen slung her bag over her shoulder and nodded toward the door. "I know just the place," she said. "Let's all go for a drink and something to eat."

A second location had already been cleared for them down the street, so Kate suggesting a burger was expected. Carmen was impressed by how naturally she had done it. Maybe she had underestimated this girl at first glance.

Carmen watched Kate gather up her guitar and her things, feeling optimistic about her new castmate. As they headed out into the warm Santa Monica night, it occurred to her that she might not need the quotation marks around "friend."

7

BASICALLY A NATIVE

Madison stretched out one long, toned leg and then the other, enjoying the feel of the warm sun on her skin. Beside her was a giant bottle of Voss water and a stack of gossip magazines. (She liked to fold down the corners of pages that mentioned her and keep them neatly stacked in her closet to flip through on lonelier nights.) But Gaby, who lounged beside her wearing a plum-colored bikini the size of a cocktail napkin, simply would not shut up.

"So the set is, like, totally amazing with all these lights and cameras and rotating stages and stuff," she was saying. "And I met Chase Davis already. He is soooo cute, and really nice, too. And oh my God! Did you know that all the guys wear makeup?"

Gaby was on cloud nine because she'd been hired to be a correspondent for *Buzz! News*, covering minor events around Hollywood. Trevor had obviously gotten her the gig, Madison thought, because no sane person would hire Gaby to do anything more challenging than remember her own name.

She closed her eyes and breathed deeply, the way the teacher in the one and only yoga class Madison had ever attended had instructed. (Yoga burned the same amount of calories as shopping—so why not just shop?) She and Gaby were killing time by the pool until their new neighbor, Kate Whatever-her-name-was, showed up. (Though, in truth, Kate lived two floors down from Madison and Gaby. Trevor had hoped the girls would all live next door to each other—like in *Melrose Place*—but it turned out his powers of persuasion didn't extend to people who weren't on his show; the couple in the apartment next to Madison had refused to budge.) Madison brought the bottle of water to her lips. Why, oh why, couldn't they kill time in silence?

"—so I get to go to this ribbon-cutting ceremony, and I'm supposed to talk about the history of the site, and how, like, before they built this new club there, it was a vacant lot with this huge population of, like, fearful cats—"

"I hope you won't have any trouble reading the teleprompter," Madison said under her breath.

But Gaby didn't hear her. "What is a fearful cat, anyway? Is that like a certain species or what?"

"I think you mean feral. But, yes," Madison lied. "It's a whole new species."

Gaby droned on while Madison wondered idly what this new Kate girl was going to be like. She already knew the basics because she'd called Trevor and bullied him into telling her Kate's background. Madison certainly didn't want another surprise like she'd gotten at the Togs for Tots benefit, where she'd learned that Carmen Curtis was on *The Fame Game* only by cleverly spotting her mike pack. But she was reassured to find out that Kate wasn't anything like Carmen. Her mom was a teacher and she was from Ohio or Indiana or some other flyover state. She was nineteen and relatively new to L.A. In other words, she would be no threat at all to Madison when it came to competing for screen time.

"Do you want to get in the water?" Gaby's voice broke through Madison's thoughts. "It's kind of hot out here."

Madison opened her eyes and looked at her friend as if she were crazy. "Chlorine is horrible for your skin, Gab. Everyone knows that."

"Oh," Gaby said, sounding deflated. "Okay."

Then Madison spotted, on the other side of the pool, a small figure wearing what looked like a boy's ribbed tank top, a pair of (gasp) cargo pants, and a wide-brimmed straw hat. Oh, and a beat-up pair of dollar store flip-flops.

Wow, Madison thought. *That's one way to stand out in L.A.*

She watched as Kate Hayes approached, trailed by two TV cameras. Though there were about a dozen empty chairs on the other side of the pool, the Midwesterner—no doubt acting on the director's blocking instructions—was heading for the one nearest them.

Kate dropped a canvas bag full of books and papers

onto the cement and then sank down on the chaise longue next to Gaby. And Gaby, eager for a new audience for tales of her mind-blowingly awesome new *Buzz!* gig, turned toward her immediately.

"Hi," Gaby chirped. "Hot out here today, huh?"

Kate, her face invisible under the hat (*And let's keep it that way*, thought Madison), nodded.

"I'm Gaby," Gaby said.

"Kate," said Kate. "I just moved in."

"Oh yeah? Awesome. Welcome to the building!"

Madison sat up, making sure to cover her stomach with one slender tan arm. If the angle of her body was too sharp, sometimes there was a little wrinkle of skin above her belly button, which made her appear less than 100 percent perfect. And less than 100 percent perfect was, of course, 100 percent not acceptable. Hence the arm—just in case. "I'm Madison," she said. "Gaby and I live together."

"Oh yeah? That's cool," Kate said. "I live by myself. Which is . . . nice." She seemed uncertain about that.

Madison watched as Kate fumbled with a pocket, pulled out a BlackBerry, frowned, and then removed her hat and set it beside her bag on the ground. Laurel had clearly texted her something along the lines of LET'S SEE YR FACE.

Kate didn't have sunglasses so she squinted at Madison. (It was usually a battle with the producers to wear a pair because they "shielded expression." Clearly it was a battle she had lost.) "It's nice to meet you," she said. "I loved your show."

"Which one?" Madison asked. "I starred in two, you know."

"Both," Kate said quickly.

Madison gifted her with a gleaming smile. "Thanks. My fans have meant everything to me. So tell me, what brings you to L.A.?"

Kate smiled back. "Music," she said.

"Did you follow Mop Top out here?" Gaby asked. "I heard that when they relocated from Georgia, a whole bunch of their fans followed them."

Kate laughed. "I'm not a groupie, I'm a musician. A singer-songwriter."

"Ooh," Gaby said. "Wow. Do you play an instrument?"

"Guitar," Kate answered. "And a bit of keyboard and drums, if I need to accompany myself. And ukulele."

"Wow. I took clarinet lessons when I was in third grade, but—"

Madison loudly cleared her throat. The world didn't need to hear these two have a totally boring conversation. "Do you have any regular gigs lined up?" she interrupted. "A friend of mine has this club . . ." She trailed off, leaving the rest of the sentence up to Kate's imagination. The truth was, Madison didn't know any club owners who were looking for corn-fed indie rock girls, but she might as well seem like she was the helpful type. For now.

"Not yet," Kate admitted. "I've been pretty busy

working. But I, uh, recently came into a little bit of money, so I'm going to start recording pretty soon."

"Is that your dream? To make an album?" Madison said, raising her sculpted eyebrows.

Kate nodded earnestly. "I wished for it on every single birthday candle."

"Awwww," Gaby crooned. "That's so sweet." Madison sort of felt like kicking her.

"So what are you guys doing here in L.A.?" Kate asked. "Are you from here?"

"Yes, we are," Madison said, speaking for both of them. "Gaby was born and raised in Long Beach, and I've been here for five years, which makes me basically a native." She flashed another brilliant smile at Kate (and, by extension, the cameras).

"I'm a *Buzz! News* correspondent," Gaby blurted, unable to contain herself any longer. "I just started. I haven't done any reporting yet, but I know it's going to be so incredible and I'm going to be amazing. It's, like, totally my dream job."

"Wow," said Kate as she rolled up the legs of her cargo pants to reveal china-white shins. She turned to Madison. "What about you? Are you still doing *Madison's Makeovers*?"

Madison frowned lightly. Why was Kate asking her about her canceled show? "I decided to take a break from that," she said smoothly. "I helped so many girls, you know, and it was incredibly rewarding. But I felt like it was time to focus on other things."

"Like tanning," Gaby giggled, and Madison shot her a death-ray look.

"I'm exploring my options," she said, taking a sip of her water. "There are so many."

Kate looked suitably impressed. "I'm sure you'll be able to do whatever you want to do," she said. "You seem like that kind of person."

Madison rearranged herself delicately on the chaise longue. "Thank you," she purred. She wondered if Kate might actually be an ideal castmate. For one, she was clearly too nice for her own good, and for another, she did herself no favors with that awful clothing and that carrot-top hair. The camera certainly wasn't going to linger on her, that was for sure. Which meant, of course, more time for it to focus on Madison.

"So, uh, since I'm sort of new to this neighborhood," Kate began, "I was wondering if you guys wanted to, like, grab a drink or something tonight. Maybe you could show me the local hotspots. Or whatever."

Madison had known that Kate was going to propose drinks, and she was all set with her answer. "Sure, that sounds fun. I was going to go out to The Spare Room tonight, but I'm actually feeling like being more mellow. We can do The Spare Room another night."

"Great," Kate said. "My friend Carmen might come, too. I'll text her now."

Kate bent her head down to her phone, so she didn't

see the fleeting look of displeasure cloud Madison's face. So Carmen Curtis, the Hollywood golden child, was going to tag along. That was no good, because Carmen meant competition: for the notice of any fans they might run into, for the gaze of the PopTV camera, for the attention of the paparazzo who just might—on an "anonymous" tip—happen to be lingering outside the bar Madison would take them to.

She picked up an issue of *Gossip* and then put it back down immediately. She was too agitated to skim its pages. Trevor Lord, their puppet master, had wasted no time figuring out an efficient way to get all four girls together. Well done, Trev. The real question was, what did he have planned to later tear them apart?

8

STRUGGLE. DRAMA. MELTDOWNS.

Sunlight streamed into Trevor's office through two floor-to-ceiling windows. He paced through warm patches of it, his Bluetooth strapped to his ear. "Noah, we're thrilled to be moving forward on this with you," he said, nodding and giving the thumbs-up sign to Dana, who sat on his office couch, listening in on the extension.

Noah was the president of production for PopTV Films, the counterpart to PopTV, and Trevor had been working him for weeks in the hopes of convincing him to audition Carmen and Madison for *The End of Love*, the studio's upcoming dystopian romance. Noah was reluctant at first but had finally agreed to allow them to audition. "It's perfect synergy," Trevor continued. "We'll get the girls in for reads this week. On-camera. And I'm not telling you or the director who to pick, or that you need to give anyone the lead. Whoever you choose, and for whatever role, we'll make it work for the show. We just really appreciate the opportunity."

Dana was nodding in agreement and looking very pleased with her boss. This was an excellent story line, and having *The Fame Game* linked to what could be a blockbuster movie would only increase the series' popularity tenfold. PopTV Films had lucked out with this one. They'd optioned the rights to the book before it was a best seller, and now they finally had the potential makings of a hit on their hands.

"I'm not sure I can guarantee you the on-camera part," Noah said. "Getting McEntire in a room with your girls will be the only thing I can promise you, and even that took some persuading. He is not a huge fan of reality TV."

"What's not to like?" Trevor said with a forced laugh, biting his tongue so he didn't say what he was really thinking, which was that PopTV certainly wasn't staying afloat with money from its film division. Reality TV had saved the network *and* its studio, and Trevor hated when people refused to give him credit for it.

"We'll get lunch next week," Trevor told Noah. "At Shutters. A little celebration."

Noah agreed and the two said good-bye.

Trevor sank down into his chair and put his feet up on the corner of his glass desk. "Well, that's done," he said, shaking off his frustration. "And the rest will just fall into place."

"Do you think they'll actually want to cast one of them?" Dana wondered.

Trevor shrugged. "Who knows? Obviously I'll

encourage Noah to push for it. *Strongly*. But if he doesn't, well, the crying will make for decent TV. Either way it's a win for us."

He could imagine, for instance, Carmen not being cast in the lead and thus falling, grief-stricken, into the arms of that handsome Drew guy. And then maybe he could encourage Madison to develop a crush on Drew as well. And that'd make for good drama, wouldn't it? (Madison's type was usually older and richer, but he knew that her one true love—airtime—would have her throwing herself at Drew if Trevor asked her to.) It was something to think about should the movie roles not exactly pan out. But Trevor was seriously hoping they would, because the dailies of the girls were coming back a little boring, frankly. He had a couple weeks of not-very-exciting outings and far-from-scintillating conversations, and that wasn't going to give him the ratings numbers he craved. Sure, Kate was the nearly perfect everygirl (although he had been meaning to speak to her about her look—she was a pretty girl but didn't seem to even know the meaning of the word "style"), and the camera loved Carmen. Gaby was her familiar, comical, dim-bulb self, and Madison—well, Madison was a handful, which was exactly why he liked her. But still. Dailies: dull. The PopTV audience would enjoy seeing the girls struggling to make it in L.A., but they wouldn't want them to be nice to each other all the time. If kindness and cooperation were what they were after—well, they could turn on *Sesame*

Street. They needed a character to root for and one to hate. It didn't matter if whoever was in which role fluctuated.

Madison had been in reasonably good form last week, though, Trevor thought, when he had maneuvered a seemingly organic way to get all four of them out together. She was saccharine-sweet to Carmen—she didn't get where she was by not knowing how to behave for the cameras—but she couldn't refrain from slipping in a couple choice insults, which naturally Trevor had enjoyed.

In the meantime he'd been working on a few things to ratchet up the tension and create more undercurrents of irritability and frustration. He felt confident that pretty soon it would all come together. And then fall apart perfectly. And then there was that interesting message he'd received from Madison's sister, Sophia. . . . She'd hinted at a possible story line that would be amazing if it were true. Obviously the rehab that Madison had paid for had not cured Sophia of her addiction to fame.

Yes, Sophia Parker—she had legally changed it from Sophilyn Wardell, he now knew—was the gift that kept on giving. He had her on his calendar for tomorrow.

This was yet another thing that made Trevor smile to himself. Struggle. Drama. Meltdowns. He'd given his viewers that on *L.A. Candy*, and now he was going to turn it up a notch.

9

PEOPLE LIKE US DO NOT
WAIT IN LINES

Kate sipped at her vodka and Sprite and surreptitiously took in everything around her: the low, leather lounges, the red-glass tile on the walls, the dark, smoky mirrors, the DJ booth manned by some guy dressed in gold chains and a baseball cap. . . . Nope, she definitely wasn't in Ohio anymore.

She glanced down at her outfit. It was too bad she was dressed like she still was. Had she learned nothing from her previous outings with this crew? What was she thinking, wearing a pair of worn-in Levi's and a ruffled T-shirt she'd bought at Banana Republic three and a half years ago? And let's not even mention the DSW shoes! Kate sighed. She was only at Whisper, one of L.A.'s hottest nightclubs, where everyone practically seemed to *glitter* with money and glamour. The guys were all in jeans that probably cost more than a month's rent back at her old apartment, and the girls wore tiny, shimmery dresses that hugged every tanned, toned curve. They moved sinuously on the dance floor or lounged around on the banquettes, members of an entirely different and much more beautiful species.

It was a miracle the doorman had let Kate in, even though she'd been flanked by the famous Carmen Curtis and the infamous Madison Parker. (Wouldn't that have set Laurel's teeth on edge, having the doorman open the velvet rope for everyone but poor Kate Hayes?)

When they'd pulled up in their town car (Madison refused to enter a cab), the line to get in had snaked almost around the corner of the block. "Ugh," Kate had said. "Maybe we should go somewhere else. I don't want to wait in that line."

Madison and Carmen had both laughed. "Wait in *line*?" Madison had practically sneered. "Darling, people like us don't wait in lines."

People like us? Kate had thought. *But I'm not one* bit *like you.*

Carmen had reached out and patted her arm. "You'll see," she said. "I can get in anywhere. The doormen always recognize me."

Madison had snorted. "As a person who just finished a season of her own TV show, I'm pretty sure that I'll be the one to get us in."

Kate shifted uncomfortably in the backseat. She hated to watch people bicker; it made her feel itchy and claustrophobic. "I'm sure the bouncers or whatever they are will recognize both of you," she said lamely. She'd definitely been thrust into the peacemaker role between these two. She wasn't a child of divorce, but she could only assume this was how it felt a lot—*Mommy and Mommy are fighting!* Kate had opened the door then and stepped out to the sidewalk. The line was getting longer by the second. She felt sorry for the girls who had to stand so long in those high-heeled shoes.

The PopTV cameras had already been set up to film their entrance, and Laurel was there, too, drinking something from a travel mug. "Coffee," she'd said when Carmen raised her eyebrows at her.

"I hope you put some whiskey in it then," Carmen had said. "Because you look a little tense."

It was true: Laurel looked as wired and nervous as Kate felt. No doubt it was hard to be in charge of a TV shoot, but at least she didn't have to be on-camera.

"All right, girls. The cameras are set and the doorman knows to let you in. Once you're inside, wait a moment for us to get all of the cameras in, and then you can go to your table," Laurel said, quickly motioning toward a tall doorman dressed in a black suit and armed with an ID scanner.

In a group they'd gone to the front of the crowd, and of course the ropes had parted for them as the doorman nodded a greeting. (It had nothing to do with either Carmen or Madison being recognized. They'd have to fight about it some other night, when PopTV hadn't set things up so they could jump the line.) The PopTV cameras followed them into the dim, crowded room.

"What do you think of this place?" Carmen asked, jolting Kate back to the present.

"It's . . ." Kate had to think about this for a moment. It was chic and obviously super-exclusive and everything, but did she like it? She wasn't sure. "It's . . . well, it's definitely not like any club I've ever been to before." She smiled broadly, hoping that that would convey the enthusiasm she didn't quite feel.

"Well, you aren't in Kansas anymore," Madison said as she headed toward the table.

"Ohio," Kate said quietly, but Madison was already distracted by some guy with one too many buttons undone on his collared shirt.

Carmen smiled at Kate. "Yeah, I know what you mean. Sometimes I love a club and sometimes I'd rather be at home eating popcorn and watching *Clueless*."

"I love that movie," Kate said.

"So brilliant, right?" Carmen replied.

"Completely. Although it definitely messed me up for getting around L.A. when I first moved here."

"What are you talking about?" Carmen said, laughing.

"'Everywhere in L.A. takes twenty minutes,'" Kate quoted.

Carmen laughed even harder. "Oh, honey, you can't take traffic advice from Cher's dad in *Clueless*."

"Duh," Kate said. "I know that now. . . ."

She laughed, too. She was surprised at how quickly she'd bonded with Carmen. At first she'd been starstruck—after all, the most famous person she'd met before her was the guy who did those annoying mattress commercials—but by the time they'd all finished their post-Grant's burgers that night a few weeks ago when they met, Kate felt like Carmen was just another girl trying to find her way in L.A. Which, in a way, she was.

She liked Drew, too. He looked intimidating because of his height and his tattoos, but he was down-to-earth and funny. He didn't make a big deal when Kate had spilled her Coke on his sleeve (oops!) when the three of them hung out the other night, and he laughed at all her lame jokes. But it was Carmen to whom he devoted most of his attention. He seemed to hang on every word she said, and Kate had to wonder if there was something going on between them. But she didn't know Carmen well enough yet to ask.

"Aren't you hot in that?" Madison asked, leaning over to catch her attention. She plucked at Kate's long sleeve.

Kate smiled, embarrassed. "Uh, yeah. No one told me that it's like, a violation to cover more than thirty percent of your skin around here."

Madison laughed as if this was one of the funniest things she'd ever heard. "Oh, you can cover up whatever bits you want. You just have to do it in high style." She took a sip of her drink, which was something pink served in a martini glass. She squinted over the rim, taking in Kate's outfit. "Yes, I think it's time you got yourself a new look. Do you have any favorite designers?"

Kate gripped her drink tighter and shook her head.

Designers? Why in the world would Madison think she knew anything about designers? Madison should ask her about guitars. Gibson, Maton, Les Paul: Now those were names that meant something to her.

"Time to show off those legs, girl," Carmen said.

Madison nodded without looking in Carmen's direction. She obviously wanted this to be a two-way exchange; that way the cameras could catch her being sweet for once. "You're cute as a button, Kate. We have to maximize your assets. Which means"—and here she raised her glass, toasting Kate—"we have to make a date for my very favorite activity: shopping."

"Sounds great," Kate said brightly. Now it was clear why Madison was being so nice to her: Trevor had written them a shopping date. She'd seen it in her filming schedule.

Kate and Madison—Shopping
Time: 11 a.m.
First Location: American Rag

She'd assumed that if they were going to have her shopping it would have been with Carmen. Of course, Carmen hadn't just spent a season on TV doing makeovers. Surely Trevor wanted to showcase one of the things Madison was now famous for.

And she'd play her role in this story line as best she could. Barneys! Kate Somerville! Lunch at Joan's on Third! Gossip with Madison! It would be fine. She was much better already at living on-camera. The first night she was filmed, when she'd moved into her new place—complete with a fake phone call her to mom—she kept looking right into the lens, whereas now, she sometimes found herself forgetting the camera was there (but only for a moment).

Oops! She'd just looked. *That's what you get for being too cocky*, she thought.

But then she noticed something strange: Even though she, Carm, and Gaby were all on one side of the small, round table, the cameras were trained only on Madison.

Huh? she thought. *Do the PopTV people find Madison as fascinating as she finds herself?*

And then, materializing out of the club's dimness, Kate saw a familiar shade of platinum approaching the table. She was stunning in a flowery, floaty dress, strutting in gold wedge sandals. She was none other than Sophia Parker.

Oh, thought Kate. *Wow. That's what the cameras were waiting for. And maybe that's why Laurel was acting so weird earlier.*

In that moment, Kate was no longer a cast member. She was at home, in her pj's, watching this all unravel in the docusoap she had grown to love. Only this was so much better. This was the unedited version.

One lens was focused on Sophia now, and one on her sister. Sophia let out a high-pitched squeal.

"Oh my God, sis!" Sophia cried, holding out her hands. "What are you doing here?"

Madison paled. The hand holding her pink drink

trembled a little, and she quickly set the glass on the table. Kate saw her willing herself to smile. "Sophie . . . ah! I might ask you the same thing!" Madison stood up and gave her sister an air kiss on each perfect cheek. Then she stepped back. "You look good," she said. "But what's that in your glass?"

Sophia beamed. "Nothing but Pellegrino, sis. Scout's honor." She drew an X over the plunging neckline of her dress.

"Well, sit down with us," Madison said, sinking to the couch.

From her vantage point, Kate could see how rattled Madison was. But she was a pro—she acted as if running into the fame-seeking sister who'd humiliated her in front of the whole world was no big deal at all.

"Don't mind if I do." Sophia sat next to Madison and crossed one lovely leg over the other. "I'm Sophia," she said to Carmen.

Carmen introduced herself and everyone else, but Kate could see that Sophia didn't care what their names were. Her blue eyes were bored, glassy. The only thing Sophia cared about was the cameras and whether or not they were turned toward her. When they were, her eyes came to life again.

"So—how've you been?" Sophia asked her sister.

"Amazing," Madison said. "Totally amazing. But let's talk about you. How was rehab? Did you get really good at Ping-Pong?"

Sophia leaned back, laughing, so the cameras could get a good view of her ample cleavage. "Only the mental patients play Ping-Pong. The addicts—we read magazines. Speaking of which, I kept looking for you, Mad, but I never saw you." Sophia's smile was sly now.

"Oh, I was in them, all right," Madison said. "One of my fans must have cut out all the articles about me to put in her Madison Parker scrapbook. I'm told that happens a lot."

Nice, thought Kate. Madison was well trained in the art of the rejoinder, that was for sure.

Sophia snorted. "Yes, I'm sure that's exactly it. So—come on, tell me. What are you up to these days?"

"Loving life," Madison said simply. She finished her drink and then stood. "Well, it's been fun, you guys. Soph, so great to see you again! But I'm going to head home. I've got a big day tomorrow. Gaby, you want a ride?"

"Okay," Gaby said, which was pretty much the first thing she'd said all evening. She'd been too busy scoping out the crowd for unaccompanied guys to flirt with.

Madison air-kissed Kate, gave Carmen a wave, and then she and Gaby exited, one of the cameras following them. And of course once all the cameras left (after they got a sad-looking reaction shot of Sophia), Sophia did, too. She didn't even bother to say good-bye; she just evaporated into the crowd.

"Wow," Kate said. "That was kind of uncomfortable."

"Yeah . . ." Carmen agreed. "Couldn't have happened

to a nicer girl. Now, come on. Let's get rid of the mikes and have some fun." Both girls tugged off their microphones and spotted a PA to hand them off to. Then Carmen grabbed Kate's hand and pulled her toward the bar. They hadn't gotten more than ten feet before someone reached out and grabbed Carmen in a big bear hug.

"Jake!" Carmen squealed, hugging the tall, dark-haired guy back. "Long time no see! How are you?"

"Better now," said Jake, winking. He was handsome in the way that so many Hollywood guys were: strong cheekbones, strong jaw, and strong arms. He was wearing a shirt that said *Virginia Is for Lovers*.

As the two of them tried to catch up, yelling over the noise of the crowd, Kate shifted restlessly from foot to foot. Carmen had introduced her to Jake, but Jake only had eyes for Carmen. And Carmen was lapping up the attention, Kate thought. Maybe she'd been wrong about her and Drew.

Jake bought them both drinks and they headed back to their table, where they were joined by another handsome, dark-haired guy named Drake (really), who could have been—but wasn't—Jake's brother. Drake kissed Carmen and shook Jake's hand. "Bro," he said, "haven't seen you since that roast of whatshisname. How's it going?"

Drake settled in and Carmen once again introduced Kate, who smiled mildly, not expecting him to give her the time of day.

"Kate's my new friend," Carmen said. "She's an

amazing singer. You guys have to see her."

"Cool," Drake said. "By the way, I finally saw *The Long and Winding Road*. You were awesome."

And that was how it went for an hour: handsome but interchangeable guys rotating through their booth to greet Carmen and flirt with her, and Carmen happily flirting back. She kept trying to include Kate in the conversation, but she was the only one who seemed to care what Kate had to say. Eventually, bored of being the third (or fifth or sixth or whatever) wheel, Kate got up and went to find fresh air.

Toward the back of the bar was a patio area, which was uncrowded and quiet. White lights twinkled in the jacaranda trees, and she thought she heard the murmur of a fountain somewhere. She breathed deeply, enjoying the solitude. The bass from the club registered with a dull thump behind her. She finished her drink and set the glass down in a planter filled with succulents.

"They like it better when you give them a bit of the sauce," said a voice behind her in a charming accent.

She whirled around, mortified at being caught hiding her empty in a plant. "Uh—well—" She cleared her throat. There was yet another handsome dark-haired guy standing there. Seriously, was there a special on them tonight? "I was just setting it there for a minute."

He laughed and his white teeth flashed in the darkness. "Don't worry, I won't tell the manager. But it does look like you could use another drink," he said.

She shrugged. "Yeah, maybe."

"Don't look so thrilled to be here," he said, reaching out and giving her shoulder a friendly little poke.

She took a step back, unnerved to be poked by someone she'd never met. "Do I know you?" she asked.

He threw back his head and laughed for what seemed like a full minute. When he was done he said, "Maybe you don't need another drink."

"Why?" she asked, puzzled.

"I met you ten minutes ago. We were sitting at a table together? You know, with Carmen?"

Kate flushed a deep red and was glad it would be too dark for this guy, whoever he was, to see that. "Oh my God, I'm sorry," she said. "I didn't realize—"

"I'm Luke," he interrupted, holding out a hand for her to shake.

"Oh, right, sure," Kate said. "I'm—"

"You're Kate," he said. "Kate from Columbus."

"That's me," she said softly. She was still mortified.

"Well, Kate from Columbus, you wait one second. I'll be right back." He turned and went back into the club, and Kate was free to kick herself repeatedly for her stupidity. Luke was freaking cute—how was it that she didn't remember him? Was he really so identical to Jake and Drake and Cayden and Jaden?

In a moment, Luke returned, bearing a vodka soda for her and a beer for himself. "Don't give this one to the plant," he said, handing it to her.

"Thanks," she said. "I'm sorry I didn't recognize you. Clubs like this aren't exactly my thing."

"Mine either," Luke said. "But a friend of mine promotes this night and he made me promise to come." He took a sip of his beer. "So what are you doing these days, my old friend Kate? Still in the biz?"

"Pardon?"

"Show business. Acting. Writing. Directing. Make-up . . ."

"Stunts," Kate heard herself say.

He raised his eyebrows. "Really?"

"I was Megan Fox's stunt double in *Transformers*." She tried to say it with a straight face but she could feel a smile pulling at the corners of her mouth. "Do you think *she* jumped out of that burning building?"

"You had me going there for a minute," he said, laughing and toasting her. "You're an actress."

"No, definitely not," Kate answered. "I'm a musician. I mean, trying to be." She blushed again. "Really I'm a, uh, food services technician." He smiled at that. "That's much more accurate to say, because that's what pays the bills." For some reason—perhaps because the cameras were gone—it didn't even occur to her to mention *The Fame Game*. She hadn't totally adjusted to her new life; she still felt like last month's Kate. "Are you in 'the biz'?"

Luke nodded. "Yep. Just like ninety percent of the people inside this ridiculous club. I'm an actor." He grinned. "Perhaps you've seen me in my star turn as Doctor Rose on

Boston General?" The comic, needling way he said this told Kate, who had never seen *Boston General*, that he wasn't actually one of its stars.

"I'm not much of a TV person," she admitted.

"That's okay," he said, "I won't hold it against you. But let me try another one: Did you see me in the bar scene in *Inception*? No? Okay, how about as that young lawyer from a competing firm in *The Good Wife*? No. Okay. Um, I usually don't like to bring this one up, but since I'm striking out with everything else: Did you see me in that GEICO commercial, the one where the gecko goes to Disneyland?"

"Yes!" squealed Kate. "You were the handsome prince!"

"Guilty as charged," Luke said, ducking his head modestly.

"Well, you were a very convincing prince," she said. "I'm sure all the princesses were in love with you."

"Kate Hayes! There you are!"

Kate looked over to see Carmen standing in the doorway to the patio, smiling tipsily at her. "I've been looking at you for forever," Carm said. "I mean, looking *for* you. I thought you, like, got locked in a bathroom stall or something." Carmen's eyes flicked to Luke, who was leaning against a railing, looking relaxed and happy. "Um, I was going to go home. But you look like you're having fun! So you should stay!"

Kate opened her mouth. She was having fun talking to

Luke, it was true, but she was worried that she was reaching her limits of witty banter. What if they ran out of things to say to each other? Would Luke say good night and leave her standing alone on the patio? "No, I should—"

"Oh, stay!" Carmen cried enthusiastically. "Luke can take you home, can't you?" She glanced over at her friend.

"Of course," said Luke. "It would be my pleasure."

"Great! 'Night, you two!" Carmen said, looking pleased with herself. She blew them both kisses and vanished.

Now what? wondered Kate.

Luke grinned at her. "I guess you're stuck with me," he said.

Stuck with Doctor Rose, she thought. *Every girl should be so lucky.*

10

MORE THAN JUST A STORY ARC

Madison watched as her roommate poured a stream of disgusting, sludgy juice into a tall cocktail glass. Gaby had recently started some new juice cleanse that was originally prescribed as a therapy for people diagnosed with cancer. She'd heard it helped reduce bloating, though, and apparently she was on board for anything that promised to help her drop a few pounds.

There was a little left in the blender. "Want some?" Gaby asked, holding it up.

"No thanks," Madison said. "It looks like raw sewage."

Gaby frowned as she came over to join Madison in the living room. "It has kelp in it." She put her feet—in big fuzzy bunny slippers—up on the coffee table. "And spirulina."

"Still a pass," Madison said. She leaned back against the custom-made silk cushions. The truth was, she was feeling out of sorts. She'd been blindsided by Sophie's appearance at the club the other night, and she wasn't happy about it. She knew that she'd have to grin and bear it, since it was obviously all part of Trevor's plan. And even she knew her story line wasn't exactly scintillating so far. Trevor had filmed her going to some events, taking a day trip to Vegas to appear at a Wet Republic pool party, and having a meeting with the woman who runs the Madelyn Wardell Foundation for Girls (her charity, which was still good for a photo op every now and then, and a tax write-off). Not exactly ratings bait. But Sophie was just as concerned with camera time as Madison was, if not more, which meant they were going to be elbowing each other out of the frame, metaphorically if not literally, for the foreseeable future. Maybe Madison could get a cover story out of the return of Poor Little Sophia Parker— *"I just want the best for my little sister!"* After all, Madison was perfectly capable of playing nice. And if Sophie wanted to play dirty, Madison was armed with plenty of stories about what a delinquent she was when they were growing up, and how Madison always came to the rescue.

Trevor had tried to fan the flames of Madison's rivalry with Carmen, whom Madison admittedly thought was a no-talent silver-spooner. But if Trevor thought she was dumb enough to make an enemy of Carmen Curtis on national television, then he seriously underestimated her. The first move would have to be Carmen's, and that bitch wasn't budging.

"What time is it?" Gaby asked, sipping meditatively at her sewage juice.

Madison glanced at her phone. "Almost ten."

"Oh, I've got to get to bed," Gaby said. "Tomorrow's

my first on-camera interview for *Buzz!*"

"Who are you interviewing?"

"Lacey Hopkins," Gaby said excitedly. "She just got out of jail."

"What for this time?" Madison asked. The L.A. County Jail seemed to have a revolving door policy for Lacey Hopkins, a once promising young actress who'd gotten on the path to train wreck and was staying the course.

"I forget. But she was only in there for two days, even though it was supposed to be like twenty. I'm supposed to ask her what she ate and how she slept and if she made any friends and stuff."

"I'm sure she's besties with all those people by now," Madison remarked. "Well, good luck tomorrow."

"Thanks," Gaby said, padding down the hall to her bedroom. "See you in the morning."

Madison got up and went to stand by the window. Outside she could see the traffic lights on the street far below changing from green to yellow to red. She reflected briefly on Lacey Hopkins, whose life had seemingly spiraled out of control. Lacey was weak, Madison thought. But *she* wasn't. No, Madison Parker wasn't the type to give one ounce of control to anyone, was she? And with that thought in mind, she texted Laurel.

There's going to be a change in schedule. . . .

Madison slipped into her seat at Barney Greengrass and signaled the waiter to bring her some sparkling water. She was careful to keep her chair in the right position, which had been marked with a piece of neon gaffer tape on the floor; this would ensure the cameras had the perfect angle of her. Madison didn't have a bad side, of course, but she did have a favorite one, and she made sure the camera guys knew it.

She was early, and she took the time to check her makeup, even though the cameras were rolling. She knew the footage would end up on the editing room floor, since solitary primping was not exactly the drama Trevor craved. She also quickly tweeted what lipstick color she was wearing. She'd started that habit a few months ago, after she did it on a whim one morning and then got retweeted by a bunch of beauty blogs. Her followers went up a lot that day. So now she made sure to give her fans all sorts of info about her look du jour.

Madison wondered, as she slicked another coat of gloss on her lips, how late Sophie would be. (She still couldn't think of her as Sophia, although she usually remembered to call her that on-camera.) She'd been chronically tardy as a child: to school, to detention, to dinner, whatever. But maybe rehab had worked some miracle and taught her how to pay attention to a watch, Madison thought. Maybe there was some program about the Twelve Steps of Not Being a Rude Bitch.

She smiled to herself. If Sophie was bitchy to her, maybe Madison would use that line on her. See if she thought it was as funny as Madison did. She used to have a sense of humor, that kid, before she got so bitter about being left behind in Armpit Falls. No, she reminded herself. Always take the high road . . . at least while others are watching.

And who knew what sort of mood Sophie would be in today, or what her current game plan would be; besides Sophie's appearance at Whisper, it had been six months since they'd seen each other. Madison had gotten a few random emails from Sophie, where she talked about embracing her inner sister spirit or something like that, but she hadn't replied. Madison was going to try to play the benevolent big sister. She was going to express concern, family loyalty, blah, blah, blah.

She glanced up, hoping to catch the waiter's eye again. But the restaurant was packed, filled with super-agents having lunch meetings and Beverly Hills housewives in too-sheer shirts picking at frisée salads, and the waiter didn't notice Madison at all. She was all set to get huffy when she saw Sophie coming toward her. Sophie was smiling triumphantly, pulling someone along in her wake.

Madison squinted. *No. Effing. Way.* Her heart began to thrum in her chest.

The man Sophie was hauling through the restaurant like a six-foot-tall piece of luggage? The one in baggy khakis and a raggedy blue button-down that had seen its best days back in 1975? It was their father.

"Madison!" Sophie called from halfway across the restaurant, her arms outstretched. Dozens of gold bangles clinked musically along her wrists.

Heads turned in Madison's direction—something

Madison usually relished. But oh no, not now, not today. She wished, for the first time, to be completely invisible.

Sophie was practically skipping toward her in a brightly colored maxidress that looked like it came from Haight-Ashbury. "Hey, big sis!" she cried.

"Little sis!" Madison leaned in to hug Sophie and pulled her close. After three seasons of reality TV, she knew just how quiet she needed to be to make sure her mike didn't pick up a word. "I will destroy you for this, you pseudo-hippie bitch," she whispered.

Sophie backed away from Madison, smiling as if she'd heard nothing. But her eyes were like shards of blue ice. "I brought you a surprise," she said, turning a little to her left, looking entirely too pleased with herself.

"Hello, Charlie." Madison didn't reach out her hand or move toward her father. Instead, she examined him the way she might look at last season's cocktail dress on the 75-percent-off rack: without visible emotion. Charlie Wardell had salt-and-pepper hair, a sharp, strong nose, and eyes that were the same vivid blue as Madison's, as Sophie's. It was the only thing he left them with.

Madison hadn't seen him since she was nine years old, unless you counted the faded photos she'd kept in a shoebox under her bed. She and Sophie had looked at those pictures obsessively on the afternoons that their mother went out to the bar and forgot to come home for dinner, or for bedtime, or sometimes even for breakfast the next morning. It was like they thought that if they looked at pictures of him hard enough, he'd actually come back and rescue them.

"Can you believe our dad is here?" Sophie asked, pointedly emphasizing the word "dad."

Madison stiffened. She'd never refer to this man as her dad. She hadn't had a dad for ten years, and she wasn't about to pick one up now. "Well, this is a surprise," she said, keeping her voice low and even. "I came here expecting lunch and a new pair of Manolos. Family reunion wasn't on the schedule today."

She glanced over at Sophie, who was beaming with fake benevolence. Her little sister would pay for this. She would absolutely fucking pay for bringing this man here, to ground zero of the L.A. power lunch, and while the cameras were rolling.

Charlie sat down next to her, and suddenly Madison was nearly brought to her knees by the old, familiar smell of him. *Oh my God*, she thought, *he still wears Old Spice*. She used to sit in his closet after he left, among the flannel shirts that smelled like his aftershave. She felt her throat constrict.

But she was *Madison Fucking Parker*. She did not—she would not—cry.

"So what brings you to L.A.?" Madison asked, miraculously mastering her trembling voice. "I mean, besides the fact that you're a broke ex-con with two daughters on TV? I'm assuming that's why you're here, right? For the paycheck?"

"Madison," Sophie said, shaking her head. "That's a little harsh."

"What's harsh is deserting a nine- and six-year-old to be raised by an unstable alcoholic." Madison turned and met her father's eyes. "I mean really. What kind of person *does* that?"

Charlie looked away from Madison and fiddled with his napkin. Good. She hoped he felt embarrassed and ashamed. She hoped he'd feel so disgusted with himself that he'd crawl back under whatever rock Sophie and Trevor had turned over to find him.

"You changed your name," Charlie finally said. His voice was soft.

A quick thrill flashed through Madison. She remembered that voice. Reading her stories before bed. Singing her to sleep. Holding her tight when her mother was in a drunken rage.

"The name I gave you," he went on.

She laughed harshly. "Right. That was about all you gave me, wasn't it?" *That and some serious abandonment issues*, she thought melodramatically.

He looked down at his hands, which were gripping the napkin so hard his knuckles were white. "I know you probably hate me," he said. "And Sweetpea, I'd hate me too if I were you."

Sweetpea, Madison thought. *Why doesn't he just take a fork and stab me in the heart?* That was his old pet name for her, and how she had loved it when he said it! But this was the man who was supposed to take care of her, protect her, make everything all right. And he hadn't done any of that. He had simply up and vanished.

"You've grown up so much," he said.

Madison wanted to scream. He might seem repentant, but he was just like Sophie: He was looking for a quick payday.

"I'm not here for the money," Charlie said. "If that's what you're thinking."

"Oh, and why would I think that?" Madison asked. "You've had years to try to find me, and now when I've got my third show and some money in the bank this is the first time you try to contact me? You want me to believe it's coincidental?"

"The first time?" Charlie looked from Madison to Sophie in confusion. "This isn't the first time I've tried to contact you."

Madison held up a hand. "Save it. No phone calls, no visits, not even a fucking *birthday* card—"

Charlie paled. "You didn't get my letters?"

"No, I didn't."

"Well, honey, I sent them every month at least. I never missed, except for that month I was in the hospital with pneumonia. That time I only managed a postcard."

Madison stared at him. And then she turned toward Sophie, who looked genuinely clueless, too. Their dad was a liar and a deadbeat, and she knew he would say anything right now to win her over, which he'd obviously already managed with Sophie. But this was cruel. "Well I never got any letters."

"Is he in there?" Madison demanded. The girl sitting at the desk outside Trevor's office opened her mouth, but Madison didn't pause for her answer. She strode past her, toward the closed double doors. She was not to be screwed with. Not like this, and not on national TV. No sir, she was not getting paid enough for this Wardell family shitshow.

"I'm sorry." The assistant jumped up from her chair and raced around her desk toward Madison. "But you can't just go in there, you can't—"

"Like hell I can't." Madison shoved the door open.

Trevor's back was turned. He was gazing out one of his giant windows, his Bluetooth blinking in his ear.

"How *dare* you pull that shit with me?" she started. "You want to make me a laughingstock? 'Poor little Madelyn Wardell with her ex-con father and drunken mother and psycho sister.' That is *low*, Trevor, even for you."

"Joe, can I call you back?" Trevor asked mildly. He watched Madison as she stood there fuming. "Great, talk to you later." He clicked off.

"You're using me," she barreled on. "I told you I'd go to that stupid audition for you, but my past is not some toy for you to play with, and it isn't something I want dragged out in front of all of America. Didn't we go over this with

L.A. Candy? I am not Madelyn Wardell. I am Madison Parker. My family is not at your disposal whenever you feel like a ratings boost."

Trevor smiled at her. "Sit," he said, gesturing to a leather armchair. "Take a breath, Madison."

She shook her head. She was going to remain standing, thank you. She was going to make Trevor understand that what he'd done was wrong. For one, it was an emotional ambush. For two, it reminded people that she was not the upmarket, uptown glamour girl she seemed to be, but instead, the ambitious, self-promoting daughter of upstate New York trailer trash.

"It's one thing to bring back Sophie," Madison said. "But my, my—" She absolutely couldn't get her lips to wrap around the word "dad."

Trevor shrugged. "You wanted to be the star of *The Fame Game,* didn't you?"

"Yes, but—"

"Well, guess what? The star has to be surprised." He ambled toward his desk, that infuriating, mild smile still on his face. As if he had not a care in the world, he sank slowly into his chair and looked up at Madison. "Surprise," he said.

Madison turned toward the window that overlooked Santa Monica. She felt the anger begin to deflate in her chest. Why did he always have to be right about these things? "You did this to Jane," Madison said, shaking her head. "Of course." And, ironically (and oh-so-fittingly), many of the surprises that Jane Roberts had faced were those that Madison herself helped create. How was that for karma?

"Makes for great ratings," Trevor said. "I don't have to tell *you* that, Madison. We don't even have the footage back, but I know already that this episode—with you and your long-lost dad—will be one of our biggest. This story arc . . . Well, I couldn't have written it better." He pressed his fingers together under his chin, looking very pleased with himself.

But this is my life, Madison wanted to say. *It's more than just a story arc to me!*

"This is how these shows work," Trevor went on, his voice smooth and oily. "It's a foolproof format. Find one seemingly sane girl and surround her with a whole lot of crazy. You want to be the star? You have to be the victim, too. Look, you've had a great year. You rebounded from the *L.A. Candy* finale. And, lawsuit aside, *Madison's Makeovers* was a success. You've got thousands of fans, Madison. And they don't just love to hate you anymore. They actually love you. Take advantage of that."

Madison closed her eyes. Take advantage of it? Trevor wanted her to use her ugly past to create her perfect future. Was that even possible?

"Look," Trevor said. He got up again and came over to place his arm on Madison's shoulder. "You just worry about looking good. Let me worry about the story lines. I promised you'd come out on top, didn't I?"

Madison nodded. The rage that she'd felt had disappeared, and now all that was left was confusion. And sadness.

"Well, do you trust me or not?" He gave her a little squeeze.

Without meaning to, Madison flinched. Knowing Trevor as well as she did, she could answer that question with two words: Definitely not.

11

ALL GROWN UP

"What about these?" Madison asked, thrusting a pair of slim, indigo jeans in Kate's direction. "These are J Brand."

They were in American Rag, the first stop on their scheduled shopping spree, which Kate now knew was also step one in a Kate makeover plotline, although that wasn't exactly how the day was panning out. The cameras had filmed Madison modeling a spangly frock and a pair of Rochas leopard-spotted mules, then a silky Chloé jump-suit with strappy gold sandals. According to Laurel's texts, it was time for Kate to do a little shopping herself.

IT'S SUPPOSED TO BE *YOUR* MAKEOVER, REMEMBER? Laurel had written. HAVE SOME FUN. ☺

Kate took a few steps closer to inspect the jeans. The wash was so dark it was almost black. She touched the seam lightly, then saw the price tag. "Oh my God," she said. "They're like two hundred dollars."

"I know! They're a steal!" Madison repeated, brushing a golden lock of hair from her face impatiently.

"But they're just *jeans*," Kate said.

Madison barked out a laugh. "You're so funny, Kate."

"I don't see what's so funny about that," she said, turning to look at a pretty printed blouse. The price tag on it was a mere $135. A bargain!

Madison came around the rack of clothes and snatched the blouse away from Kate. "No prints," she said firmly. "Not yet. We're going to start with the classics, but updated, with a twist."

"You sound like *Lucky* magazine."

"Mmmm," Madison replied. She was distracted, thumbing through the racks of shirts and skirts. "I actually consider leopard print to be a neutral," she mused, more to herself than Kate. "And you're supposed to be sort of a rocker. . . ."

Kate hadn't ever thought of herself as a rocker, that was for sure. But she didn't protest. She took a long, fuzzy sweater off the rack and held it up. It was cream-colored and impossibly soft, and Kate could imagine curling up in it on her couch. She pressed it to her cheek. It felt like a teddy bear.

"Gaaah," cried Madison, snatching it away. "What is this? A Snuggie?" She tossed it onto the padded daybed in the corner of the shop.

"But it's a neutral," Kate pointed out.

"It looks like a potato sack," Madison said. "You're not buying it."

"Okay," Kate said meekly. She decided not to touch

anything else. She'd just let Madison, who was clearly the expert, handle the selections.

She was actually kind of enjoying herself, though. She was drinking a delicious chai latte, it was a lovely July day, and she was relaxed from the pedicure they'd gotten before the shopping began in earnest. Madison was being bossy, but in a helpful way, and frankly it was about time someone got Kate to shop somewhere besides the Gap. If Trevor thought the world would want to see a nice Midwestern girl go Hollywood fashionista, well, she was reasonably happy to oblige him.

"Just get me stuff that I can wash," she called to Madison. "I don't want to have to deal with dry cleaners."

Madison looked up over the racks of clothes just long enough to roll her eyes.

Kate snickered. No one would ever accuse Madison of not having an opinion.

As Kate watched her castmate amass an armload of clothing for her to try on, she wondered if Madison was being nice because she felt like it or because she was supposed to, for a story line. Could her friendliness be genuine? Carmen would argue no. But Madison hadn't been getting texts from Laurel, as far as Kate could see, telling her to pretend like she cared about someone besides herself. (Meanwhile Kate was getting them with embarrassing regularity: SMILE! And CAN YOU LOOK LESS BORED? And PULL HAIR AWAY FROM FACE.)

She'd surreptitiously glanced over at Laurel, who

grinned and gave her a thumbs-up sign. Kate liked Laurel. And even more than that, she liked feeling that she had an ally behind those big black cameras.

Madison pranced over and thrust a silky navy sweater, skinny jeans, a gold belt, and a pair of dove-gray ankle boots at Kate. "Here," she said. "Try these first."

Obediently Kate rose and slipped into the dressing room. She pulled on the various pieces of the outfit and twisted her hair up in a loose knot to avoid any future blocking issues. When she pulled back the curtain and stepped out of the little room, Madison clapped her hands gleefully.

"Look at you! I wouldn't recognize you. Skinnies and some booties and oh my God, it's like you're all grown up all of a sudden." Madison looked pleased with herself.

Kate turned toward herself in the mirror and saw that Madison was right: She looked strikingly different. Sophisticated. Polished. Pretty. "Wow," she said. "I feel like Carmen or something."

Madison sniffed. "You're much prettier than Carmen. It's just that she knows how to maximize her assets, and you don't. Not yet. But I'm going to teach you." She held out another outfit. "Now try this one."

Madison definitely had a good eye, Kate thought. As the clothes piled up on the dressing room benches she began to feel a mix of elation and dread. On the one hand, she was finally going to look like she had a sense of fash-ion. On the other hand, her bank account was going to take a serious hit.

And so it went for another two hours, with Madison selecting the clothes and Kate dutifully putting them on. After the first hour, Laurel and the crew were satisfied they'd gotten what they needed and had packed up to go film Gaby walking out of her dressing room a dozen times. Laurel said that was approximately how many takes it took for Gaby to get something right. To Kate's surprise, Madison hadn't bolted as soon as the cameras were gone.

"The boys are going to love you in that," Madison said, nodding at the sea-green shift dress that Kate had donned. "It makes your legs look amazing."

Kate blushed—both at the mention of boys and her legs.

"Why are you looking at me like that?" Madison demanded, smirking. "Did you meet someone?"

Kate sighed. "I might have met someone at Whisper the other night. After you and Sophia left."

Kate looked to see if the mention of her castmate's sister elicited any kind of reaction, but Madison simply raised an eyebrow in interest and said, "Do tell." God, she was good at pretending like nothing fazed her. Kate guessed that a couple seasons of being on reality TV could do that to a person.

Kate shrugged. "I don't know that much about him, really," she said. "But he's an actor and he plays the bass, and he might be the cutest guy I've ever seen. His name is Luke, and he has these green eyes. . . ." She lost herself in remembering Luke's charms. The way they'd found themselves talking and laughing about their childhoods. The way he gleefully agreed when she said that Justin Timberlake's best work was that Liquor Mart song he'd performed on *Saturday Night Live*. The way he had put his hand on the small of her back when they were leaving the club. The way he—

Madison waved a hand in her face. "Whoa, hello?" she said, smiling. "I think we lost you there."

"Sorry," Kate said. "I was just thinking. . . ."

"Is he famous? Would I know him?"

"Not likely," Kate said. "Sounds like he's still trying to make it."

"So you only met him once," Madison said, and Kate nodded. "Well, we'll have to change that immediately." She paused. "Did you tell him about *The Fame Game*?"

"No. It didn't occur to me," Kate admitted. The cameras had been gone by then, and Kate hadn't given them another thought. And it was such a weird thing to tell someone. *Yeah, I'm a runner at this restaurant Stecco but secretly I'm about to be a reality TV star.* She could never imagine saying something like that.

Madison nodded approvingly. "That's definitely for the best. If he knew, he might not be into it. I mean, actors sometimes think that what we do isn't legit. They think that memorizing lines makes them better than us." She shook her head, as if in disbelief. "And if he *is* into it, then you have to wonder: Does he like you for you? Or does he like you for the camera time that you represent?"

Madison was kind of blowing Kate's mind—and

bursting her bubble. As if meeting guys in L.A. wasn't already difficult enough!

"Trust me, Kate, you want to let this develop naturally."

Let *what* develop naturally? Kate wanted to know. She wasn't even sure she'd ever see Luke again. He might not call her, and she was definitely not the type to make the first move. "Okay," she said uncertainly.

"You're still a nobody," Madison said gently. "And I mean that in the nicest possible way. But when the premiere airs? Say good-bye to anonymity and everything else you thought you knew about your friends and your family and your life."

"Wow," Kate said. "You make that sound sort of . . . scary."

"It's not," Madison assured her. "It's amazing. But it's crazy, too. Anyway, do you have this guy's number?"

"Yes, he put it in my phone before he dropped me off."

"Good," Madison said. "Can I borrow your phone for a second?"

"Uh, yeah, sure," Kate said. "What for . . . ?"

"Thanks." Madison quickly snatched the proffered phone, typed into it for a moment, and then returned it to Kate. "You have a date," she said. "Tonight."

Kate felt her mouth drop open. She had to hand it to Madison. That girl did not mess around.

When the knock sounded on her door, Kate still wasn't ready, even though she knew her time was up since she'd just buzzed Luke into the building. She'd spent two hours trying to figure out which one of her new outfits to wear, but she couldn't remember which jeans Madison had paired with which top and shoes. Did the ankle boots go with the skinnies, or was she supposed to wear the ballet flats? She just wanted everything to be perfect. She should have had Madison make her a cheat sheet.

The knock came again, louder this time.

"Come in," she yelled. "I'll be out in one second—" Maybe she should just give up and wear that old Gap sweater, the one with the stripes.

"I'm a little early," Luke called. She could hear him coming into the living room. "Sorry."

"It's okay," she called back. She loved the way he talked. Was there anything cuter than an Australian accent? A baby koala, maybe. "Really, I'm almost ready."

She hurried over to the mirror and was surprised to see that she'd actually managed to pull one of her new outfits together. She quickly ran a comb through her hair (Madison told her their next outing would include a trip to the hair salon), and then she went to find her date. Or whatever he was. She wasn't actually sure.

"Hey," Luke said, smiling at her. "You look great."

"Thanks," she said. "So do you." He had on faded jeans and a leather motorcycle jacket. His longish brown hair looked tousled and windblown.

"Do you have a coat?" he asked.

"What for? It's, like, eighty degrees outside."

His grin stretched wider. "You'll see. Just grab something warm."

She went to the closet and grabbed an old leather jacket. (Too bad today's shopping extravaganza had not included any new outerwear.) "Okay," she said, pulling it on and hoping it didn't totally ruin her look. "Jacket donned."

She followed him down the hallway and out to the front of the building. The sun was beginning to set, and a warm breeze was rustling through the leaves of the potted bamboo that bordered the parking lot.

"Where are you taking me?" Kate asked.

"You'll see." He stopped and turned back to her. "Your chariot awaits," he said.

She looked at him in confusion. Where was his car? Was he talking about the cab across the way? Then she noticed that he was standing in front of a gleaming black BMW motorcycle. "That?" she said. "You came here on *that*?"

He laughed. "Sure did." He reached into a compartment on the bike and pulled out two helmets. He handed the smaller one to her. "Here you go," he said.

She shook her head. "No way."

He made a pouting face, revealing dimples. "Surely you're not afraid of a motorcycle."

"No, but I'm afraid of my mother, and her number-one house rule was no motorcycles," she said.

"Let me tell you something interesting about a

motorcycle," Luke said. "You asked me where we were going. And I'll tell you that it doesn't even matter where we're going, because you're going to have the time of your life getting there."

Kate felt her heart pounding lightly in her chest. It could have been the bike or it could have been Luke, it was hard to say. She took a deep breath, reached out, and reluctantly took the helmet from him.

"Now climb up and hold on tight," he directed, slinging his leg over the leather seat.

Kate scrambled on behind him and leaned forward. Her arms wrapped around his waist. It felt strange and thrilling to be this close to him. She tightened her grip as he pulled out of the parking lot and into the street.

The wind whipped her hair as Luke took winding curves upward into the hills, and the sky turned brilliant shades of pink and violet as they passed Spanish mission–style homes and classic California bungalows surrounded by pockets of rustling palm and madrone trees. At first she tried yelling questions at him over the noise of the engine and the wind, but each time he turned his chin toward her, shook his head, and yelled, "I can't hear you!"

She was nervous for what felt like ten miles, but by the time he turned right, pulled through a cluster of trees, and slowed the bike to a stop, Kate was ready to invest in a motorcycle herself. Although, she reflected, her own motorcycle would unfortunately not come equipped with a gorgeous driver.

Luke put the kickstand down and turned toward her. "Ever been up here before?"

"I don't even know where we are."

"Look behind you," he said.

Kate turned around, and there, glowing in the fading light, was that iconic symbol of fame: the Hollywood sign. "Oh!" she exclaimed.

"Here, come on." Luke grabbed her hand and they made their way to the edge of the turnout. The hill dropped steeply away toward the valley, but makeshift stairs had been carved into the rocky dirt and led to the giant white letters.

"There's a place to sit down that way," Luke said.

A few moments later they were close enough to the H to reach out and touch the whitewashed metal.

"This is so cool," Kate said, turning her gaze between the giant letters and the sparkling grid of Los Angeles below them. She could see the Capitol Records Building and the lights from The Grove. She couldn't see the ocean, but she knew where it was, because that was where the lights stopped and the darkness began. "Do you come up here a lot?"

"Not much anymore," Luke said. "I used to, when I first moved to L.A. four years ago. Being up this high makes it all seem—I don't know"—Luke scrubbed his hand through his hair—"more *manageable* or something."

Kate nodded in complete agreement. Even with some success (and especially without any), L.A. could seem so overwhelming. Everyone here wanted something: money, fame, success; a starring role, a record contract; a chance at making his or her dreams come true. And it seemed like most people would do just about anything to get it.

"Do you ever wonder what it would have been like if you'd stayed in Australia?" she asked.

"You mean, what if I was okay with being Australian successful instead of trying to be Hollywood successful?"

"I guess," she said.

"I do wonder. My mother certainly doesn't, though. She's completely sure I made a horrible decision coming here. She thought that after things didn't work out with *Fight or Flight*, I should've gone back home immediately."

Kate had never heard of that movie when Luke told her about it the other night. Luke explained that of course she hadn't because before it was released the star (who Kate definitely *had* heard of) was arrested for drunk driving and apparently said some completely misogynistic stuff to the female cop who'd pulled him over. And someone had filmed it. His name was poison after that and the movie went straight to DVD.

"Sometimes I even wonder what it would be like if I'd just gone to university, gotten a job, got a promotion, and settled down."

"Yeah?" She sat on a step and Luke crouched next to her.

"It does seem like it would be easier sometimes," Luke said. "Don't you think?"

"Maybe, but you don't get a view like this in Ohio."

Luke was gazing intently at her, his green eyes smiling. "Yes, the view is definitely better around here," he said.

She gave him a little punch on the arm. "Shut up," she said.

He laughed. "I was just testing you. I want to make sure you don't fall for any corny old line."

"I'm not a total innocent," Kate said. But she wondered how true this was. Ethan had been her first and last boyfriend; it wasn't like she was chock-full of romantic experience. But did this, right now, count as romantic experience? Luke was flirting with her, but maybe he was just that way. She had Googled him earlier and saw him on the red carpet with a few different girls. Maybe he was one of those guys who got off on making girls like him. She really had no idea. She'd wanted to ask Carmen about him, but she didn't want to bother her—Carmen had told her she was sequestering herself for a few days to prepare for some big audition.

Kate gazed out over the glittering landscape. "I want to be somebody," she said suddenly, as if informing the lights of L.A. itself. "I want to write songs that matter to people."

"Do you hear that, L.A.?" Luke yelled. "Kate Hayes is going to take you by storm! And so am I!" He stopped and smiled, then added, "Whenever I can get away from the GEICO commercials, that is."

Kate laughed. "There's no shame in a commercial," she said. Thinking: *And there's no shame in reality TV, either.*

Right? "I mean, whatever pays the rent. And keeps your agent returning your calls."

"Something like that." Luke reached over and took her hand. He looked at her fingers as he spoke. "So, I didn't ask before, but is there someone back in Ohio?"

Kate flushed, thinking of Ethan, whom she still emailed almost daily. When she was lonely, she missed him. Or was it just that she missed her home and everything that was familiar?

"That's sort of a long pause," Luke said, interrupting her thoughts. "Does that mean—"

Kate shook her head vehemently. "No," she said. "There isn't anyone."

Luke smiled. "Good," he said. And then he leaned forward and kissed her, with all of L.A. laid out at their feet.

12

CARMEN CUPID CURTIS

Carmen felt like she was floating out of the building. She'd *nailed* her reading for *The End of Love*. She could feel it in her bones—the way her dad could feel a future *Billboard* chart-topper, or her grandma could sense rain coming on. It was as if, the moment she took the script in hand, every ounce of Carmen Curtis had evaporated. She had *become* Julia Capsen. She'd spent the last few days holed up in her room re-reading the script and the book the movie was based on, stopping only to take notes on Julia, the star-crossed heroine of the story (and, okay, to eat and sleep . . . and grab a quick brunch with Fawn that turned into brunch and a once-around the Runyon loop and a mani-pedi—Fawn was a terrible influence!). She had so believed in Julia's futuristic, war-torn world that when the reading was over, Carmen was almost surprised to find herself in relatively peaceful 2012, in a simple bungalow on the studio lot.

Whether or not her excellent performance would

result in a role, no one could say—but at least she'd shown Colum McEntire, the director, and all those PopTV Films people that she wasn't just some entitled brat riding the coattails of her famous parents. After today, they'd have to acknowledge that her talent was all her own.

A few short weeks ago, Colum had been completely uninterested in auditioning her; rumor had it his eye was on Bryn Malloy, a distant cousin of his who'd starred in a bunch of teen-superhero movies and was ready for more gritty roles. But when Carmen had gone in for a meeting with her agent last week, Johnny had told her that there was a change in plans; she was going to read for the part after all. Because the PopTV cameras were rolling, she didn't ask Johnny what had made Colum McEntire decide that she wasn't just an L.A. party girl who liked to swipe clothes from designer boutiques. Besides, she was pretty sure she knew: the incredible persuasive powers of Trevor Lord.

Not that she'd minded one bit. In fact, she was downright grateful to that manipulative ratings hound. All she'd needed was a foot in the door, because once she was in, she knew she would blow them away. That was the thing: Everyone assumed she'd just decided on a whim to be an actress, and that she'd get bored and flit on to wanting to be a fashion designer or have her own record label or whatever. They didn't realize she'd been taking acting classes for years, had always gotten the lead in school plays (except the musicals), and sometimes spent Saturday nights reading Shakespeare so she could parse the words and get at the emotions behind them.

The cameras had naturally accompanied her to the audition, and she'd tried not to show how nervous she was. She kept biting her lip, though, until Laurel texted her: EAT SANDWICH, NOT OWN MOUTH.

As she entered the bungalow, flanked by the PopTV cameras, she was surprised to find Madison in the waiting area, script in hand and her own camera in the corner. Madison looked up, and her brow furrowed almost imperceptibly. *It would probably be a full-on frown if it weren't for the years of Botox injections,* Carmen thought. "Fancy meeting you here," she said, sitting down across from her castmate.

"Small world," Madison said coolly. She was looking through an issue of *Gossip*, no doubt searching for some mention of herself in it.

Carmen hadn't ever imagined that Madison had thespian desires. But maybe it wasn't so surprising. The girl would do anything to be famous, and if hosting a makeover show wasn't doing it for her, maybe being on the big screen would. Well, Carmen wished her luck with that. She was pretty sure she'd need it.

After a few more tense, silent moments, a short, grayhaired woman called her name, and Carmen went in to kick some acting ass. The cameras were relegated to the reception area.

Another surprise? She'd be reading with Luke Kelly, who was looking gorgeously ragged as Roman, her character's love interest. They hadn't talked since the night at Whisper, but apparently he had the role sewn up. She wasn't sure what happened with Luke and Kate last week, but if Kate wasn't interested, maybe Carmen could have a little fun with him. She'd made out with him one night a few months ago and wouldn't mind doing it again. He smiled at her as she sat down, so nervous at first that her palms were icy and damp. "Bryn's going to have nothing on you, mate," he'd whispered.

She had hoped he was right.

And, as it turned out, he was.

"I mean, I could be crazy," Carmen said, fiddling with the straw in her iced coffee. "Maybe I totally sucked."

Luke shook his head. "No. You were amazing. Seriously, I had chills."

"Oh please," Carmen snorted. "They just had the AC up too high. Did you see my goose bumps?"

"Hey now," Luke said, nudging her elbow playfully. "You can talk about how great you were, but then when I try to back you up you pretend like I'm full of shit? That's low, Curtis."

She laughed. "Sorry," she said. "You know us actors. We're all crazy."

"Speak for yourself," Luke said, feigning offense. "You're the one with a reality show, which is its own special brand of crazy, right? I'm as sane as they come."

"Whatever you say." Out of the corner of her eye, Carmen could see a couple of girls staring openmouthed at

Luke, trying to decide if he was in fact Doctor Rose, from *Boston General*. She wasn't offended in the slightest that they didn't seem to recognize her; in fact she preferred it that way. Carmen had always found it exhausting to be stared at by strangers. If it went on too long—whether it was in a grocery store or on a red carpet—she always felt the urge to run home and jump in the shower. Which, she knew, made her recent career choices somewhat suspect. "Don't look now," she said, "but I think you have some fans."

Luke hunched his shoulders a little, as if this could shield him from their adoring gazes. "Are they coming over here?"

Carmen shook her head. "Don't think so. They look kind of shy. I think they're tourists."

"Good," he said. "I'm not up for it today. Can you frown at them a little? Look, I don't know, possessive and intimidating?"

"I could kiss you again," Carmen offered. "A little Roman and Julia reprise."

"Uh—" Luke said, looking uncertain.

"What?" she demanded. "It's not like we've never kissed before. Was it so horrible that you can't bear to—?"

"No, no. Not at all. It's just . . ."

"Wait! Oh my God, you're blushing. You *like* someone!" She grabbed his hand and squeezed it happily. Her own love life was nonexistent, so she might as well live vicariously. (Making out with him would have to be strictly professional then.) "Tell me this instant or I will break your finger."

Luke hesitated, then spoke. "That friend of yours. Kate."

Carmen sat back and crossed her arms. "Shut. Up."

Luke shrugged. "She hasn't said anything to you?"

Carmen shook her head.

"Maybe I kept her too busy this week. What can I say? We hit it off. She's down-to-earth. She's talented. She's totally *not* a typical Hollywood girl. And she's beautiful, too, but she doesn't seem to have any idea. Which I appreciate."

"I will overlook the fact that she didn't tell me and just be excited. Oh, this is awesome!" Carmen clapped her hands, genuinely thrilled. "I love her, and I totally put you guys together! You can just call me Carmen Cupid Curtis."

Luke laughed. "All right, Carmen Cupid Curtis. How do you know her, anyway?"

Carmen looked at him in surprise. "She didn't tell you?"

"Tell me what?"

Carmen was chewing an ice cube, and Luke tapped his fingers impatiently until she could speak again. "She's on *The Fame Game* with me," she said.

Luke's eyebrows shot up and disappeared under his dark bangs. "You're kidding," he said. "Wow." He scratched at the scruff on his chin, looking confused and slightly perturbed. "Why didn't she tell me that?"

"I don't know," Carmen admitted. "Shyness? Embarrassment? Midwestern reticence?" She poked him with her straw. "You don't mind, though, right?" she asked.

Luke thought about this for a minute. "No," he said finally. "I guess I don't. But I still think it's kind of weird that she didn't say anything."

"Fine," Carmen said. "It's weird. But so is a platypus."

Luke shot her a look. "What in the world are you talking about?"

Carmen laughed and reached out to pinch his cheek. She was pretty convinced that Luke was really no slicker than Kate when it came down to it. They could be wide-eyed foreigners in L.A. together, making a successful go of it but being slightly baffled the whole time. "I'm just saying, what seems weird to you seems fine to someone else. No doubt the platypus thinks a kitten looks totally bizarre."

"I seriously have no idea what you're talking about," Luke said. "Did they put something illegal in your coffee?"

Carmen grinned. She was feeling punchy but it was from her post-audition adrenaline. "Nope. Just high on life. But hey, let's get out of here. I need to hit the gym, and you, Doctor Rose, have got a few autographs to sign." She paused. "And Kates to kiss. Get it? You know, *Kiss Me, Kate*?"

Luke rolled his eyes. "You are crazy," he said.

Carmen sighed dramatically. "Yes, but you love me anyway."

13

A LITTLE OLD
FOR STUFFED ANIMALS

Madison wanted to know which PopTV genius had the idea to film at Santa Monica Pier, that tacky, run-down tourist trap jutting into the Pacific Ocean. Was Trevor trying to torture her by sending her to a place with gross food and grosser people? Or had he farmed out this shoot to Laurel, who seemed to enjoy watching Madison squirm?

Of course, the location wasn't even the worst of it. Maybe, if she held her nose and wore her biggest, darkest sunglasses, she could tolerate being among the unwashed masses, their stupid carnival games and their greasy funnel cake carts. But could she face it with her sad-sack father and her sociopathic sister in tow? She wasn't feeling her typical confidence.

Part of her bad mood came from her audition for *The End of Love*, which was weighing on her. She knew that some people accused her of having an overly inflated opinion of herself. Fine. But she wasn't the type to lie to herself.

In many things, Madison Parker was downright awesome. But in her reading with Luke Kelly, she had completely and totally sucked. The only saving grace was that the PopTV cameras were only permitted as far as the waiting room.

When Trevor pitched her this story line (it was more like he told her to go to the audition if she wanted screen time *not* with her freeloading family), she knew it wasn't going to end well for her. She would look like exactly what she never wanted to be: an oblivious wannabe. Even if she could emote like Meryl Streep, there was no way in hell any director would take a chance on Madison. Nobody who came from reality TV had gone on to be taken seriously as an actress. (That girl from *The Real World* didn't count—that was the '90s, which was practically another lifetime.) But somehow she'd forgotten all that while she was learning her lines and rehearsing with Gaby. She'd let in a sliver of hope that she didn't suck and that she'd have a chance, and for that she'd never forgive herself, or Trevor.

She cringed at the memory of stumbling over her lines. When she mispronounced the name of a minor character, she'd heard a snicker at the back of the room. She couldn't relax at all; it was as if she'd split into two people, one of whom was trying desperately to do a decent job of reading the script and another who was hovering nearby, witnessing her failure. She wished she'd gotten her hands on some beta-blockers, or at the very least a Xanax, before the reading.

Now, as she turned around so the sound guy could attach a mike box to her bra strap, Madison tried to convince herself that she'd have another chance to do it better. She'd never acted before—surely Colum McEntire didn't expect her to be perfect her first time!

Though, admittedly, in a way she'd been acting ever since she'd moved to L.A. Even before she was on *L.A. Candy* or *Madison's Makeovers* or *The Fame Game*, she'd been pretending to be someone she wasn't. She'd dyed her hair, spray-tanned her skin, and nipped and tucked in the places that needed it. Ever so carefully, she had constructed a new person; and, just as carefully, she had given that new person a fitting history.

Madison had dreamed up glamorous, wildly successful parents who were camera-shy, old-money jet-setters (which explained why no one could ever find them and put their pictures in a tabloid). She had told stories of a childhood spent mansion-hopping and teen years spent abroad.

Madison had been imagining better parents for herself ever since her days in Armor Falls. And, when she stopped to think about it, that was when she began her acting career, too. She'd acted as if she wasn't embarrassed to be wearing the same pair of dirty jeans to school day after day. She acted as if she'd forgotten her lunch, when in fact there was no food in the house. She acted as if her mother was sick with the flu, as opposed to puking her guts out from a massive hangover (which Sophie, at least, always believed). She acted that she didn't mind being unpopular, when every single day her loneliness was like a tiny knife piercing her heart.

Yes, Madison Parker was a born actress. Too bad she could only deliver lines that she herself had written.

Her BlackBerry buzzed, and she read Laurel's text: LOOK TO UR LEFT.

Doing as she was told, Madison saw Sophie in the distance, slowly wending her way through the crowd. She knew she had a few more minutes before the cameras began to roll.

SO WHOSE IDEA WAS THIS? Madison texted back.

IT WAS A JOINT EFFORT, Laurel wrote. ☺

Madison took that to mean that she'd come up with it and Trevor had approved. She also assumed the smiley face was sarcastic. Bitch.

She put her BlackBerry back into her purse. "You better not have us on any rides," she yelled. "Those things are filthy."

"Only the Ferris wheel," Laurel called back. Then she quickly ducked behind the cameraman, as if she thought Madison might throw something at her.

Great. Madison hated heights. But this wasn't something she wanted Laurel or Trevor to know, otherwise they'd schedule some outing where all *The Fame Game* girls went skydiving.

"And after the Ferris wheel we'll do cotton candy and the shooting range," Laurel added.

Madison rolled her eyes. Processed sugar and firearms. Perfect. Sophie was getting closer, and she squared her shoulders. It was time for some family bonding, maybe a trip down memory lane. She couldn't think of anything she'd like less. Except for maybe riding the Ferris wheel.

"Maddy!" Sophie yelled, belatedly spotting the cameras and bounding toward them. She wore a giant floppy hat, another maxidress, and a pair of Birkenstocks. Her look was boho—hold the chic.

"Namaste," Sophie said and wrapped Madison in a patchouli-scented hug.

Madison peeled her sister's arms off her. She hated patchouli. And what was with the yogi act? The cameras weren't even on yet.

"Where's—you-know-who?" Madison said. She didn't exactly want to call him Charlie, but she still had a hard time with Dad.

"Parking the car."

Laurel walked toward them, grasping her earpiece. "Okay, on it," she was saying. She turned her attention to them. "I'll be right back. Stay here, and we'll start in a few minutes." Laurel jogged toward the far side of the pier, her ever-present travel mug of coffee in hand.

Sophie reached out and clutched Madison's arm. "Dad desperately wants your forgiveness. This anger you're carrying around really puts off bad energy. It's affecting everything around you."

"Cut the crap," Madison said, tugging her arm from Sophie's grasp. "That might play on-camera, but it's just you and me right now."

Sophie blinked at her with her beautiful, long-lashed

eyes. "This is who I am," she said. "I've spent a long time becoming this person—"

"Six months?" Madison scoffed.

"A person of forgiveness and love. It's really good. You don't have to be filled with rage and pain."

Madison rolled her eyes. "Screw you."

"I can see the anger in your aura. It's bright orange."

Madison barely stifled a guffaw. "Oh really? My aura? Well, I'll be sure to get it bleached along with my roots next time I'm at the salon. Seriously, Sophie, give it a rest."

Sophie pressed her palms together in front of her chest and bowed her head. "What are you doing?" Madison asked.

"Seeking the love of the Divine Goddess for you," Sophie said, without looking up.

Madison turned away in disgust. Either Sophie had taken some acting classes or she was insane. Or, Madison thought, both.

She saw a hand waving eagerly at them then: Charlie. He still looked like he'd dressed himself out of the Goodwill reject box, but he was trying. His shirt was pressed and his khaki pants looked cleaner.

"Good morning, Madison." He rubbed his palms together and appeared uncertain about whether to hug his oldest daughter or shake her hand. He didn't have to make the choice, though, because Laurel came bustling up with two more mike packs in hand.

"The gang's all here," she said brightly, "so let's get started."

Madison clutched the seat bar of the Ferris wheel as it shuddered to a halt. She might vomit. She might pass out. Or—if she was capable of speech—she might call Trevor and give him hell. She didn't care if the cameras were rolling or not. They'd been pointed straight at her for the last painful hour, as three-quarters of the Wardell family from Armpit Falls, New York, spun around and around on a giant rickety wheel above the Pacific Ocean. Sophie was giddy, squealing. Meanwhile Madison had been clutching her stomach in a combination of nausea and fear. She prayed that Laurel wouldn't add a roller-coaster ride to the shooting schedule, because if she did, Madison might not make it.

"I loved it!" Sophie cried, leaping from the still-swinging seat. "Do we have time to go again?"

Laurel shook her head no, and Madison breathed a sigh of relief. She steadied herself against the gate as a dirty-looking carnival worker leered at her.

"You all right?" Charlie asked, touching Madison's elbow. "Here, come here."

She was too queasy to protest as her dad led her to a bench and gently sat her down. "I'll get you some water," he said.

"You know what I want?" Sophie asked, her eyes wide as a little kid's. "I want some cotton candy!"

Madison put her head in her hands. Wow, Sophie was (a) oblivious to her suffering, and (b) hitting every mark and location with the subtlety of a hammer. How much were Trevor and Dana working with Sophie on the Wardell family story line? From the looks of it, a lot—which did not make Madison happy.

Charlie returned and handed her a bottle of water. "Four bucks for that," he said to no one in particular.

Madison took a few sips and eventually stood up. She felt a little better now; the ground wasn't moving beneath her feet. "How about we skip the cotton candy and try the air rifle." She slipped her arm through her father's. It was a small thing, changing the shooting order, but it said that she was in control of the situation. Without waiting for Sophie's response, she began to walk through the crowd, Charlie Wardell at her side. It seemed like the right time to play the role of the forgiving daughter to the repentant father.

At the air rifle booth, cheap stuffed animals—hot-pink pandas, blue kangaroos, acid-green turtles—hung from the rafters in sad-looking clumps. The carnival worker wore a striped apron and desperately needed a shave.

Charlie stepped up to the booth. "You remember the Harvest Festival in that little town on the Hudson, the one I used to take you girls to?" he asked.

A dim memory of cool evenings, carnival rides, and baby animals that you paid ten cents to pet flickered at the edges of Madison's mind. She kept it there at the edges, though, and said nothing. She watched as her father handed over a five-dollar bill to the worker and picked up an air rifle.

"This was always your favorite part," he said.

"Shooting a gun was my favorite?" Madison said skeptically.

"Nope," Charlie said. "Me shooting the gun and you winning a stuffed animal was your favorite." He bent over the counter and let three air pellets fly. Miss. Miss. And . . . a miss. He stood up and shrugged sadly. "I guess my aim's not what it used to be."

"Well, I'm a little old for stuffed animals," Madison said, inexplicably wanting to comfort him. "I like shoes now. Do you think there's a booth where you can win me a pair of the new Marc Jacobs wedges?"

Charlie smiled wistfully. "You're so grown-up," he said. "So sophisticated. You probably don't even remember that old purple unicorn I won you."

"What?" Madison looked at him closely.

"There was this unicorn," Charlie said.

"Yeah, I got that part," Madison said. "It was purple."

"You were only three or four, and you named it Bitsy," Charlie went on, smiling at the memory. "You carried it with you everywhere. I seem to recall wrapping Bitsy in a plastic bag so she could take a bath with you."

"How funny," Madison said. But it wasn't actually funny. Because she still had Bitsy in her apartment, tucked in the back of her sock drawer. She hadn't remembered who'd given her the thing; she only knew that the unicorn was one of the few possessions she took with her when she left Armor Falls. Most of her memories of home were bad, but somehow some old good feelings had been attached to that cheap, made-in-China unicorn. And now she understood why.

She was torn between wanting to hug Charlie and to hit him in the face. (Which would Trevor like more? The punch, probably.) She had loved that unicorn instinctively because it was all she had of her father. Her heart felt tight in her chest.

"Bitsy probably ended up in the Dumpster years ago," Charlie said. "Well, she was your best friend for a long time."

My only friend, thought Madison bitterly. What a joke her life had been! She'd had a drunk for a mother, a convict for a father, a headcase for a sister, and a stuffed animal for a best friend.

But now she was Madison Parker, star of three (well, it'd be three soon enough) hit TV shows. Here on the Santa Monica Pier, amid the bustle of tourists and the stink of fried food, she straightened her spine and tossed her hair back. Thank God things were different now.

"So, it's been great," she said, "but I should really—"

"I thought if I left, then things would get better," Charlie said, as if they were in the middle of discussing a topic neither of them had even gone near today. The sun was in his eyes and he squinted at her. It made him look much older than his forty-two years.

"Well, they didn't," Madison said coldly.

Sophie, who had briefly vanished, reappeared with a

giant snow cone. "Yeah, Dad, it was bad." She shook her head as if lost in a horrible childhood memory. "Really bad." She didn't seem angry so much as baffled. Maybe that was part of her new goddess-of-love trip: She wouldn't blame him for leaving them with a mother who drank Wild Irish Rose for breakfast and whose best efforts in the dinner arena amounted to a few slices of wet ham on sale-rack Wonder Bread.

Well, Madison wasn't Sophie. She was *pissed*. Her mother couldn't even keep a jar of mayonnaise in the fridge for the awful sandwiches! So what if she hadn't realized how much she missed her father until right this very moment—it didn't matter. She was still furious.

"I'm so sorry," Charlie whispered. "I tried to explain in my letters."

God, those stupid letters again, Madison thought. As if they *mattered*, as if they even *existed*. And if they did? Well, you could have a stack of letters ten feet high and they still didn't add up to a father.

She turned on her heel and walked to the edge of the pier. Leaning over the railing, she took a long breath of ocean air. Any dad who vanished for a decade and then showed up only after his daughter had made it was obviously in it for the money. Two could play that game, couldn't they? She, Madison Parker, was in it for the ratings.

Ratings, she whispered. *Ratings, ratings, ratings.*

It was a mantra that kept her from flinging her mike pack into the Pacific Ocean. It gave her strength to turn back around and smile her megawatt smile.

"So," she said to her family, "how about that cotton candy?"

Standing in her colossal walk-in closet, Madison brushed her fingertips along the sleeves of her silk tops, arranged by color from deep jewel red to coral, from lime to lavender. Even in her wildest dreams, she'd never imagined a life like this. That she would own these nice things. She'd been an eight-year-old scrubbing her jeans by hand in the kitchen sink because her mother couldn't be bothered to take them—or anything—to the Laundromat. And now she didn't have to even *touch* her dirty clothes: She tossed them into a basket from which they magically disappeared, and days later they reappeared, wrapped in plastic: crisp, fresh, and clean.

Madison didn't open the dresser toward the back of the room, but she didn't need to. She knew what was in there, nestled in the top drawer: a soft form, its synthetic fur faded and slightly matted, its horn drooping. She felt silly for keeping it all these years.

But, said a nagging voice in the back of her mind, *what if he meant what he said? What if there really were letters? Did that really mean* nothing?

Almost without thinking, Madison pulled her Black-Berry from her pocket and punched in her mother's number. It rang for a long time, and Madison was just about to hang up—probably Sue Beth had lost her phone one night at a bar—when her mother answered.

"Hello?" Sue Beth's voice sounded weary and old. But not drunk: surprisingly sober.

"Mom?"

"Who is this?"

"It's Madison."

"Madison . . . ?" Her mother sounded confused.

"Mom, it's Madelyn." She tugged on one of her platinum extensions. It had been years since she had heard her mother's voice.

"Nice of you to finally call," Sue Beth said, not unkindly. There was a long pause and Madison knew her mother was taking a drag on a Parliament cigarette. "I've seen you on the TV. You look really nice."

Madison's heart clutched with that comment. A compliment was not what she'd expected. "I wanted to tell you that we heard from Charlie," she said. She waited for a response, but none came. "Mom, you still there?"

"I'm here," her mother said. "What exactly do you want me to say? It's not nice to speak ill of a girl's father, even if you think he's a lying rat bastard."

"Right," Madison said. "I just didn't want you to be surprised when you saw it on TV—when you see him on the show, I mean. I didn't ask him to come here. He just showed up. Well, after Sophie reunited with him during rehab. You knew Sophie went to rehab, didn't you?"

Her mother sighed. Or maybe it was just an exhalation of her cigarette. "Yes, Madelyn. I may not have been mother of the year, but I did know that Sophie was in rehab.

In fact, I spoke to her several times while she was there."

"You did?"

"I did," Sue Beth said.

"Wow, if I'd known the fastest way to get my parents' attention would be to crash on booze and drugs maybe I would have tried it," Madison said drily.

"Didn't figure from the looks of your life that you needed me much anymore," Sue Beth said. "That why you called then? To tell me you saw your dad?"

"He mentioned something I wanted to ask you about. Some letters." Madison scrunched her eyebrows together and tilted her head. She wasn't sure which answer she wanted. "He was lying, right?"

Her mother waited a long time before answering. "No, there are letters."

"There are? How many?"

"I don't know. A few dozen, I guess."

"For me? And for Sophie?"

"For both of you, I think," Sue Beth said.

"And you didn't feel like sharing them with us?"

"I didn't want to give you false hope. That man never did anything right in his whole life. I figured those letters were full of promises he never would've kept."

Madison's fury at her mother was matched by her surprise. Charlie wasn't lying. Yes, he'd abandoned her. But he'd tried to stay in touch. He really had. And now he'd come back. He'd finally, after all these years, come back to take care of her.

14

THE BEST IDEA YOU EVER HAD

Kate was curled on the couch, her guitar in her lap and a mug of green tea steaming on the coffee table in front of her. She hummed quietly to herself as she strummed: E minor, D, A minor, C, E minor—but then what? She was stuck on the bridge. She tried a few chords and then shook her head in frustration. She frowned down at her fingers as if it was their fault.

She considered giving up for the night. Maybe she should bake a batch of cookies or something. Presumably the oven worked—not that she'd ever turned it on. (There were just so many good restaurants in L.A., so many convenient take-out joints. It wasn't at all like her little suburban slice of Columbus, Ohio, where the dining choices were either Chili's, the Olive Garden, or the all-you-can-eat Super Buffet.)

She was halfway to the kitchen when she reminded herself that one did not forge a successful music career by baking Nestlé Toll House when times got tough. One *persevered.* She turned, sighing, and headed back to the couch. E minor, D, A minor, C . . . What was that stupid poster her first guitar teacher used to have on his wall? "Success is 1% inspiration and 99% perspiration"?

She picked up her guitar again but kept stealing glances at her phone. She hadn't talked to her sister in a few days. Maybe she should call her. Or maybe Luke would call. They'd hung out a lot in the last week, mostly at the little cottage he rented in Venice. They had taken long walks along the water, people-watched on the boardwalk, and watched old Gregory Peck movies. They'd talked and talked, about all sorts of things—but Kate never said a word about PopTV. She had done just as Madison instructed.

E minor, D, A minor, C, E minor, D, A minor, C . . . Ugh, she was going crazy.

When her buzzer sounded, she tossed her guitar onto the cushions and ran to the intercom. Madison, Sophie, the cable guy—she'd be happy to see anyone, as long as it meant she could take a break from that damn chord progression. "Hello?"

"It's me," Carmen said. "Buzz me in, *chica.*"

Kate happily obeyed and in a few moments Carmen was in her doorway, smiling and holding out a white box tied with pastry string. "I brought cupcakes."

Kate had to stop herself from snatching them from her friend's hands. "You have no idea how badly I was craving sugar. It always happens when I'm stuck on a song."

Carmen followed her into the living room, looking

polished and vaguely French in a pair of slim black pants and a sort of Marcel Marceau–ish striped top. "Rough day at the office?"

Kate laughed. "Well, it's no rougher than being in front of a dozen cameras, that's for sure. But I hate composer's block. It's the worst." She opened the box and selected a pink-frosted cupcake dusted with edible silver glitter. "Ohh, almost too pretty to eat." She smiled.

"Yeah. I actually brought these as an apology," Carmen admitted.

"For what?" Kate asked, her mouth full of delicious cake.

"I accidentally told Luke about you being on *The Fame Game*." Carmen reached for one of the chocolate cupcakes and slowly peeled off the paper wrapper. "I didn't know you were keeping it a secret from him. Why *were* you keeping it a secret from him? Also, why were you keeping *him* a secret from me?"

Kate groaned. "I wasn't—on either account. I mean, I just haven't seen you much this week because you were prepping for your audition. And with Luke, I didn't mean to not tell him, not at first. I just wasn't thinking about it the night we met."

"Fair enough. I forgive you," Carmen said, licking a bit of frosting off her fingertip. "But as for Luke, what about the nights after that first one?"

"Madison told me that I shouldn't tell him."

Carmen shot her a questioning look. "And since when

do sane people take advice from Madison Parker?"

Kate looked down at her hands. She had frosting under her fingernails and her polish was beginning to chip. "She said that if I told him, it might mess things up. Maybe he'd be totally put off and he wouldn't want to see me anymore. Or maybe he'd be so into the idea that pretty soon he wouldn't care about spending time with me—he'd only care about spending time with the PopTV cameras."

While Kate was talking, Carmen was nodding thoughtfully. "Not terrible advice, especially when you consider the source."

"Oh, Carm." Kate laughed. "She's not that bad."

"Everyone is entitled to her own opinion," Carmen said. "But seriously, if it was anyone other than Luke, I'd think she was onto something. Of course, she was probably motivated by some nefarious angle she's trying to work with your story line. But anyway, I'm sorry I screwed it up."

Kate frowned. "Was he mad?"

"No," Carmen said. "I mean, I don't think so."

"I should have just told him." Kate sighed. "I'm so lame."

Carmen reached out and patted her hand. "Hey, Hollywood is crazy. Celebrity is crazy. Trust me, I was born on the sidelines of this game and now I'm on the playing field. And it only gets crazier in there."

"Why does everyone who ever counsels me use sports metaphors?" Kate asked.

Carmen looked puzzled. "What do you mean?"

Kate shook her head, smiling. "Nothing, nothing. You were saying?"

"I was just trying to tell you that getting involved in show business, or whatever you want to call it, can really mess with a person. You have to try to remember who you are. And right now, you're just Kate Hayes, singer-songwriter extraordinaire. Enjoy it like you are enjoying those cupcakes. Seriously, is that already your second?"

Kate looked up guiltily mid-bite. "Urmm?"

"You're going to ruin your appetite for dinner." Carmen laughed. "Oh hey, I think your phone just beeped."

Kate had to search under various pillows for it. When she found it, there was a new text from Luke. Speak of the devil.

IN UR HOOD. CARE 4 COMPANY? She felt a jolt of excitement. Yes, she wanted his company. She wanted to climb on the back of that motorcycle and ride up into the hills with him. But Carmen was on her couch, and pretty soon the two of them were going to have to head over to film an "impromptu" dinner party at Madison and Gaby's place.

"It's Luke," she said to Carmen. "He wants to come over."

"Well, by all means," Carmen said. "I'll make myself scarce until dinner."

Kate texted him that he didn't have much time, so he'd better hurry, and it seemed like she'd hardly said good-bye to Carmen before Luke appeared in her doorway, wearing that motorcycle jacket of his and smelling like wind and sand and leather.

"I didn't hear the buzzer," she said, flustered. She was both excited and nervous to see him.

"Carm let me in," he said, leaning in to kiss her cheek. He'd shaved the stubble that he'd worn for *The End of Love* auditions, and his skin was tan and smooth.

"So, are you mad at me?" she blurted. She couldn't help it. She just had to know for sure immediately.

Luke laughed. "You're not even going to say hello?"

She looked up at him, her expression a mix of embarrassment and hope. "Hello. Are you mad at me?"

"Hmmm," he said, folding her into a hug. "Let me think about this. If I say I'm mad at you, will you be extra, extra nice to me?"

Kate nodded into his broad chest. This was a good sign, wasn't it? You didn't hug a person you were mad at. "Yes," she said, relief flooding through her. "Extra, extra nice."

He put his finger under her chin and lifted it. Their lips met in a swell of warmth and softness, and Kate wrapped her arms around his waist. She felt like she could have kept kissing him forever, but after a moment, Luke pulled away.

"I do wish that I didn't have to hear about it from Carmen," he said. "But I *think* I can forgive you."

"I'm really sorry," she said, twining her fingers in his as they walked into the living room. "I just didn't tell you when we met because it didn't seem important, and then,

I don't know, I thought you might think less of me. I'm a jerk, I know it."

Luke laughed. "No, you're not. You're just new to this kind of thing." He took off his jacket and draped it over the arm of the couch. He was wearing a flannel shirt underneath it, and it sort of made him look like the foxiest lumberjack she'd ever seen.

"Do you think it's a bad idea?" Kate asked. "Being on a show like this?" She didn't know why she was asking him; it wasn't like she could back out now. But then again, she didn't want to.

Luke picked up her guitar and idly strummed a G chord. "I say, whatever helps you live your dream. If *The Fame Game* brings you attention for your music, then it was the best idea you ever had."

Kate flopped down on the couch. "I hope you're right. But the music is . . . well, I'm stuck on this song," she said. "I've got this four-chord progression and the beginning of a melody, but then it all falls apart. I can't get the right chords for the chorus. I'm stuck on those stupid four."

Luke smiled. "Well, I know your problem," he said.

"You do?" she said, blinking hopefully at him. From what he'd told her, she gathered he was a pretty decent bassist—maybe he wrote songs, too.

"Yep. You've got one too many chords. It's like Willie Nelson said: All you need is three chords and the truth."

"Oh, shut up," Kate said, tossing a pillow at him, which he deflected, laughing.

"Ask your friend Carmen," he said. "Her dad's Mr. Pop Music. He knows I'm right and so does she."

"Whatever," she said. "I'm going to stick with my four chords until I wrestle them into submission."

"Uh, you can wrestle me into submission," Luke noted.

Kate threw another pillow, and it hit him in the chest.

"You know what they say about aggression," he said, smirking. "It's a sublimation of intense sexual desire." His green eyes glittered playfully at her.

She laughed and scooted across the cushions to him. How could he be so sexy and so goofy at the same time? She kissed his neck and then his lips. "Mmmm," she said. "But you're the one who said you were mad at *me*, remember?"

"Well, last I checked, sexual desire is often a two-way street."

She crawled onto his lap and threaded her fingers through his, sighing. "But I have to go soon," she said. "It's almost time for my 'spontaneous' dinner party." She sat up suddenly, a thought striking her. "Hey, you don't want to come, do you? Like, to take down the estrogen concentration a notch?"

Luke shook his head. "*The Fame Game* is going to be great for you," he said. "But it wouldn't be so good for me. Not at this point in my career."

She sighed. "I know, you're right. I just thought—"

"It was a sweet thought," he interrupted, kissing her again. "But let's keep us . . . between us."

"Well, Carmen already knows," Kate reminded him.

"No, I mean, let's keep us away from the cameras and all that. Cool?" He continued kissing her.

She closed her eyes. She was glad he didn't want to be on PopTV. A moment like this was perfect and private.

And if they were to keep their relationship a secret? Well, there'd only be more perfect, private moments like this one. Which was fine by her.

15

THAT WAS AWKWARD

"This is delicious, Gaby," Carmen said, carefully dotting the corner of her lips with a napkin. "Too bad I don't cook, or else I'd ask you for the recipe."

"Thanks," Gaby said brightly. "I just sort of whipped it up. You know, a little sea salt, a little olive oil . . ."

Of course Gaby couldn't sear tuna any more than she could tell you what the capital of California was. But Trevor wanted to make it look like Gaby was capable of making something besides sludge-colored smoothies, so they'd ordered the dinner from M Café and hidden the takeaway containers.

The room was hot from all the extra lighting that shooting required, and Carmen wished she'd thought about that before selecting her A.P.C. henley sweater ensemble. She looked around the table, noting somewhat resentfully that the burden of making conversation seemed to have fallen on her thus far. Kate was picking at the salad (those cupcakes had ruined her appetite, just like Carmen said they would), Gaby was now gazing vacantly into her water glass, and Madison was emailing her publicist on her bedazzled iPhone. (Rhinestones were so four years ago.)

"So," Carmen said, turning to Madison, "how did your audition for *The End of Love* go?" Laurel had instructed her to ask this; personally, Carmen didn't really care. She knew Madison wasn't any competition for her.

Madison tossed her hair back and smiled faintly. "It was fine," she said. "I thought Colum McEntire seemed sort of arrogant, though."

Arrogant? Now that's the pot calling the kettle black, Carmen thought. But of course she kept that observation to herself. "I know what you mean," she said. "He's tough."

"I'm not sure I'd even want to work with him," Madison said. "If he offered me a good role, I don't know . . ."

Way to lay the groundwork for not getting the part, Carmen thought. *Way to pretend like you don't want what you can't have.*

"I'm sure you'll get a great role," Gaby said loyally. She smiled, but the expression seemed slightly painful for her. She'd gotten more fillers since Carmen saw her last, and her skin looked shiny and puffy. "Pillow face": that was the tabloid term for it. And it was really unfortunate, because probably all Gaby needed to do to fill out her face naturally was eat something besides the odd lettuce leaf now and then. She hadn't touched her tuna; she'd just cut it up and moved it around to different places on her plate.

"Totally," Kate said. "You'll *totally* get something."

But Madison just shrugged and took a drink of Prosecco.

"What about you, Carmen?" Kate asked. "How did your audition go?"

Carmen had already told Kate all about it, of course, but the cameras hadn't been rolling. "It went really well, I think," she said. "I was pretty nervous, but it was great that I know Romeo. I mean *Roman*. Being able to read with someone you know and like makes it a lot easier."

"That makes sense," Kate said, blushing a little, probably because she knew "Roman" too. Carmen had considered mentioning to Kate that she and Luke had hooked up all those months ago, in the interest of full disclosure and being a good friend, but then decided it wasn't even worth mentioning. It would only make Kate feel weird—and obviously Luke hadn't said anything about it to her.

"Whenever I performed with my ex, Ethan, I hardly had stage fright at all," Kate added.

"Maybe you should be part of a duo," Madison said, obviously eager to change the subject. "Like Zooey Deschanel and whatever his name is."

"She & Him," Kate said. "They're good."

A new text from Laurel reminded Carmen that Kate was supposed to play her guitar in this scene. Kate's next open mic was still a ways off, and Trevor thought the audience would need to be reminded just what she did with her time. So Carmen, ever helpful, said, "Do you know how to play that song of theirs—'Change Is Hard'?"

Kate looked startled. "What? Oh, yeah." She got up from the table—she wasn't eating anyway—and sat on the loveseat in the corner with her guitar. Slowly she began to strum the chords to the song Carmen had requested.

Carmen smiled as she watched Kate play. She was really good. Dana'd had a lucky strike the day she ducked into that Coffee Bean & Tea Leaf. Carmen felt like it had been lucky for her, too. It'd been a while since she'd made a new friend. After all, when you were the semi-famous daughter of two very famous parents, figuring out who was interested in you and who was interested in your connections could be tough. That was why Carmen tended to stick with Drew and a handful of other people she'd known forever. They had no tabloid-fueled preconceptions of her (celebutard; party girl; shoplifter), and she felt normal with them. Free. Before Kate, Fawn had been her newest friend. But they'd met two years ago now (in an acting workshop with Carmen's favorite teacher, well before Fawn developed an interest in taking things that didn't belong to her).

"*I was never no / never no / never enough, / But I can try / I can try / to toughen up,*" Kate sang softly.

Carmen could see the camera's focus tightening in on Kate and hoped she wouldn't notice. Kate's stage fright occasionally extended to the camera lens. But Kate seemed oblivious, quietly singing and playing while in the background Gaby began to clear the table.

Laurel made a slicing motion across her throat; the sound of clinking silverware was overpowering Kate's singing. Gaby stood uncertain for a moment, a plate in her hand, and then sat back down again. Laurel looked relieved.

When the song was over, Carmen and Gaby clapped. "Another," Gaby cried.

Madison raised an eyebrow. "I didn't know we were in for a sing-along."

"No one's singing but Kate," Carmen pointed out. She was expecting some kind of snappy comeback, but Madison didn't say anything; she just drained her wineglass and reached for the bottle. What was this new meekness about? Carmen wondered. She considered exploring how far it went. Could she tell a dumb blonde joke? Could she talk about the hazards of tanning beds? Could she ask Madison about her sister, Sophia or Sophie or whatever her name was? She was weighing her options when Gaby spoke.

"So," Gaby said, too loudly, "Madison, have you heard from your dad since the other day?"

Madison flinched at the question, which Laurel had obviously just instructed Gaby, via text, to ask. Kate looked up from her guitar, her hair shielding half of her face but her expression of curiosity nevertheless evident. Madison never willingly brought up her family, so now that she was forced to, everyone wanted to hear what she had to say.

"No, I haven't," she said stiffly.

"Oh, did you run into him again?" Kate asked. "After that lunch?"

"Oh, it's so boring," Madison said, stifling a fake yawn.

"I really don't want to talk about it."

"It didn't sound boring to me," Gaby said. "It sounded fun." She turned to Kate and Carmen. "Madison and Sophia and their dad went to the Santa Monica Pier, just like tourists," she told them. "They rode rides, they got cotton candy—"

"So, like six-year-old tourists," Carmen interrupted. She couldn't help herself. Madison shot her one of her trademark evil glares, and Carmen smiled sweetly back.

Gaby nodded and breathlessly began to recount the Wardell family day. "It sounded to me like her dad was trying to be nice, but Madison was all against him or whatever, but then she found out that he'd sent her all these letters over the years, like he hadn't totally abandoned his kids to their drunk mother, and—"

"Gaby, shut up," Madison hissed.

Gaby looked hurt. "What?"

Madison's eyes blazed. "Do I go around airing your dirty laundry? Do I tell the world how you never eat anything but celery sticks and spirulina? Do I talk about how you're practically a pincushion for your aesthetician's Botox needle? Do I mention that when you go to get your nonexistent fat 'warmed off,' or whatever your plastic surgeon calls it, you look like you're being roasted under a fast-food heat lamp?"

Gaby's mouth dropped open. "I was just—"

"Well!" Kate exclaimed. "Anyway!" Then she walked over to Madison and touched her shoulder. "Hey, it's okay.

I know that must have been hard, having all that intense family time."

Smart of her to ignore the tirade, Carmen thought. "Yeah, that really sucks, Mad," she added. She meant it, too. And she felt a surge of gratitude to her own parents for being there for her, emotionally, geographically, and financially.

Madison brushed off Kate's hand and stood up from the table. "I said I didn't want to talk about it," she said. "So drop it, all right? I don't need your pity. In fact, I don't need any of this." She gestured wildly to the whole room and then stormed off down the hall.

"Well," Carmen said after a few moments. "That was awkward." She glanced at Kate, who looked worried, and then over at Laurel.

Laurel looked thrilled.

16

WALK WITH ME

Madison wanted answers. Not diversions or evasions. Not a lame "Aw, Sweetpea, I just wanted to see you," or a "Well, I happened to be in the neighborhood." No: She wanted real, honest answers about why Charlie had shown up now and exactly what he wanted from her.

The momentary flush of love and gratitude she'd felt when she learned about the letters had dissolved and become tinged with suspicion. It was time to uncover the truth.

The parking lot of the E-Z Inn was littered with fast-food wrappers and empty glass pint bottles still camouflaged in paper bags. ("Give me Rosie in a skirt," her mother used to say to the clerk at the 7-Eleven; it meant Wild Irish Rose in a paper bag, which she could take to the park while she watched Madison and Sophie climb all over the jungle gym.) A man with tattoos on his neck, his hands, even on one cheek sat on a folding chair outside room 3, smoking. He asked Madison, as she stepped out of her gold Lexus, if she'd like to join him for a drink.

Madison shuddered and hurried past, down the row of forlorn-looking doors toward the one that was marked OFFICE.

The last time she'd been in this neighborhood was when she got off the Greyhound from Armpit Falls. She'd made it out of downtown L.A. in under an hour, though. On the bus she'd befriended a guy named Travis who was going to visit his sister at UCLA. When the sister picked him up, she offered Madison a ride. Madison took it and never looked back. A week later she'd found a job at a little salon, and her transformation began with some free highlights and a spray tan.

A bell jangled on the lobby door as Madison entered. There was a man passed out on an avocado-green couch near a fake potted palm. Fluorescent lights flickered overhead. The room smelled like stale cigarettes and mildew.

Madison walked over to the Plexiglas window that separated the owner of the motel from his guests. "Hello?" She tapped her knuckles against the greasy glass and wished she'd brought a bottle of hand sanitizer. Who knew what kind of infection you could get in a place like this?

"Be right with you." The owner's back was to her, and Madison could see that he was playing online poker. The man on the couch turned over and snorted wetly in his sleep. Madison shuddered once again. Maybe this had been a bad idea.

After a moment the owner turned around, and his expression turned from boredom to predatory interest the moment he saw Madison. "Well, hello and hello," he said to her breasts. "Are you looking for a room?"

Madison nodded curtly. "Yes, I—"

The man smiled. "We don't usually see your caliber of girl around here. You want the room for an hour or for the night? Money's due up front, of course. Cash only."

Madison paled. "Excuse me?" she said. "Do you think I'm"—she looked both ways and angrily whispered—"a *prostitute*?"

The man shrugged.

"Sir," Madison scoffed. "This is Stella McCartney," she said, motioning to her dress.

"Okay, not your line of work. No problem. So you want the room for the night, then."

"I'm not here to book a room," Madison said with more than a hint of disgust.

He held up his hands in surrender. "Hey, don't act so offended. You know we're all prostitutes in this life, baby. We just make our monies different."

"Says the philosopher of the fleabag motel," Madison remarked acidly. "Thanks so much for your wisdom. But I'm looking for a Charles Wardell. I believe he's staying here?" She glanced over her shoulder at the guy on the couch, who was now upright and leaning by the door.

"Ready when you are, darlin'," he said, leering. It was 11 a.m., and he was already (or still) drunk.

"Oh my God." Madison clutched her YSL bag closer to her body. "Ew. Can you just tell me where Charlie

Wardell is staying?" she said to the owner.

"Room nine," he said. "I'm Earl, if you should need . . . *anything.*"

Madison rolled her eyes. He was talking to her breasts again. "Thank you," she said coldly.

She turned on a heel and almost ran into the drunk. "Hey," he said. "Aren't you that girl on the billboard on Sunset?"

But Madison was already pushing past him. She couldn't get out of there fast enough. She passed the tattooed man again, who waved, and hurried toward the far end of the building.

Her dad's room was located between the fire escape and the Dumpsters. Madison knocked on the metal door and waited, feeling uncomfortable and out of place in her heels and short summer dress. She should have tried a little harder not to stand out. Too bad she'd thrown away the clothes she'd brought from Armpit Falls long ago; cheap denim and pleather shoes would have been just the ticket for today's excursion.

Sometimes she wondered what her life would have been like if she hadn't run away from home when she was fifteen. Would she still be miserable and alone, a fish out of water? Or would she finally have accepted her hardscrabble existence? If she had, she'd be settled down with one of the guys from the paper mill by now, the mother of at least two little brats and the proud owner of six Ford pickup trucks, only one of which ran.

She shook the thought from her mind and knocked again.

"I'm coming," Charlie yelled. "I told you I won't have the money until—" The door flew open and he stopped speaking.

"Oh! Mads, I thought you were Earl."

"No, not Earl. Nice place you picked out." Madison looked past her father into the dim, tiny motel room. She could smell cigarettes and bleach. The TV was on in the corner but its picture was blurry. There were two beds, both of them neatly made. She supposed he'd developed that particular habit in prison.

"Oh, where are my manners?" Charlie said and stepped aside. "You want to come in?"

Did she want to? No, absolutely not. But did she need to? Yes. She told herself that she was just trying to find what a therapist would call "closure," but she sensed there was something deeper involved. Something weaker.

"Sure," Madison said, and entered the room.

Dirty yellow curtains covered the windows; only a sliver of light came in. The comforters were probably mustard-colored once, but they had faded to a dingy shade that looked like the room smelled. There was a small Formica table and two chairs next to the built-in wooden dresser. The door to the bathroom hung ajar, one of its hinges broken.

"It's temporary," Charlie said, sounding apologetic.

"Of course. The Standard must have been booked." She tried hard to keep the revulsion she felt from being visible on her face. She examined one of the chairs and determined it looked clean-ish enough to sit on.

"How are you?" Charlie asked.

"Fine," said Madison stiffly. "You?"

"I got a job," Charlie said, settling himself into the chair opposite her. "Well, I mean I had the interview for the job, and the guy said he liked me. He's supposed to call later this week."

"Doing what?" Madison asked. She had no idea how he'd made the little money he had.

"Mechanic," Charlie said. "I was always good with my hands. Sometimes it seemed like I only had to open the hood and the car would just tell me what was wrong with it."

"Really?"

"Really. Except for that damn Mustang. I spent years of my life lying under that thing and I never could get it to run right." He laughed, remembering. "I swear, on a cold clear night you could just hear it rusting."

A slight smile found its way to Madison's face. "I remember that car. It was cherry red."

Charlie nodded. "Yes, it was. Beautiful, but useless. Though I did get it up and running once." Charlie reached into a Styrofoam cooler beside his chair and pulled out a Dr Pepper. "I took you around the block a few times before it shit bricks." Charlie shook his head at the thought and popped open his soda. "You want one? I can get you something else, if you'd rather. They got a vending machine. Ice, too."

"No," Madison said. "Thank you." She leaned forward a little and clutched her hands tightly in her lap. It was all well and good to share what few childhood memories they had, but she still needed answers. "Why, exactly, are you getting a job as a mechanic? I mean, Trevor is paying you. Isn't he? To be on the show?"

Charlie gazed over toward the window, and a shaft of light lit up one stubbled cheek. "Mr. Lord did make an offer, yes." He took a drink of his soda. "But I wouldn't take it."

Madison looked at him in surprise. Charlie had declined money to be on the show? But he so obviously needed it; he was living in this horrible place, and he didn't even seem to own more than one pair of pants.

"Don't look so shocked, Sweetpea." His voice was soft.

"I'm not shocked," Madison said, although of course she was. "I'm confused. Why did you say no?"

Charlie's blue eyes met hers. "I told him I wasn't here to cash in on your success, only to get to know you. Sophie said she didn't think you'd see me unless it was on-camera."

Sophie had been right about that, Madison thought. At least at first.

"That made sense to me, because this is your life now," Charlie went on. "But profiting off it just didn't seem right. I'll be okay. I'll get that mechanic job, find a studio apartment. It'll be enough. Hell, it'll be more than perfect if I get to see you and your sister. I've waited more than a decade to be able to do that."

Though she might have been tempted, Madison didn't ask him what it was that had kept him away so long. (He wasn't in jail the whole time, so what was his excuse? Had he been shipped to Siberia? Had he suffered from temporary amnesia? Or was he always nearby, just not near enough for her to see?) She kept her mouth shut because she didn't want to hurt his feelings. She just wanted him to keep talking.

"Of all the things I regret in my life—and believe me, there are a lot," Charlie said, "the biggest is not getting to watch you turn into the young woman you are."

Madison smiled wryly to herself. From the breast augmentations to the syringes of Restylane, from the hair dye to the personal training regimens, it had taken a *lot* to turn her into this particular young woman. She didn't think Charlie would have actually wanted to witness any of that.

He reached across the chipped, slightly sticky table and touched her arm. "I'm so proud of you," he said. "You made it out of there. And what's more, you made it *here*."

Madison turned away and looked through the dirty slice of window toward the freeway. Why was she tearing up?

He left you, she reminded herself. *He left you, and don't you forget it.*

But she could tell herself that a thousand times and still there would be the small, hollow part of her that cried out to forgive him. To love him and be loved by him. He had come all the way to Los Angeles, and he had not taken any money for it. He wanted a relationship with Madison and her sister, and he was willing to live in a shithole like this to prove it.

"I have to go," Madison whispered. She stood and ran her hand over the back of her dress, smoothing out the wrinkles.

"I'll walk you to your car," Charlie said. "It's not a great neighborhood around here, as you may have noticed. It's not a good idea for a young lady to walk alone."

Against her better judgment, Madison paused to wait for him, and her heart opened a bit more. Yes, she wanted a father. She wanted a father to compliment her and protect her and worry about her and be proud of her. "Okay," Madison said. "Walk with me. I'm just down the parking lot a little ways."

When they got to her Lexus, Madison unlocked it and folded her legs inside. Charlie stood in front of the car, still holding his Dr Pepper can.

"I don't suppose you have much need for a mechanic with a new thing like this," Charlie said. He ran his fingers along the gleaming hood. "Drive careful, all right?"

Madison rolled down the window. "I wanted to tell you . . ." She paused, knowing what she had to say but unsure she was a big enough person to say it. "I need to tell you that I'm sorry I didn't believe you." She exhaled and the tightness in her chest released. "I spoke to Sue Beth and she told me about the letters."

Charlie nodded, and then he patted the hood of the car.

"I didn't know that you tried to see us or contact us."

"I wasn't much of a father," Charlie said. "And I've got to live with that the rest of my life. I wouldn't expect you to really ever forgive me, but I just wanted you to know I tried. It was a poor try, a weak one, but it was all I could do back then." Charlie lifted his arm and rubbed the sleeve of his shirt across his eyes.

Madison nodded and turned on the ignition.

Charlie took a step backward. "Will I see you again?" he called. "Maybe when you aren't filming?"

Madison smiled out the window. "Yeah," she said. "You will."

17

THE TV–READY NEXT BIG THING

"Can I bring you something to drink while you wait for your friend?" Kate asked the woman in hot-pink yoga pants.

The woman blinked at her, smiling vaguely. She was obviously having a very hard time not looking at the PopTV cameras. No doubt Laurel was annoyed, but Kate thought it was funny: You could order people to pretend the camera crew wasn't there; you could beg them to "act natural"—but as soon as the camera was rolling they stared into the lens like deer in headlights.

Kate wondered if people were like that everywhere, or if it was a fascination unique to Los Angeles. "Pellegrino?" she suggested helpfully.

The woman thought about this for such a long time that Kate was starting to think she hadn't heard her. It was ten minutes before the end of her shift, and from the looks of it they were going to be the longest ten minutes of her life.

"Um, what about the lemonade? Is that sugar-free?"

"No, but it's delicious," Kate chirped.

The woman threw up her hands. "What the heck! It's Friday," she said.

Simone, one of her coworkers, sidled up to Kate as she poured a glass of lemonade. "If lemonade is her idea of letting loose on Friday, I do not even want to know what the rest of her week is like." She smiled.

Kate noticed that Simone was blocking her line to the PopTV camera and that she kept coming up to her to make what she thought were snappy remarks. She also noticed that Simone had touched up her makeup and put her glossy black hair into a flattering updo. So, here was yet another person who couldn't act natural in front of a camera. Because Simone's niceness wasn't natural in the slightest: Her true personality lay somewhere between casually snooty and downright bitchy.

Kate smiled, artificially bright. "I know, right?"

She was wondering how much longer they could pretend to like each other when she saw Gaby enter the restaurant, waving excitedly. She was wearing an extremely short skirt and a demure, long-sleeved top; the effect was nunnish above the waist and slutty below it. Kate wondered who'd thought up that bit of sartorial confusion. Gaby? Her new publicist? Or Madison, trying to be funny? Poor Gaby. Someone could tell her to go out dressed in tin foil and newspaper and she'd ask, *L.A. Times* or the *Daily News*?

"So," Gaby said, mincing up to the bar on her platform heels. "You about ready to go for drinks?"

"Oh, gosh, I'd love to," Kate said. "But I have to go home tonight and work on some songs. I've got studio time next week and I want to be prepared."

The funny thing was, she and Gaby *were* going out for drinks tonight. But the PopTV producers were excellent at getting multiple scenes out of single locations, which saved them a lot of time and money and hassle.

"Oh, bummer," Gaby said, twiddling a piece of her dark hair. "I wanted to go to that new club over on Vine."

"We can go next week," Kate assured her. "I'm free every night."

This wasn't technically true—she had made numerous half-plans with Luke—but since the PopTV people didn't know about him, he didn't officially exist. He'd been surprisingly agreeable about working around her shooting schedule. She smiled at the thought of cooking dinner with him in her apartment, taking another ride up into the hills on his motorcycle, or just lying around on the couch, wrapped in each other's arms. . . .

"Next *week*?" Gaby looked authentically disappointed. Either she'd been working on her acting or she'd forgotten the very next shoot, in which she would ask the same question and Kate would say yes. "Well, all right," Gaby said. "See you later, I guess." She teetered out to the sidewalk and stood for a moment in the sun.

The camera trailed behind Kate as she headed to the

kitchen to clock out. Then there was a ten-minute break while Gaby changed into different clothes, and Kate braided her hair back and changed her earrings.

She took her place behind the bar, this time only pretending to watch the clock for the end of her shift as she did some sidework. *Might as well help out whoever's on the next shift,* she thought as she folded cloth napkins into perfect triangles.

She worked for another few minutes before Gaby entered again, this time in a pale yellow tank dress that clung to her thin body.

"Hey, girl," Gaby said, "are you getting off soon? Let's go get drinks!"

Kate acted as if this was a wonderful proposal, and one she hadn't just turned down. "Totally," she said, wiping her brow dramatically. "I could seriously use a cocktail."

As her filming schedule noted, she and Gaby would be heading to Wood & Vine for happy hour. Laurel had told Gaby to ask Kate about her latest song, and Kate had been instructed to ask Gaby about her *Buzz! News* gig. The producers weren't writing their words for them. They were simply suggesting a subject. And a location. And an activity. The producers, Kate had discovered, had a lot of suggestions.

Once again the camera followed Kate as she clocked out. It filmed her as she brushed her hair out and applied a bit of makeup to brighten her rather tired eyes. Like an obedient puppy, it trailed Kate as she made her way out into the seating area to get Gaby.

Gaby held out a pair of dangly gold earrings. "I brought you these," she said.

Kate was surprised. They were lovely, with cascading tiny golden leaves. "Really? What for?"

Gaby grinned with slight embarrassment. "I bought two pairs by mistake," she said.

Kate raised her eyebrows. Was Gaby so mentally challenged that she would buy the same pair of earrings twice? "How come?" she asked.

"Well, I thought I lost them," Gaby explained. "And they were my favorite, so I bought a new pair. And then I found the old pair in my jewelry box."

"Such a strange place for a pair of earrings," Kate remarked.

"I know, right?" Gaby said, without any apparent irony.

Kate swapped her earrings once more. "I love them," she said sincerely. "Thank you."

"No sweat," Gaby said. She stood and linked her arm through Kate's. "Now let's go get drinks and find cute guys."

Kate and Gaby sat at the bar at Wood & Vine. Kate had ordered a French 75, and after a few sips she already felt it was going to her head, so she asked for a cheese plate, thinking that it'd help soak up some of the Champagne.

"A cheese plate?" Gaby said, after the bartender had taken the order. "You live dangerously."

"What do you mean?" Kate asked. "What's dangerous about cheese?" She thought of Jack, one of her coworkers at Stecco, who'd just come back from a two-week illness after eating strawberries tainted with E. coli. Had there been some cheese-related outbreak of salmonella or botulism or something?

"The saturated *fat*," Gaby whispered. "That's what's dangerous."

Kate couldn't help it; she burst out laughing. "God, Gaby, I thought you were talking about a food-borne illness."

Gaby's expression was still serious. "Obesity is a food-borne illness, Kate." She took a sip of her cocktail and then a sip of ice water. Drinking a pint of ice water, she'd told Kate, burned fifteen calories.

Wow, Kate thought. *Just wow.*

Come to think of it, she couldn't remember ever seeing Gaby eat. Certainly not at their "impromptu" dinner party for the benefit of the PopTV cameras, but not any other time, either. When the rest of the girls sat around eating popcorn or chips and salsa, Gaby drank ice water and chewed gum. No wonder she was so thin. And with those fake breasts? She looked like a twig with two cantaloupes attached to it.

Now you sound like Madison, Kate chided herself. *Be nice.*

"I don't think a bite of Brie will make you—or

170

anyone—obese," Kate pointed out.

Gaby looked unconvinced. "I'll stick to drinking my calories," she said.

"Suit yourself." Kate smeared a slab of a goat's milk double cream onto a cracker and took a delicious, rich bite. She knew Trevor would love it if she confronted Gaby about her eating habits on-camera, but she wasn't up for it. For one thing, it was possible Gaby ate when no one was around because she couldn't help chewing with her mouth open or something; also, it was private business. And Kate was sensitive to that aspect of the matter, since she was involved in some private business of her own with Luke Kelly.

"So," Gaby said, "how is that new song of yours coming? The one you played for us the other week?"

Kate had already given some thought to how she'd answer. Would she play the role of the inspired and hopeful singer-songwriter, the TV-ready Next Big Thing? Or should she confess that she'd been so turned upside down by her new life that she was having a hard time writing about anything? She hadn't decided. Honesty came naturally to her, but in this case she was pretty sure that Trevor would prefer the fiction. (Another strike against "reality" in reality TV.)

She took a sip of her drink to buy herself a moment. Pause. "It's coming along really well," she heard herself say.

"I can't wait to hear it," Gaby said. "What's it called again?"

"'Lonely Doll,'" Kate said. "I think."

"It's just so cool what you do," Gaby said. "I mean, I couldn't write a song to save my life."

No, thought Kate (not without affection), *you probably couldn't.*

Her phone buzzed to life on the bar, and when she picked it up she saw that there was a message from Carmen. WHERE ARE YOU? HAVE NEWS AND WANT TO SEE YOU. Carmen knew where she was, of course, but hey—pretending she didn't was all part of the game.

She texted back and then told Gaby that Carmen would be joining them.

"Oh goody," Gaby said. "It'll be like a real party."

"What, I'm not enough excitement for you?" Kate pretended to pout.

"More guys come up to us when Carmen's around," Gaby said. When she saw the look on Kate's face she added, "Not because you're not totally hot. It's just that she's—you know, famous?"

"Yeah, I know, I know," Kate said. "I'm just a girl from Columbus, Ohio."

"Not for much longer," Gaby said, seemingly sincerely. She adjusted the thin straps of her dress. "Do you think this dress works? It's a Mario Nuñez, but I kind of think it looks a little Forever 21."

Kate laughed. It *did* look like it was from Forever 21, but could you say that about a nine-hundred-dollar dress? Luckily Carmen came racing up just then and planted giant kisses on both of their cheeks. Her own cheeks were flushed and her dark eyes were glittering.

"Wow," Kate exclaimed. "You look over the moon. Did you just fall in love or something?"

Carmen settled herself onto a stool next to them. "Better," she said. "You guys aren't going to believe this, but . . ." She paused, biting her lip and smiling hugely at the same time.

"But you've finally taken my advice and booked your first Restylane treatment," Gaby said. "I'm telling you, it's going to change your life. Say good-bye to nasolabial folds!"

Carmen looked at Gaby as if she'd lost her mind. "What? No!" She was all but bouncing up and down on her stool. "I got the part in *The End of Love*."

Kate flung her arms around her friend. "Oh my God! I knew you could do it! Congratulations!"

"That's amazing," Gaby said. "What part?"

"The lead," Carmen squealed, and Gaby clapped her hands excitedly.

"This calls for a bottle of Champagne," Gaby said, signaling the waiter. "Bring us some Dom," she called. "We're celebrating!"

Kate saw that Carmen's entrance and the flurry of their excitement had brought attention their way; there was a trio of girls staring at them now, their faces revealing a mix of awe and longing. Kate gave them a little wave, even though, as far as they were concerned, she was a nobody.

One of the girls raised her eyebrows in a *Who the hell are you?* expression. Kate smiled. Maybe, in a few weeks, after *The Fame Game* premiere, that girl would remember this moment and realize that Kate was someone famous, too.

Famous. She shook her head at the thought. It really was just too weird to imagine.

"—and so Colum was like, 'You really surprised me. I wasn't expecting to be so moved,' and I was like, 'You have no idea how thrilling this is,'" Carmen was saying. She was talking a mile a minute. The waiter had poured them all Champagne by then, but Carmen hadn't even noticed.

"What about Madison?" Gaby asked hopefully. "Did she get a part?"

This stopped Carmen's breathless monologue. She frowned lightly. "Oh, I don't know," she said. "I didn't think to ask."

Kate glanced surreptitiously in Laurel's direction. She would know, wouldn't she? Laurel met Kate's eyes and shook her head.

Poor Madison, Kate thought. Wherever she was now, she was *not* enjoying a bottle of celebratory Champagne.

18

SPARKS

Trevor Lord was feeling very pleased with himself. This was not exactly a rare occurrence—he tried to find reasons to be pleased with himself on a daily basis—but this afternoon's sense of self-satisfaction was a particularly sweet one.

The Fame Game premiere was a month away, and already he had the seeds for a full season's worth of plotlines: Madison's family drama, plus her desperate and occasionally misguided attempts to make it to the next level. Madison's ongoing makeover of girl-next-door Kate. The blossoming friendship between Carmen and Kate, which he could complicate (at least on-screen) by playing up the tension between Carmen and Madison. Carmen's new role in what was sure to be a hit movie. And of course there was Gaby, who was ever a source of comedy (*Did she really say that?*) and speculation (*Has she gotten even more work done?*). Although it was getting harder to fake continuity with her, since her face and body were constantly changing. He had sat her down last week and requested she hold off on any more face work until they wrapped the season.

Yes, there were many things to be happy about. "We're missing something, though," he said to Dana, who was typing madly on her BlackBerry and didn't look up. He cleared his throat. "We just need one more element."

Finally Dana looked up. "Pardon?" she asked. "We need what?"

Trevor smiled at her. She worked so damn hard. He should give her a vacation someday. But he probably wouldn't. "Romance," he said. "The only thing this series is lacking is a love interest."

Dana nodded. "Right. What about that Drew guy? Carmen's friend?"

Trevor shook his head. "I thought he'd do something for us, but he's a nonstarter."

"Well, Jordan said—"

"Who the hell is Jordan?" Trevor interrupted.

"He's on the crew," Dana said. "He's a location assistant. Anyway, he just mentioned that he saw Carmen looking pretty chummy with that Australian actor."

"Australian?"

"You know, what's his name? He's going to be in the movie with her. God, all these actors look the same to me. Nick—no, wait—Eric—no, *Luke*. Luke Kelly."

"Luke Kelly, huh? Very interesting."

In fact, it was much more than interesting. It was all Trevor could do not to rub his hands together with glee.

Luke Kelly, the next It guy and the lead opposite Carmen in *The End of Love*. Come to think of it, Colum McEntire *had* mentioned that the chemistry between those two had been undeniable. He smiled wolfishly at Dana. This was brilliant. If this was true (and frankly, even if it wasn't) he had his romance angle, complete with a charming accent.

Yes, things were going well, for him and for the girls. Kate had done great at her second open mic, and Carmen had been so good in her audition that Trevor hadn't even needed to twist an arm for her to get cast. Gaby was Gaby; she'd always say the wrong thing at the right moment and be fine. Then his thoughts shifted to Madison, the one he'd told would be his shining star.

Her audition had been terrible, and she and everyone else knew it. He'd had to beg for her to get a role, and he really did hate begging. But he'd gotten her one. It was small, but it was enough. Enough to keep Madison happy? Probably not, especially since he had to practically twist *her* arm to get her to that audition. But enough to keep fueling the rivalry between Madison and her more talented castmate, Carmen? Yes. And that was all that really mattered in the end.

One way or another, Trevor would make sure that sparks would be flying on *The Fame Game*.

19

THINK BEAUTIFUL THOUGHTS

"These are almost perfect," Madison said. She plucked a minuscule piece of lint from the charcoal wool slacks her father wore and flicked it onto the floor. "I want a cuff on them, though," she directed.

The salesman, his mouth full of pins, nodded and began to fold up the hem. Charlie stood stock-still, but he smiled at Madison in the mirror.

They'd spent a lot of time together since her visit to his motel, both on- and off-camera. Sue Beth had finally sent the box of his letters that she'd kept hidden, and Madison had read them all in one tear-soaked sitting. *(Dear Maddie, It's fall so you must be getting ready to start sixth grade. I hope you have a pretty new dress to wear on your first day of school. . . . My dear Mads, Your old man misses you so much! I bet you're getting taller by the day. . . .)*

After that, she'd been more willing to listen to his explanations and apologies. There was still a part of her that wanted to remain furious and unforgiving—but a larger part than that just wanted to have a father, no matter how imperfect he was.

After all, it wasn't as if he'd left them to have some wonderful life of his own. He'd bounced around upstate New York and Pennsylvania, looking for work as a mechanic, which wasn't easy without a trade certificate or a high school diploma. He'd made a go of it outside Pittsburgh for a while, but then he'd fallen in with a bunch of roughnecks. He'd been in a car with a couple buddies one night, just sitting in the back, drinking a Pabst and listening to Lynyrd Skynyrd, when the other two decided to rob a convenience store. He hadn't even known what they were doing. He'd just been waiting for them to come back when they came dashing out with a bag full of cash. Before he knew it they were racing down the highway with two state troopers in pursuit.

"What could I do?" he'd asked her then, his eyes searching her face. "I copped a plea. I mean, I was there! No one was going to believe that I was just some innocent bystander. So I pled guilty and I served my time. And while I was in jail? Every single moment of every single day, I thought about you. You and your sister."

The heart Madison had worked so much to harden softened yet again, and one of these days she was afraid it would just crack open. She knew that her dad had been in prison, but Sue Beth had never said that he'd been innocent. Poor Charlie: He'd paid for his stupidity with jail time and he'd paid for his absence from their lives with pain. He wasn't a deadbeat dad; he was just the unluckiest guy she'd ever met.

"I should have taken you two girls with me when I left," Charlie had said, "but I didn't know how. Seemed impossible for me to take care of two little girls without their momma, and Sweetpea, I just couldn't stay. Your mother—me—we fought a lot. I was afraid of what one of us would do to the other." He shook his head sadly. "If I could do it all over again . . ."

After that, Madison began contemplating a life with her father. Maybe it could even include Sophie, who was still working that peace-love-harmony act. What if, after all these years, Madison could have a family after all?

She'd made up her mind: She was going to show Charlie that since he'd come back into her life, she'd let him stay there. For good.

The salesman stood and slipped the suit jacket over the blue dress shirt that Madison had picked out to match Charlie's eyes. "Yes, the fabric is perfect," she said.

She missed this type of shopping excursion. She used to go to men's stores with her older boyfriends— well, the single ones; the married ones didn't like to be seen in daylight with her—but she was in between boyfriends right now. She hadn't been in Ted Baker for months.

"Very good," the salesman said and began to pin the sleeves of the coat.

"Sweetpea," Charlie whispered, motioning for Madison to lean closer. He lifted his arm and a tiny tag attached to the jacket sleeve fluttered near his fingertips. "Tell me this is the year that the suit was made and not the actual price."

Madison smiled. The four-figure number was indeed the price, but this suit would last Charlie for a long time. "Don't worry. I've got this one," she said. Pride swelled in her chest that she could buy it for him.

"Doll, it's a looker, but I don't have anyplace to wear it," Charlie said.

"I don't know." Madison watched his reflection in the mirror. "This suit would be perfect for a premiere."

Charlie looked puzzled. "What premiere?"

"I was thinking that maybe you'd want to go to *The Fame Game* premiere with me."

Charlie smiled then—a huge, infectious grin. When he didn't look so pitifully beaten down, he was a handsome man. "Oh, Mads," he said. "I'd love that."

"Good," Madison said and smiled at her father.

Madison handed her AmEx to the hovering salesclerk. "The suit," she said to him, "and these three ties and shirts. Have them sent to this address." She handed him one of her business cards with an address scribbled on the back. "How long will it take?"

"A week," he said.

"Perfect," Madison said. And that word felt truer than ever.

★ ★ ★

Her next surprise was the really big one. Though she'd thought about inviting the PopTV cameras along, or at least a paparazzo or two (*Madison and Dad kiss and make up!*), she had decided, in the end, to keep the moment private.

She was supposed to drive Charlie back to the E-Z Inn, but instead she turned off La Brea onto Rosewood.

"Doll, I don't know Los Angeles too well, but this doesn't look like the way back to my place." Charlie had lit a cigarette. Madison hated smoke (and the wrinkles it caused), but they'd agreed that he could smoke as long as the top was down.

"It isn't?" Madison said, all fake innocence.

She pulled down a residential street lined with trees and manicured lawns. Her fingertips drummed the steering wheel with excitement. The place was absolutely perfect: a quiet neighborhood of modest, well-cared-for houses, close to Charlie's job, Sophie's apartment, and Madison's own place. She turned into the driveway of a tiny brown bungalow. There was a white fence half-covered in roses and a front porch trellis practically dripping with bright fuchsia bougainvillea.

"Cute place," Charlie said and took another puff on his cigarette. "One of your friends live here?"

"You could say that." Madison smiled as she turned off her car. "C'mon."

They climbed the front steps together and Madison pulled a key from her purse. She opened the front door to a sunlit room. The living room was modestly but tastefully furnished with a couch, an oversized chair, and a flat-screen TV. The dining area, attached to the bright kitchen, was big enough for a table of six. On the mantel, she'd placed an old photograph of her and Sophie and Charlie together. They were laughing, eating ice-cream cones.

"Do you like it?" Madison asked. Her dad wasn't getting it. She smiled and a feeling of warmth flashed through her. Her father's happiness was what she wanted right now most of all.

"What?" Charlie looked around the room. "Yeah, it's really nice, but—" And that was when he saw the photograph. "Wait a second. Whose place is this?"

"Well, technically it's mine," Madison said. "But I want you to live here."

Charlie gazed around the room in disbelief. "Here? You want me to live here?"

Madison nodded. "If it's okay, I mean, if you want to, and you like it and—"

Charlie looked at Madison and then back at the picture of the three of them that he now held in his hands. "Nobody's ever done anything like this for me. Not ever."

His eyes glistened, and Madison watched as tears welled in them and then slipped down his cheeks. He ran the sleeve of his blue shirt over his face.

"Oh, don't cry, Dad," Madison whispered. "It's just a little two-bedroom house. But it's got two bathrooms, too, and a washer and dryer, a yard, a kitchen—"

"Wait," Charlie said. His voice sounded almost sharp. Madison stopped and turned back to him. Oh no. He wasn't happy—he didn't like it after all!

"What is it?" she asked.

"Sweetpea, did you just call me 'Dad'?"

A smile slipped over Madison's face. She'd just called Charlie "Dad" without even thinking about it. "Yeah," she said. "I guess I did."

Madison's good mood lasted for all of about fifteen minutes after arriving at the photo shoot for *The Fame Game* ads. Seeing Carmen perched in her chair, getting her makeup done and looking so damn nonchalant with all the primping and fussing, made Madison clench her fists in resentment. That little celebuspawn had probably had her first hair and makeup session before her first birthday. She was just so *entitled*.

Even worse, seeing Carmen reminded Madison of the auditions for *The End of Love*. That particular day had involved the sort of humiliation that Madison Parker did not want to experience again. Sure, she'd gotten a role, but it was as The Girl Who Gets Killed in the First Five Minutes. (*That* was really going to beef up her IMDb page, wasn't it?) She glanced over at Carmen again: the *lead*. Of course they'd given that role to her. Madison had never had a chance against Carmen "My Parents Own Hollywood" Curtis, and Trevor Lord had known that when he pitted the two of them against each other.

She smiled grimly. That was probably why he called his show *The Fame Game*: Like in a round of poker, there were winners and there were losers. Carmen Curtis had been born with a full house, while Madison Parker had to fight for every lousy pair and bluff her way through the game.

"Madison," Laurel called. "We need you in makeup." She pointed to a chair to the right of the set they'd be shooting on. "Have a seat."

Madison sighed and walked over. Normally she would have had her own team do her hair and face—she didn't trust the PopTV people to get her look right—but she hadn't had time because she'd been with Charlie. She'd just have to cross her fingers and hope for the best.

As some gum-popping dingbat blew out her hair, Madison watched her castmates in the mirror. Kate and Gaby were dressed and ready to go. Wardrobe had put Gaby in a chiffony coral dress, probably to hide how thin she was. Kate was wearing a little red number that was sleek without being particularly sexy. (Wouldn't want to knock her too far out of her cargo-pant and Gap tee look!) There was an orange dress hanging on a rack for Carmen. And Madison—the *star*—would be wearing gold.

Trevor arrived then, flanked by two assistants. "Ladies," he said, "are we excited or what?" He took off his sunglasses and gave Madison a wink. Madison offered him a sultry smile in return. No, she didn't think Trevor was attractive, but he didn't have to know that, did he?

"We're going to shoot you against this plain backdrop," he informed them. "And then in the posters, we'll make it look as if you're standing in front of the Hollywood sign. Like you're way up above the city, looking down on it all—but you're also standing with your heels in the dirt. It's a study in glamorous contradictions."

Kate nodded, wide-eyed. She was eating up his BS. Gaby wasn't paying attention, but there was nothing unusual about that. Madison glanced over at Carmen, who was getting a final touch-up.

"I like it," Carmen said as her makeup person dusted her cheeks with a bit of shimmery powder. "Good concept."

Suck-up, Madison thought. Her own makeup person was lining her eyes with a smoky shadow. "Careful," she warned. "Keep it close to the lash line. I don't want to look like a raccoon."

Carmen popped out of her chair and went to change into her dress. A moment later, she and Kate were over at the craft services table, picking at a giant tray of fresh fruit and laughing about something. Laurel joined them, and then all three shared some stupid giggle session.

Trevor walked over to stand behind Madison, and his eyes met hers in the mirror. "So, after the shoot, we'll do the voice-over recording," he said.

"Of course," Madison said. "I'm totally prepared."

"Great. I'm actually going to have everyone read—"

"What?" Madison interrupted.

"I'm going to have everyone read. I want to see whose

voice makes the most sense—whose inflection is the most relatable."

"You want to see whose inflection is the most relatable?" Madison repeated, aghast. "What the hell does that mean?"

Trevor gazed at her calmly. "It means I want to see who does it best," he said.

Madison was speechless. He'd promised her the voice-over back when he'd asked her to be on the show. Whoever did the voice-over was the de facto main character—the *star*. The person through whose eyes the rest of the world would see Hollywood. Which meant that *it had to be her*.

"But Trevor," she began.

Trevor held up a hand like he knew what she was going to say, and he didn't want to hear it. Like he didn't care that he was reneging on a promise. Honesty meant nothing to a TV producer.

Madison wanted to scream at him. She wanted to leap from her chair and tackle him. She wanted to tighten that ugly navy tie around his neck until he could no longer breathe. But she knew that this would get her nowhere. When he'd approached her back in June, Trevor had made it sound like *The Fame Game* was her show. But at the end of the day, it was always his show. And there was nothing she could do about it.

"Let's get our pictures taken, shall we?" he said. His tone was light but his eyes were steel. They said to Madison: *Do not fuck with me.*

Her makeup and hair were done, so she slipped on

the golden dress that wardrobe had laid out for her. It was small comfort, having the prettiest dress out of all the cast members.

Laurel positioned the girls in various groupings, and the camera shutter clicked madly.

"Kate. Remember, no smile," the photographer told Kate at some point. "This isn't your senior class photo."

Madison snickered and Carmen shot her a look. Madison reciprocated. Pretty soon the two of them were all-out glaring at each other.

"I like that," Trevor called. "Does it play?"

The photographer shook his head. "It makes their eyes look small. Come on, girls, think beautiful thoughts. They will make you look beautiful."

After a few more minutes, Laurel hustled up and rearranged them: Madison and Carmen standing back to back, arms crossed in the center. Then Gaby on one side and Kate on the other.

"Love it, Carmen. Awesome, Kate," Laurel said. "Gaby, can you try to move your face a little bit? Madison, can you look a little more alive?"

More *alive*? What was she talking about? Madison was a pro at this. She'd been at more photo shoots than that little troll would ever be. She stood up straighter and gave the camera her best look: a mix of sultriness and defiance.

"Mmm," Laurel said, sounding less than thrilled. She was drinking from that stupid travel mug again.

Madison repositioned herself slightly. She was still

staring right into the camera lens, but now she was gazing down her nose at it. The look was meant to say: *I am the shit and don't you forget it.* The shutters clicked. The lights were hot and Madison felt a touch of perspiration on her lip. Within seconds someone yelled, "Shine! Can someone powder Madison?" and the makeup assistant was patting her face.

"My feet hurt," Gaby whispered.

"Smile through it," Madison said. "It's the only way."

The photographer called for a break—all the girls needed a makeup touch-up—and Madison watched as Laurel fluttered right over to Carmen and Kate, smiling. When did they get to be such besties? Madison wondered resentfully. She never thought she'd miss having Dana around, but now she did. Dana was always stressed and bitchy, but at least she was equal-opportunity bitchy.

To take her mind off her interpersonal annoyances, Madison ran through the voice-over narration in her head. *There are four of us, and we're all trying to make it. We know it's going to be a rough road; we know fame isn't easy. But this is our time. And we're ready to get in the game.*

Madison tossed back her platinum hair and readjusted her posture. Her spine was ramrod straight. She was ready for the cameras at all times. *Because really,* Madison thought, *really it's just* my *time. And I will win this game.*

20

SECRET LOVERS

The *Buzz! News* studio looked sort of flimsy in real life, Carmen noticed, but then again, that was the way it always was. She'd been on enough sound stages to know that in Hollywood, nothing was really as glamorous as it looked on TV.

Gaby was looking nervous, but also weirdly grown-up and professional in some kind of chic little silk blouse and tweed skirt ensemble. She kept popping pieces of sugar-free gum into her mouth.

"Don't worry," Carmen assured her. "This is going to be easy. It's just me, remember? Just me and one extra camera."

Gaby smiled tremulously. Her first on-camera interview, the one with Lacey Hopkins, hadn't gone very well, and since then the *Buzz!* people had kept her behind the scenes. They'd made her kind of a PA, even though she was pretty useless for that, too. Although she did do a decent job of fetching people coffee.

But as Laurel had reported to Kate and Carmen when they'd all met for drinks the other night, Trevor told *Buzz!* that they could film Kate making espressos over at Stecco. "The show doesn't need two baristas. So get Gaby back on-camera, okay?" he'd said. And apparently they'd done what he asked.

Some semi-handsome PA settled Gaby and Carmen into uncomfortable armchairs and took away Gaby's gum wrapped in a tissue. They were surrounded by cameras, and even Carmen felt a little weird. She was being filmed being filmed, acting out an interview (for a reality TV show *and* a real TV show) about an acting job for a movie. Huh? It was like looking at endless repetitions of yourself in a mirror.

"Okay, girls. We're rolling in three . . . two . . . one," someone called.

Gaby looked down at her question cards and then back up at Carmen. Carmen could see her take a deep breath before she spoke. "So, you've just been given the role of Julia in *The End of Love*. It's your first picture with a major studio. How are you feeling about it?"

Carmen smiled glitteringly. "I'm so incredibly excited," she said. But of course she didn't want to seem too excited—she wanted to ooze poise and sophistication. "It's such an incredible opportunity to work with Colum McEntire and the whole PopTV Films family."

Gaby glanced down at her questions again. "Are you

excited to be working with Colum McEntire?" she asked.

Carmen kept her smile even. Hadn't she just said she was? Poor Gaby: No one had told her that if your interviewee answers a question spontaneously, you don't have to ask it again. You can skip ahead to the next one. "Yes," she said. "I thought he did an amazing job with *One Way Out*, and I think this movie is going to show the world what an incredible artistic vision he has."

Gaby nodded. "What about Luke Kelly? His star is ascending."

Carmen was pleased to hear Gaby pronouncing "ascending" correctly. "Yes, I think people are really going to sit up and take notice once they see him on the big screen. He's a fantastic actor and an all-around great guy."

"He's cute, too," Gaby noted.

Wow, Carmen thought, *an actual ad-lib*. She laughed prettily. "Yes, he's a handsome guy," she said.

Then Gaby read a question card for a very long time as Carmen shifted tensely in her seat. She'd like to see how *Buzz!* managed to edit this into a reasonably competent interview.

"Can you tell us a little bit about the story?" Gaby asked.

"Of course," Carmen said brightly. And she went off on a riff she'd practiced: about how, in the distant future, Roman and Julia are the children of warring families in a society where love is a crime. And how she and Luke fall in love despite adversity, and how they vow to restore the world back to the way it was. "And you'll just have to see it to find out more," she finished.

Gaby's eyes were wide. She was trying to process this information, but it seemed as if the cranial wheels were just spinning, going nowhere.

"Ask a question," someone hissed.

"Do you think the story has any revelance—I mean *relevance*—for our time?"

"I think love is always a good subject," Carmen answered. "It's part of everyone's life—either its presence or the lack of it. Though I hope not lack, of course." She smiled in a way she hoped would suggest she had more love than she could possibly deal with. In truth, there was a distinct lack of love in her life these days. But maybe she'd get to live vicariously through her character, Julia. Of course, she hoped she wouldn't die from it, the way Julia did. (Spoiler alert!) "When the movie begins, Julia's love is unrequited," she went on.

"What's 'unrequited' mean?" Gaby whispered.

It was as if Carmen could *hear* every eye in the room rolling. "See, Julia loves Roman, but Roman doesn't even know she exists at first."

"Oh," Gaby said, "I get it."

Carmen doubted this was actually the case.

After another awkward ten minutes of discussing Carmen's parents, her favorite summer vacation spot, and her new reality TV show, the *Buzz!* people emerged from the shadows and told Carmen and Gaby to take a break.

"We're going to see what we've got," said a pinched-looking blonde. "We might do a few more questions, but I'm not sure there's time."

Gaby followed Carmen to the side of the set, where a ring of folding chairs had been set up. "I was bad, wasn't I?" she said.

"No," Carmen assured her. "You were fine! You're just nervous, and that's okay. They'll edit it so you seem as professional as Barbara Walters."

"Who's Barbara Walters?" Gaby asked.

Seriously? "She's a very famous interviewer," Carmen said, pulling a water bottle from her purse.

"I don't want to be an interviewer," Gaby whispered.

"What do you want to do then?"

"Honestly, I just liked getting people their coffee."

"Don't sell yourself short, Gab," Carmen said firmly. "You'll figure it out. I promise." She wasn't actually convinced of this, but Gaby could use a little more confidence and ambition in her life. (Unlike her best friend, Madison, who had too much of both.)

Laurel yelled, "Great job, ladies!" reminding Carmen that the PopTV cameras were still rolling. She had honestly forgotten since they were in a roomful of cameras that at least one of them was still pointed at her. "You're done for the day," Laurel continued.

After the girls handed over their mike packs and Laurel and the crew started packing up, Carmen plucked her phone from its pocket so she could check her email. There was a new message from Fawn. *Something you aren't telling me?* it said.

What are you talking about? she wrote back.

Seconds later, she received a link, which, when she clicked on it, took her to a gossip blog splashed with a huge picture of—what? Her and Luke at the coffee shop the other day? NEW LOVE ON-SCREEN AND OFF!!!!! the title read, and the blog's author had drawn hearts around their heads with Photoshop.

"No way," she whispered.

"What?" Gaby said, leaning closer.

Carmen tilted the screen toward her so she could see the picture.

"You're dating Luke Kelly?" Gaby asked. "Why didn't you say anything?" Then she smiled slyly. "Oh, I get it. You're *secret lovers*, like in the movie. That's so awesome! That's, like, perfect publicity once it all comes out."

"No, no, no," Carmen said. "I'm not dating Luke!"

Gaby raised an eyebrow as far as the Botox would allow her, which was not very far. "You sure look like you are. I mean, you're holding hands."

Carmen shook her head. "No, we're not. I just grabbed him right then because I was trying to make a point."

"A point about how much you looove him?"

"Gaaah," Carmen said, slapping her forehead. "No."

She looked again at the silly hearts around her head. It was almost funny, the way the gossip sites could make something out of nothing. And it was almost funny that even Gaby refused to believe that she and Luke weren't together and Fawn assumed it was true ("back for seconds," she'd written, since of course Fawn knew they'd hooked up—they were all at the club together that night).

But less funny? Imagining Kate's reaction. She hadn't been exposed to the Hollywood rumor mill yet. She didn't understand the way photos and videos and even direct quotes could be manipulated. And she'd seen the way Carmen liked to flirt. How could Carmen persuade her that things weren't at all how they seemed?

Welcome to reality TV, Carmen thought. Where, as the Beatles put it—and her father often sang it (badly)—"nothing is real." She just hoped it wouldn't be too hard to convince Kate of that.

21

LITTLE MISS HOLLYWOOD

"Met you, then forgot—what a crazy night that was / Amid the glitter and the music and the champagne buzz," Kate sang softly. *"Now days and nights and afternoons / Aren't even all the times I think of you. . . ."*

She let the notes of the chord fade into silence. Did that song suck? She sighed. Yes, it probably sucked.

She got up and walked over to the window, gazing down at the pool that flickered, aquamarine and inviting, in the late August sunlight. The tune felt familiar, like maybe she was stealing it from somewhere she couldn't quite recall. And then there was the questionable choice of writing a song about Luke. Things were going great between them, but still—they hadn't even been going out for a month. Luke might be flattered, or he might think she was completely psycho and trying to move things along a little too quickly. Or both.

He could have his pick of girls in L.A., Kate thought. He

could be with someone like Carmen, and yet he'd chosen to be with her. She didn't want to do anything to screw it up.

Like write a terrible song about him.

She peeled herself away from the window and returned to her spot on the couch. She picked up Lucinda and plucked out a melody, slightly different from the one she'd been working on before. What if the song was about heartbreak, or growing up, or being lonely? What if it was about the new shoes she'd gotten at Fred Segal? What if it was about how good the tacos were in L.A.?

Kate leaned over and buried her face in frustration in one of the couch pillows. She had to get her act together, because she was going to go into the studio next week. Swing House Studios, to be exact, where everyone from The Donnas to Shakira had recorded. There was going to be a giant mixing board, a million fancy microphones, a badass sound engineer . . . not to mention all the PopTV cameras and crew. She couldn't go in there and sound like any other nineteen-year-old with a guitar and a dream. The world was too full of those already; she'd been in line with them for the *American Idol* auditions, and most of them had failed. Just like her.

She wished she could spend one hour with Carmen's dad talking through some of her songs. Even ten minutes would do. He would know exactly what was missing and would help her lame attempt become the next big hit. But she would never ask this of Carmen. That would feel inappropriate.

She looked at her watch and realized that it was time to

stop beating her head against the wall (or the pillow, in this case). Her old roommate, Natalie, would be arriving in half an hour. Kate was going to figure out this song before she walked through the door, even if it killed her.

She sat back up and wrapped her fingers around her guitar, then closed her eyes and began to play.

"Sorry I'm late," Natalie said, kissing Kate on the cheek. "I got lost. Cute haircut!"

Kate laughed. "Thanks. And don't worry—I still get lost all the time. Come on in."

Natalie whistled as she stepped into the foyer. "Wow, this is all yours?"

"Well, not mine. PopTV's."

Natalie ran her hand along the curved, glossy white wall that led into the living room, with its sleek, modern furniture and floor-to-ceiling windows. "Is that an Eames chair? Is that an Alex Katz print? Dang, if I'd known the digs were going to be this sweet, maybe I would have tried to be on the show, too."

Kate laughed. She had no idea who'd designed the furniture or who'd made the art, but Natalie was right: Her place was pretty awesome. There was a jetted tub, a huge walk-in closet, and a state-of-the-art kitchen she had used primarily to microwave frozen dinners on the nights she didn't go out. (How much was the rent? she wondered. Twice the mortgage on her mom's house? More?) The only unfortunate thing about the apartment was that it never felt like home to Kate. They had done their best to camouflage the large Kino lights that had been built into the ceilings of each room and were careful to keep all of their extra equipment in its designated room, but it always felt like more of a set than a home.

Natalie flopped onto a low settee. "Oof," she said. "It's not as soft as it looks."

"Sorry, I should have warned you. You want something to drink? I've got V8, lemonade, Pellegrino . . . and some milk that's probably expired."

"I'll have the sour milk," Natalie said. "Please."

Kate poked her head out of the kitchen and said, "Seriously?"

"Fine. Pellegrino, then, thanks. So tell me, what's it like, having cameras around all the time? Living a new lavish lifestyle? Hanging out with celebrities? Et cetera."

Kate padded into the room with two tall glasses of sparkling water. "Well, a lot of it is amazing," she said. "I mean, I'm going to record at Swing House Studios. Do you know how long it'd take me to pay for one hour of their time with just my old paychecks? Probably the rest of my life. I can get into any club I want. I got this haircut for free because it was part of the Madison-fixes-the-hick plot so the salon will be prominently featured in the episode. And every month I get a paycheck that's more than anyone should make for ad-libbing in front of a camera, but it's helping me get out of debt, so . . ."

She knew she was focusing on superficial things, but

she didn't want to rub her new friendship with Carmen Curtis in her old friend's face. And Luke? Well, she'd get to him later. "And I'm getting used to the cameras. I hardly even notice them anymore."

"That's great," Natalie said. "Who knew you'd be such a natural?"

"Yeah, right?"

"So, do they actually follow you around twenty-four/seven? Are there cameras in this apartment?"

Kate laughed. "You'd know if they were here, trust me." She readjusted herself so she was sitting cross-legged on the couch. "No, I usually talk to the producer, this woman Dana, and let her know what I've got going on, then I get a schedule at the beginning of every week, telling me what my 'reality' will be. Some of it is stuff I'm actually doing that they want to film—like they filmed me at work the other day, which was of course fascinating"—she rolled her eyes— "but a lot of it is stuff they set up for me, like the studio time and going to dinner or lunch or clubs with the other girls."

"That definitely sounds more fun than Draping and Garment Construction," Natalie said. "I mean, you get paid to socialize and sit around and make up songs!"

Kate rolled her eyes. "Believe me, it's not as fun as it looks." Although she had made some improvements to her new song, so that was something.

"What about your castmates? What are they like?"

Kate thought about this for a moment. "Carmen is awesome—she's totally not some spoiled celebrity child like everyone thinks. Gaby is sweet and kind of dumb. And Madison is . . . well, she's complicated."

"How tactful of you," Natalie said. "What was her tagline for *Madison's Makeovers*? 'Beauty's a bitch'?"

"Yeah, something like that. And it's not exactly inaccurate. But look—she helped me pick out this top!"

"I *thought* you were looking a little less discount bargain-y," Natalie said, and laughed as Kate pretended to take offense. "Well, it sounds like everything is going kind of perfectly for you."

"I wouldn't go *that* far," Kate allowed.

"Really? What's not perfect?"

Kate felt the sudden desire to whisper, even though there were no mikes around. She didn't want to seem ungrateful. "Well, take this apartment. I feel like I'm living on a TV set. I keep waiting for someone to pop out of a closet and tell me to call my ex-boyfriend and tell him how much I miss him. You know, for romantic drama."

Natalie raised an eyebrow. "Do you miss him?"

Kate smiled, thinking of Luke and the way he had surprised her the other day with a trip to the Getty to see an exhibition of Helmut Newton's photography ("He's a fellow Aussie," Luke had said proudly). "No, actually."

Natalie gave a little hop on the settee. "Oh my God, I know that expression! You have a crush on someone, don't you?" she squealed.

Kate flushed but didn't answer. "Let's go down to the pool," she said. "I'll tell you there."

And she wouldn't say another word until the two of them were stretched out by the water, baring their fair skin (how un-Hollywood!) to the sunshine. Kate had brought her laptop in case the muse of song lyrics should choose to pay her a visit.

"All right," Natalie said as she smeared SPF 45 on her arms. "Go."

"So I met this guy," Kate confessed. "At a club a few weeks ago. It was embarrassing, because Carmen had introduced us, but then ten minutes later I ran into him again, and it was like I'd never seen him before in my life."

"Sounds like he makes a great first impression," Natalie said drily.

"I mean, it was just all sort of hectic and crazy. But we started talking and we have all this stuff in common. He plays bass and he's teaching himself the mandolin—"

"So he's a musician?"

Kate bit her lip. This was the weird part: admitting to her friend that she was dating an actor who she now realizes is semi-famous. Someone Natalie might see in *Stars—They're Just Like Us!*, putting gas into his motorcycle.

"He's an actor, actually," she said.

"Ooh, have I heard of him?"

"Maybe? I mean, I hadn't, when I met him, but you know more about this stuff than I do."

Natalie looked at her in surprise. "Check you out, Little Miss Hollywood! Who is it?"

Kate couldn't keep the goofy smile from her face. "His

name is Luke Kelly," she said.

But instead of squealing happily, Natalie looked puzzled, and then slightly disturbed. "From *Boston General*?"

"Yeah—what, do you think he's a bad actor or something? I've never seen the show."

Natalie shook her head. "I'm sure he's a fine actor. I just think—how do I say this? Uh, I thought he was dating your new BFF Carmen Curtis."

Kate paled. "What are you talking about? He and Carmen are in the movie together. You must have misunderstood the headline."

"No, I read about the movie, but it also said—"

Kate was already whipping out her laptop.

"You brought your computer to the pool?" Natalie muttered. "So if I'm too boring you can scroll through Facebook or something?"

"I bring it everywhere," Kate said, banging at the keys. "In case musical genius strikes." Her email program popped up, and there was a message from Carmen.

It's not what you think, read the subject line.

Then Kate went to D-Lish and saw a picture of her new friend and her new boyfriend in a coffee shop, looking mighty—suspiciously—chummy.

She read her friend's subject line again. *It's not what you think.*

Kate slowly closed her computer. *Oh, really?* she thought. *Then what exactly is it?*

22

BAD ROMANCE

"I'm telling you," Trevor said, meeting Veronica Bliss's eyes across her desk at *Gossip*'s West L.A. offices, "there's romance in the air."

The editor of the magazine batted her eyelashes at him. "Oh, Trevor," Veronica said, "you're a married man."

Trevor smiled grimly. He didn't have time to play this little game with Veronica today, but he was obliged; he needed to stay on her good side. With *L.A. Candy,* he'd had to pretend as if tabloids and gossip blogs didn't exist—but with *The Fame Game*, they played a crucial part of the story (and in the success of the show). In fact he was hoping for a cover in the next few weeks leading up to the premiere (or at the very least, a nice two-page spread). He was cutting the trailer this week, the *Buzz!* interview with Carmen was in the can, and this was the next piece of the puzzle.

He raised his glass to Veronica, who was obviously waiting for the expected compliment. "Well, if I were still single, you'd be at the top of my list. Because you look amazing in that dress." He winked, and she grinned at him, satisfied now. Then he pointed the arm of his Dior Homme aviators at her. "But really, now, Veronica— there's love on the set of *The Fame Game*. That's got to interest you just a little bit. You've run Brangelina crap for four issues in a row. You could use some fresh blood."

Veronica smirked as she took a sip of tea. "Oh, really? Last I checked your show hadn't even aired yet. Which means the vast majority of the world doesn't know it exists, and those who do know don't really care."

"They'll care soon enough," Trevor assured her. "The show is going to be a hit."

Veronica eyed him skeptically. "Pretty sure of yourself, aren't you? Listen, your show *might* be a hit. But you're dealing with a different world now. PopTV no longer corners the market on reality. Every network and cable channel has plucked some nobody from Wherever, USA, and tried to build a show around them."

"But I don't have nobodies," Trevor reminded her. "I've got Carmen Curtis—"

"Has she nicked anything lately? I thought that top she stole was ugly, personally."

Trevor chose to ignore this. "We've got Madison Parker, and—"

"Madison Parker!" Veronica interrupted again. "She is an absolute joy. I'm sure you're just loving the chance to deal with her again. Though, of course, I did have some successful interactions with her during *L.A. Candy. . . .*"

She smiled slightly, and Trevor knew that she was remembering how Madison had sold racy pictures of her supposed best friend, Jane Roberts, to *Gossip* and then swept poor Jane away to Mexico, where she had tried her hardest to turn Jane against her true best friend, Scarlett.

"*Anyway*," Trevor said pointedly, "what I'm here to talk to you about is Luke Kelly, the star of Colum McEntire's future blockbuster, *The End of Love*."

"Operative word being 'future,'" Veronica said.

Trevor had had enough of her bullshit. "Yes, *future*. Why don't you try to be ahead of the curve on this one, Veronica? Or would you rather run the same old stories a week after the blogs break them?" He watched her expression turn cooler; yes, he'd gotten to her. Finally.

"All right," Veronica said. "I'll bite. What do you have?"

"The movie is based on Romeo and Juliet—it's the original bad romance, right? And Luke Kelly and Carmen Curtis, his costar, are together. Lovers on-screen and off." *I think*, he said to himself. Trevor had put in a call to Luke's agent, but it had not been returned.

Veronica nodded ever so slightly. "I saw something about that—do you think it's true?"

"On D-Lish, yes. But he only had one picture. I'm sure you've got something in your files somewhere. Are you interested in taking a look?" If Luke Kelly was dating one of Trevor's stars and wouldn't come forward or sign a release to be on the show, then Trevor would simply flush him out. And publicity—whether this guy wanted it or not—would do the trick.

Veronica thought for a moment, then pressed a button on her phone. "Stacy, find me those motorcycle shots. You know, the ones with Luke Kelly and that BMW he's so proud of?" She turned to Trevor. "Let's take a look at these. We almost ran them in a 'stars on bikes' feature, but it got traded out at the last minute when Lacey Hopkins got that hot-pink bike. She even got that thing bedazzled."

"These" turned out to be photos of Luke and a girl bundled up in a jacket and wearing a helmet. In the background was the Park Towers building where Madison, Gaby, and Kate lived. And where Carmen did a lot of filming.

Veronica squinted at the photos. "You think that's Carmen?"

Trevor nodded. "I do. I mean, I've seen her wearing that leather jacket." He wasn't sure, but it was the best story for the show so he was willing to run with it anyway.

"Huh," Veronica said, folding her arms. "Huh." She stared at the photos a little bit longer. "It's only a story if it's Carmen. But I can't tell. . . ."

"What, like *Gossip* has never speculated before?" Trevor laughed drily. "I seem to recall that cover story where you announced the impending divorce of a certain British pop star who two weeks later renewed her vows in an intimate Hawaiian ceremony."

Veronica shrugged. "We all make mistakes. Besides, our cover was the only reason they felt the need to renew."

"Live a little," Trevor said. "Run with the story! This is your chance to be first. And to be on TV."

She raised her eyebrows. "So you'll be filming the *real* reality this season? You're not going to continue to pretend we don't exist? Because that was beginning to hurt my feelings, you know."

"We're going to have the tabloids—the *magazines*—delivered to the girls the moment they come off the presses," Trevor said. "Your publication will be featured prominently."

Veronica gave this a little thought. "We could speculate, I suppose. We could do a spread of all your girls. Luke Kelly in the center. Question marks all around."

"'Which reality star has captured the heart of Doctor Rose of *Boston General*?'"

Veronica nodded. "Something like that. When did you say the premiere of *The Fame Game* was?"

"I didn't." Trevor leaned back, certain he'd just found another way to make his girls famous. "But it's in three weeks. You want a ticket?"

Veronica smiled. "For me and a photographer. And an exclusive. For that, I'll run these."

Trevor reached across the desk and patted her hand. "You're the best, babe," he said.

"I know," she said. "Too bad you're taken."

He smiled his best fake smile. Nope, that joke never got old.

23

KEEP TABS ON YOUR COSTARS

Madison sat in her agent's office, tapping her foot in a combination of boredom and annoyance as the PopTV camera crew finished setting up. Nick was on the phone with another one of his clients, conducting business as if she weren't even there. "No, of course we'll get you that spot," he was saying. "They want someone who's a little curvy, a little—no, that's not an insult, not in this particular case. It's a *good* thing. Whatever you do, do *not* go to the gym this week."

Madison sighed. She'd rather be anywhere than here right now. It was nothing against Nick; usually he had good news for her. But not today. Today she was here so that he could tell her, again, that she didn't get a good role in *The End of Love*. This, of course, was so the viewers of *The Fame Game* could see her crushed reaction. She hated this story line—it made her seem desperate and sad, as if she was stupid enough to believe she'd had a chance in the first place.

"All right, we're ready," Laurel called. "Mad, your mike on?"

"It's *Madison*," Madison said. "And yes."

The director gave the signal, and filming began: Nick turned to her, his hands folded on his desk and a sympathetic look on his face. "Not good news on the movie front," he said. He scratched at his temple and waited for her response.

Oh, really? Madison thought. *You don't say.* "What is it?" she asked, allowing the slightest hint of a tremor to creep into her voice. That'd make the viewers feel sorry for her. "What did they say?"

Nick cleared his throat. "Uh, they said that you were *great*, of course. . . ." He paused. "But they were looking for someone with a little more on-screen experience."

Madison nodded silently. Oh, reality TV: where you got to live the most humiliating moments of your life twice. "But I've been on TV a hundred times by now," she said. "Doesn't that count as a screen?"

"Yes, yes," Nick agreed. "But movies are a different animal, as you know."

Madison said nothing. She felt the camera lingering on her silent, still face. She hated the thought of being publicly rejected.

"I mean, let's face it," Nick said, suddenly looking more cheerful. "Can we find a better character than Madison Parker herself? No, because there's no such thing. If you played anyone besides exactly who you are, it'd be a letdown for your fans."

Madison smiled wryly at the way Nick could turn

rejection into a compliment. That was an agent for you.

"But I do have some good news for you," Nick went on.

She sat up a little straighter. She hadn't expected anything good out of this meeting.

"I've got you in the running for a guest spot on *The Big Bang Theory*," he said.

"Recurring?" Madison asked.

He nodded. "Yep. A hot new neighbor."

Madison smiled. "Excellent. You know I do 'hot' very well."

Nick said, "Yes, of course you're hot, darling. You're the hottest. So hot that I think I've got you a new endorsement, too. KleenSkin is looking for a new celebrity spokesperson and—"

"KleenSkin?" Madison interrupted. "The zit cream?"

"The . . . uh, skin-care system," Nick said, shifting uncomfortably in his chair.

Madison reached up to feel her flawless cheek. She was not about to go on TV and tell people she'd once had a face that looked like a pepperoni pizza. She might as well become a spokesperson for liposuction or Botox or laser hair removal and sell a picture of herself from ninth grade to *Gossip*.

"Well, I'll have to think about it," she said. "Is there anything else?"

Nick shuffled through some papers on his desk. "The L.A. Humane Society would like you to come to their benefit. You're scheduled for a ribbon-cutting at the new

Sephora in Glendale. Secret deodorant wants you to come to a lawn party they're having to launch a new scent. . . ."

Madison nodded, smiling as if these things sounded good to her. But they didn't. She needed to get some better exposure, stat. This was *The Fame Game*. Not *The Wannabe Game*. Not *The Almost-Famous Game*. Not *The You-Promised-Me-the-Next-Level-So-What-the-Hell-Am-I-Doing-Going-to-a-Deodorant-Party Game*.

"So let's do lunch next week," Nick said. "All right? We'll have more to discuss. We should talk about a party for the Madelyn Wardell Foundation, for instance."

"Great," Madison said, standing. "Call me." She blew him a kiss and let the cameras follow her out of the office.

"Got it," someone called, and Madison whirled around mid-stride and headed back into Nick's office.

"Seriously," she hissed, "zit cream?"

He looked up, not at all surprised to see her. "It's a big check, Madison, and we all know you like those. And so do I. Katy Perry did it, and she's done all right, don't you think?"

"Deodorant? Fucking *animals*? Where are the endorsements for spring water, or hair color, or something respectable? Even freaking Snooki has a perfume!"

Nick held up his hand to stop the tirade. "Babe," he said, "I'm working on it. I do nothing but work for you." Madison scoffed, but he chose to ignore it. "I'm telling you, something huge is around the corner, I can feel it."

"You'd better be right," she said.

"Sit back down," he said. "Tell me how you're doing. Really. You seem a little stressed."

She sat back down. "I'm fine. Except for my bullshit movie role and my crap endorsement deals. I mean, other than that, life is great."

"How's the show going?" He raised his eyebrows in that way that said *I know something about something*. Madison hadn't told Nick about her dad, but of course he knew—he got her weekly shooting schedules, too.

Madison reached back to switch off her mike and glanced over at the crew breaking down the camera equipment. They were too busy to pay attention to her answer, and Laurel was in the hall, talking on her phone. Madison could be honest. And a week or so ago, the honest answer to Nick's question would have involved a true Madison-style tirade: The way Trevor had sprung her dad and her sister on her had been completely out of line and totally uncalled for. Did he really need to keep reminding the world that she wasn't who she said she was?

But having Charlie show up the way he did had turned out to be a blessing in disguise. Suddenly she had a father again, no matter how imperfect. So, in fact, Madison felt like thanking Trevor (not that she ever would).

"The show's going well," was all she said, because Nick was her agent, not her friend, and although it was fine for him to know the facts, there were *some* things Madison wanted to keep private.

Nick waited expectantly, but when nothing more was

forthcoming he said, "All right, you don't want to talk about the show. Fine. Then you should at least talk to your agent about your new Hollywood romance."

"Pardon?"

"Playing dumb, are we?" Nick pointed a pencil at her. "That's so unbecoming. You're the one seeing Luke Kelly, aren't you?"

"What are you talking about?" Madison asked, thoroughly baffled.

"Oh, come on. You mentioned something about him after that Togs for Tots benefit you went to. You had your eye on him, didn't you? Then your publicist, Sasha, called me this morning—someone at *Gossip* called her to get the dirt on you and Luke."

Madison was still having a hard time understanding what he was talking about. Sure, she'd noticed Luke Kelly on the red carpet. But he was just Doctor Rose back then— he was hot, but he was still kind of C-list. Then she'd had that horrible reading with him and was too mortified to even look him in the eye. So she hadn't made a move, and she'd just gotten so distracted by her sister and her dad. . . .

"So is there going to be an article or something?" she asked, mentally kicking herself for not returning Sasha's calls for the last two days.

Nick shot her a look of annoyance. "*Gossip*'s running something about Luke Kelly's romantic entanglements with one of *The Fame Game* cast members. I thought it was you. It *should* be you."

Madison ran through the last few weeks in her mind, knowing there was something she was forgetting. Who was he dating? Not Gaby—Luke lacked the Neanderthal gene that Gaby seemed to find so irresistible, and if her own roommate had been dating him she'd definitely know. That left Kate and Carmen. Kate was too vanilla, too Iowa or Ohio or wherever she was from. So it had to be Carmen.

She was so sick of Carmen, and the season hadn't even begun yet.

"How did you not know about this, Madison? You're always so on top of your own press. Is it this stuff with your dad showing up?"

Madison gritted her teeth at his dismissive tone and for the first time felt a little stung that she was just a character on a show to her own agent, too. *Not your friend,* she reminded herself.

"You're supposed to keep tabs on your costars," Nick continued. "You're supposed to stay two steps ahead of them. You can't do that if you have no idea what's going on off-camera."

Madison nodded. He was right of course. When they were shooting *L.A. Candy,* she'd known everything about everything. She had crafted her own story line, giving herself almost as much control as Trevor had. She'd kept Veronica Bliss, the editor of *Gossip,* on speed dial. She had made sure people saw things the way she wanted them to be seen. And now? Now it wasn't like that at all. Now she kept getting surprised. Regardless of what Trevor had told her, that was not a good thing.

"It's got to be that bitch Carmen," she said. "She must have sunk her claws into him at the audition."

"I'm telling you, 'that bitch Carmen' is going to be a problem for you if you don't start paying attention. Everything you've busted your ass for, she was born with. She's used to getting things her way. She's going to walk all over you if you don't wake up."

Madison bristled. "I'd like her to try. Carmen Curtis is the dullest, most talentless person I've ever met. If she weren't the product of famous DNA, no one would give a shit about her."

"That's the point, babe. She *is* the product of famous DNA."

"She's a shoplifting troll with hairy forearms."

Nick grinned. "Now there's the Madison I know and love. Always so diplomatic."

She shrugged. Whoever said diplomacy was such a great trait? Personally she felt that brutal honesty got the conversation going much faster. "She's a walking yawn, Nick. She really ought to steal something again—then she'd at least have a story."

"But she has a story," Nick reminded her. "A relationship with her new costar."

Madison gave an involuntary shudder. New love! She couldn't believe she'd been so out of it. Of course *The Fame Game* needed a romance story line. And it seemed like Carmen had scored that role, too.

24

TALK ABOUT *THE END OF LOVE*

Carmen watched with amusement as Kate gazed into her coffee mug with the sugar in one hand hovering over it. "Late night?" she asked, giving the question a suggestive tone. She knew Kate and Luke had been seeing each other practically every day. She could only assume this involved some sleepovers.

"Yeah, but not that kind." Kate snapped out of her haze and actually began pouring the sugar into her coffee. "I had to close at work last night."

Carmen laughed. "Stecco still treating you right, I take it? The restaurant to the stars making all your dreams come true?"

"Oh, totally," Kate said sarcastically. "I think I want to work there forever. Even after I become a famous musician, I'll still put in a shift or two every week. You know, just to keep in touch with my hourly-wage-plus-tips roots."

"And I'll be a famous actress and I'll come in late at night with my entourage and make unreasonable demands," Carmen said. "Like, an order of truffle fries made up of only the crispiest fries or a tea made out of orchids or goat milk cappuccino or something."

"Ewww," Kate said, wrinkling her nose.

Carmen and Kate were grabbing a bite at Swingers, a former greasy spoon turned retro-hip diner (complete with vinyl booths, old-school linoleum floors, and a giant jukebox) before Carmen had to go in for a table read for *The End of Love.* Swingers was supposed to be ironic and cool, but according to Kate it looked—ironically—exactly like any number of crappy truck-stop restaurants in Ohio. Except, of course, everyone at Swingers was highlighted and slightly better looking and everything shined a little more.

Carmen giggled as she looked over the menu. "Does a chili omelet sound bad?" she asked.

Kate nodded emphatically. "Almost as gross as a goat milk cappuccino. It's like ordering a waffle taco or something."

"Well, they're supposed to be good here. And what I don't finish I can give to Drew. He said he was going to try to drop by to say hi. Actually, he called me a loser but said he missed me, which translates to him showing up here and cleaning our plates."

"What's up with you two?" Kate asked.

"What do you mean 'what's up'?" Carmen felt the hint of a blush but willed it away. "Nothing's up. We're best friends."

"Is Drew gay?" Kate asked matter-of-factly.

Carmen laughed. "No. Why? I can't be friends with him if he's straight?"

"Not saying that. I'm just saying he's cute and funny and I totally thought you guys were dating when I first met you."

"Well, we're not. Maybe *you* should go for him—oh, wait, you already have a boyfriend."

Now Kate blushed. With her complexion it was pretty easy to make that happen and Carmen loved doing it. But with the flush came something else—a look Kate tried to hide. Carmen looked down at her menu again and then up at Kate. She had to make sure the air was clear. "You're sure this whole Luke thing isn't going to bother you?" she blurted, her dark eyes searching Kate's face.

Kate sighed, and Carmen knew that she was thinking back to the photo of Carmen and Luke that had shown up on D-Lish. Kate hadn't been worried about the picture, or what it seemed to show—she'd believed Carmen's story immediately. ("They took the picture the moment he was telling me about *you*," Carmen had told her, which was the truth. "That's why I grabbed his hand. I was just so happy.")

But the aftermath, Carmen had to admit, had been a little weird. And had confirmed to her that not mentioning her makeout session with Luke had been the right choice. Clearly Luke hadn't said anything about it and now Carmen would make sure he never did.

Kate had called Luke to tell him about his apparent romance with his leading lady, and they'd had a good laugh. But then Luke's agent, Simon Leff, had called on the other line, and when Luke called Kate back, his tone had changed. Simon had told him that *Gossip* was planning to run a "Which *Fame Game* star is Luke Kelly dating?" story. The agent had been relieved that it wasn't Madison or Gaby. But he was not exactly thrilled to hear that it was Kate.

So then Luke had had the awkward job of trying to explain to Kate why dating her publicly could spell bad news for his career. *It's not you,* he'd said. *It's the show. Simon says anyone who wants to be taken seriously as an actor should stay away from reality TV. His exact words were, "Unless you're already established or your name is George Clooney, you have to shut it down."*

Kate poured some more cream into her coffee but still didn't drink it. "It's like his agent thinks I'm a second-class citizen," Kate said to Carmen. "I'm not good enough for his precious Luke." She met her friend's gaze. "But you are."

Carmen ducked her head in embarrassment. "Oh, Kate," she said. She did feel bad about it. According to Kate, Simon had informed Luke that unless *The Fame Game* girl he was dating was Carmen Curtis, then he had to deny being involved with anyone at all. Carmen was born on the A-list, Simon had pointed out, and she'd just landed the lead in what was sure to be a blockbuster. They were costars! Simon had practically yelled. It was perfect.

They could pretty much write their own cover story, and you couldn't *buy* that kind of publicity. Yes, Carmen was the kind of girlfriend Luke should have if he cared about his career.

"And he's telling me this," Kate said, "and my heart starts to beat really fast and hard and my palms start to tingle. It's just like what I feel before going on stage. It's a fear of what's to come. Usually I'm afraid of what I'll do wrong—but this time I'm afraid of what he's going to tell me, you know? Like he's going to break up with me."

"But he didn't break up with you," Carmen reminded her.

"No," Kate whispered. She didn't look very reassured by that fact, though.

Carmen signaled to the waitress that they'd take two orders of pancakes. Screw the fitting she was scheduled for after the table read, she thought; they could both use some comfort food.

"I know, it's so stupid," she said, reaching out to pat Kate's hand. "But everything in Hollywood is a competition. Where is the best party? Who is the most powerful person in the room? How do I get my name in lights? How do I get my name in *bigger* lights? People spend twenty-four hours a day worrying about the answers to those questions."

"But Luke didn't seem like he did," Kate pointed out.

"No, but his agent does. That's what Luke pays him for."

"Right. So I said, 'Your agent doesn't approve of me.' And Luke said, 'No, it's Madison Parker and her desperate attempts at fame. It's Gaby Garcia, who's become a total train wreck. Simon doesn't think I should be associated with those people.' And I said, 'Oh, but it would be okay if you were associated with them because you were dating Carmen?'"

Carmen felt the weight of her friend's wounded gaze. The whole situation sucked. Kate was the nicest, most sane person Carmen had met in a long time, and she didn't want her to be hurt. Unlike so many people Carmen knew, who either resented her for her celebrity or tried to befriend her because of it, Kate didn't care that Carmen was famous. In fact, she was practically oblivious to it. And Kate was a struggling singer-songwriter who knew exactly who Carmen's dad was and what he could do for the right struggling singer-songwriter. Finding someone in Hollywood to whom fame and connections didn't matter? It was like finding a unicorn—something you didn't even think existed.

"It's just because Luke and I are costars now," Carmen said reassuringly. "Really, it has nothing to do with you." She knew how hollow that sounded, though, and she sympathized with Kate.

"Wait—have you talked about this with him? So he's not going to deny that he's dating you?" Kate said. "Talk about 'The End of Love.' It's going to be all 'no comment' from his publicist or whatever?"

Carmen shrugged, taking Kate's flippant movie-title crack in stride. "That's okay with me," she said. "I don't have a real boyfriend, so I might as well have a fake one. I mean, if it's okay with you." Her publicist had already urged her to go with the story. (And her mom had called from somewhere across the world to ask when Carmen was bringing her new man for dinner. They had a good laugh because they both knew that if Carmen was actually dating someone, Cassandra would be among the first to know.)

Kate put her head in her hands. "I guess it's okay. I certainly don't want to get in the way of Luke's career. It's just so weird."

The waitress appeared and set two steaming plates of pancakes in front of them. Kate looked up in confusion.

"I ordered them," Carmen admitted. "I thought we could use a little pick-me-up."

"And what you don't want, I'll eat," said Drew, appearing at Carmen's elbow. He smiled at them both, looking handsome and slightly scruffy, as if he'd been up too late the night before. Which, Carmen thought, he probably had; her dad had been sending him around to lots of shows lately, looking for fresh talent ready to take the next step.

Drew slid into the booth beside her and smiled at them both. "And let's order some bacon, too. Which you are buying, since I'm mad at you." He jabbed Carmen in the ribs with a tattooed elbow.

"What for?" Carmen asked.

"For dating Luke Kelly and not telling your oldest, bestest friend about it," he said, sticking out his lower lip and making a pouting face. "I had to hear about it from your dad."

Carmen glanced over at Kate, who looked pale. She hadn't touched her pancakes.

"From my *dad*?" Carmen asked. "First of all, it's not even true, and second of all, what, is my dad gossiping about me at the watercooler?"

Drew raised an eyebrow. "Not true? Really? Various publicists and gossip sites seem to say otherwise. I had to read up on it, see, after I heard."

Carmen shook her head. "It's not true. The truth is—"

"The truth is that *I'm* dating him," Kate interrupted. "But no one is supposed to know that. In public he needs to have a better girlfriend, which is our Carmen here." She was smiling, but Carmen thought she detected a note of bitterness in her voice.

"Oh, Kate," she said.

Drew held up a hand. "Wait a second. The guy is dating you"—he looked at Kate—"but he's pretending to be dating you?" He turned to Carmen.

"He's not pretending to be dating me," Carmen said. "He's just not denying it."

"Wow," Drew said. "Wow."

"Wow what?" Carmen asked.

"That's . . . lame," Drew said flatly.

Kate pushed her plate of pancakes toward him. "Here,"

she said. "I'm not hungry."

Carmen watched as Kate gazed out the window at the traffic on Beverly Boulevard. She felt bad for her, but Carmen was only trying to do what was best for everyone.

"You could pretend to date me," Drew said to Kate. "If that would make you feel better."

Kate turned to him and smiled. "Would you get a tattoo in my honor?"

"Just name the body part and font."

Kate laughed. "Would I get special consideration at Rock It! Records?"

"Baby," Drew said, "I've got a gold record with your name on it."

And then they were both laughing, and Carmen joined in, hesitantly at first and then wholeheartedly. Everything was going to be all right, she told herself. Everything was going to work out just fine.

25

EVERYONE WANTS TO BE FAMOUS

Lugging her guitar, her ukulele, and an oversized cup of green tea, Kate entered the recording studio at Swing House, flanked by a PopTV camera and crew. Her heart felt like it was in her throat—how was she going to sing around *that*? she wondered.

A tall guy wearing various shades of denim from head to toe walked into the studio with one giant hand outstretched. "I'm Mike," he said. "I'll be at the soundboard in there, on the other side of those windows. We've got a vintage twenty-channel API along with a twelve-channel Cadac sidecar and multiple Neve and Calrec Mic Pres," he said. "We've got Sam over there to deal with the mikes and cables, and we've got an intern, Laura, to boss around, too. So we're all ready to roll."

Kate, who was the queen of low-tech, lo-fi recording, nodded as if she expected nothing less. A twelve-channel Cadac sidecar? Of course! She couldn't live without it! (*And what exactly was it?*) "Awesome," she said. "Sounds great." She hoped that Sam was good with the mikes and cables, because she certainly didn't know what to do with them.

"You can go ahead and get yourself set up over there." Mike smiled and pointed to the vocal booth. "And don't be nervous," he said, peering at her good-naturedly. "This is going to be fun."

From the corner, behind the cameras, Laurel gave Kate a little wave. Kate couldn't smile back, of course, but she did feel momentarily reassured. Laurel was rooting for her; that counted for something, right?

She took Lucinda from her case and stepped into the vocal booth, a small room off to the side of the main studio. A wooden door formed one wall and egg-crate acoustic foam lined the other three. Inside was an Oriental rug, a music stand, and a single stool. It smelled faintly like pot.

She sat on the stool and brought her guitar to her lap.

"All good in there?" Mike asked. "Comfy? You need anything?"

Kate shook her head, too intimidated by everything to speak.

"Well, if you change your mind, just let me know. We're used to the whims of you creative types, and we cater to them pretty well." Mike winked at her.

Kate wondered what he thought she'd like: the pot she was smelling? And a pile of Doritos and Good & Plentys? She did want a bottle of water, but she was too shy to ask.

And then Mike disappeared into the sound booth, and Kate was alone in her little vocal chamber. Alone, that is, until a PopTV cameraman wedged his way in and set up in the corner. "Don't mind me," he said with a smile. "Just pretend I'm not even here."

That was easier said than done, though, considering he was practically sitting in her lap.

She took a deep breath and tried to focus. She'd spent hours working on her songs, especially the one about Luke, which she'd totally rewritten. She'd kept her guitar and her laptop right next to her for days, so when it finally came together—which was, ironically, during a commercial for *Boston General*—she'd picked up Lucinda and perfected the chords in moments, the way the melody looped around before settling down into a simple, catchy chorus. Then she'd typed out the lyrics in a burst of inspiration. The day after that, two more songs had come to her, as if suddenly writing was as easy as rolling out of bed.

If only everything else were so easy, she thought.

She felt on edge, and it wasn't just being in Swing House Studios. It was Luke, and it was Luke and Carmen, and it was the way it had begun to seem as if her life was no longer truly her own to control. She thought of Ethan's most recent email: As usual, he'd sent a funny clip (two grandmothers singing Katy Perry's "Firework") and he'd asked how she was. Then he'd signed off. *TTYL*, he'd written. *Keep it real.*

Keep it real. It was a generic good-bye—something

he'd written to her a hundred times before. But this time it seemed to have a new meaning. It seemed almost like a command. Or a warning.

She was not keeping many things real these days.

Focus, she told herself. *Get in the game here.*

Inside the control room, Mike put on a pair of headphones and indicated that she should do the same. She found a pair hanging on the wall and slipped them on.

"Can you hear me?" Mike said.

"Loud and clear." His voice sounded so close it was like he was speaking right into her brain.

"All right, so why don't you just strum a little bit, get yourself warmed up while I fiddle with some things in here. No need to record anything yet. Just take some time to get comfortable."

"Sounds good," Kate said. She strummed a little warm-up progression and then did one of her fingerpicking exercises. After a few moments she leaned toward the mike. "I think I'm ready," she said.

Mike gave her the thumbs-up and smiled. Kate took a deep breath and began. The song was about her first date with Luke—when they'd ridden up into the hills. But she'd been working on it for so long that the lyrics kept changing and it was still about Luke, but it wasn't the sweet love song she'd set out to write.

We thought we'd give this town a try, the first verse
   began.

We saw the Hollywood sign up so high
And we rode up into the sky
Just you, the stars, and I. . . .

But when she came to it, she changed the second line—
almost by mistake. She sang, *"We thought the Hollywood sign
was on our side."*

No one else knew she'd made a mistake, so she kept
going, singing the chorus:

Lovestruck, starstruck, dreaming of our better days
Holding on as tight as we can before the bright lights shine
    our way
Lovestruck, starstruck, dreaming of better days

In the control room Mike was nodding along to the
beat, and Kate felt herself growing more confident, more
free. She forgot about the PopTV cameras and lost herself in the song. She played it over and over, wanting to
get it perfect but also wanting to explore all the possibilities within it: a slower tempo, a slightly different bridge,
a hummed verse, a full stop punctuated by a series of four
syncopated hand claps. She changed it many times, mess-
ing around with the chorus so at one point she sang "ready
for the game" instead of "dreaming of better days," which
earned her a thumbs-up and a smile from Laurel. But
through all the different takes that new line in the first
verse stayed the same.

When she'd done a few other songs and her time was up, Mike came into the booth. He was eating a bag of M&M's. "You're sure you're not a studio regular? Some secret session musician maybe?"

She shook her head. "The only recording I've done is on my laptop. Which is about a hundred years old."

"I saw your YouTube video, you know," Mike said. "It was really good. But you're already better than that."

She looked up at him, hope written all over her face. "You think so?" she asked.

He nodded. "I know so. That song? The one about Hollywood being complicated and confusing? That's good stuff."

Gee, thanks, Kate thought, as Laurel ran over, smiling. *Glad my ridiculous Luke situation makes for good stuff.*

"Oh my God, you were amazing!" Laurel squealed, putting her arm around Kate's shoulder. "And Mike's right about that song. Trevor's still looking for the perfect song for the opening credits and I think you may have just recorded it."

Kate flushed with pride. What if Trevor would actually use her music for *The Fame Game*? That would be incredible.

"I'll get it mixed and mastered as soon as possible and send it to Trevor Lord," Mike said.

"Well, I won't get my hopes up," Kate said, although she already had. "So we're done for the day?" she asked, indicating the cameras.

"Yep. Got what we needed."

As soon as Kate knew that the cameras weren't rolling anymore, she felt herself deflate. She sank down on top of a big Fender amp and ran her fingers through her wavy hair.

"What's the matter?" Laurel asked, peering at her with a worried expression. "You were seriously fantastic."

Kate shook her head. She wanted to bask in the glow of performing well—of not being intimidated by all the gold records on the wall or the countless blinking lights on the soundboard. Trouble was, she just couldn't.

Laurel knelt down in front of her and touched her knee. "Come on, something's the matter. Tell me."

Kate looked into Laurel's wide, dark eyes. She didn't know Laurel that well, and though they'd shared some laughs on *The Fame Game* sets, she wasn't sure she could trust her. What if Kate told her what was going on, and then she went running back to Trevor with the news? She wished Natalie were here, or her sister or her mom, or even Ethan. Someone she'd known for longer than a month.

Laurel sat down and folded her long legs lotus-style. "Look," she said, "I know this stuff can be really weird. And hard, too. It's a whole different thing when you have to live your life in front of a camera."

Kate nodded. "You know, I was thinking the other day: I used to be really into nature documentaries when I was a kid. The kind where some biologist with a camera would follow around a wolf pack for months, watching how they interacted, how they hunted, what they ate, and where they slept. I thought it was so cool. But it never occurred to me what the wolf might feel like, having a camera in his face all the time."

Laurel laughed. "Of course, they *hid* the cameras from the wolves, though."

"Right. Because they couldn't sign releases," Kate said. "And they kept flubbing their lines."

Laurel's laugh turned into a snort. "No, I think it was actually because the wolves might try to eat them."

Kate waved this away. "Sure, whatever. But seriously, it's not even the cameras. I'm getting used to them in my life. It's the way they complicate *other* people's lives. . . ."

Laurel frowned lightly. "What do you mean?"

Kate sighed. She just needed to talk to someone about it. Now. Which meant that Laurel would have to do.

"Is this about that *Gossip* story about Luke Kelly and which *Fame Game* girl he's dating? The PopTV publicist said she was sending you a PDF of it. Your picture was only smaller because people don't know who you are yet."

"PDF not received, so no, it's not about that. I mean, it is about which *Fame Game* girl Luke Kelly is dating but—"

"Yeah, we figured out it was Carmen," Laurel said.

Kate shook her head, unable to stop her mouth. "No, it's not Carmen. Luke is dating me. He's only pretending to date Carmen."

Laurel raised her eyebrows. "Shut your face!" Then, once she'd recovered, she added, "How is that working out?"

"Fine for them," Kate said. "I just . . . I don't know. I

guess I'm just bothered by the fact that I'm not good enough to be Luke Kelly's public girlfriend." Suddenly, she turned to Laurel, eyes blazing. "You can't tell anyone about this," she demanded. "Especially not any of the producers."

Laurel looked slightly taken aback by Kate's fierceness. "Okay," she said. "I won't."

Kate twisted her hands in her lap. "I'm mad, but I don't know if it's fair to be mad. And if it *is* fair, then who should I be more mad at? Luke, for pretending he's with Carmen, or Carmen for going along with it?"

Laurel smiled sympathetically. "Honestly, I don't think you should be mad at either one of them. They're just playing by the rules of the game." She took a sip from her travel mug and sighed. "Let me tell you a little secret about life in L.A. *None* of it is real, whether you're on a reality TV show or not. Everyone is scheming, and everyone is looking out for number one. *The Fame Game* isn't just the name of this TV show. It's basically the theme around here. Everyone wants to be famous. And only a lucky few get to be." She reached out and poked Kate in the shin. "Like *you*, Kate Hayes. You are one of the lucky ones."

Kate nodded slowly. Carmen had given her a speech very much like this one. Kate knew she ought to be grateful. And she was, she really, really was. But she didn't feel lucky. She felt weird. The chorus of her song circled around in her head. *Holding on as tight as we can before the bright lights shine our way . . .*

26

THE GOOD OL' DAYS

Madison scrutinized, for one last time, the lunch that the Urth caterers had laid out on the dining room table and pronounced herself satisfied. There was tomato-basil soup, organic spinach salad, and a Mediterranean platter of grilled baby artichokes, hummus, tabouli, stuffed grape leaves, and olives. Everything looked fresh and delicious, garnished with Urth's signature edible orchids. She smiled. Her father had probably never eaten this well in his whole life.

She was expecting him and Sophie any minute. The visit had been Trevor's idea, but Madison had been happy about it. She'd gone from resisting Trevor's efforts to get her family on film to welcoming them. Trevor wanted to get some footage of the family looking through old photographs? Fine! Great! Sophie had an album from the good ol' days, such as they were, and Madison had a giant couch they could all sit on to look at it. As far as Madison was concerned, it was a win-win situation: She got to spend time with her dad, and she got to play the part of the forgiving daughter and big sister for the PopTV audience.

Sophie continued to be something of a wild card. She was still working the love goddess act—so perfectly, in fact, that Madison was tempted to believe it wasn't an act at all. But her sister had always gone through phases (skateboarder, goth, rocker chick, burnout), and this was probably just a longer and friendlier phase than her previous ones.

Madison examined herself in the hallway full-length mirror (one of seven in her apartment, so she knew what she looked like in every room, in every light) and smoothed the front of her Joie top. She was going to have to see her colorist soon; there was the tiniest hint of dark roots in the part of her pale golden hair. She gave her nose a quick dot of powder and then went back to the table and plucked a spinach leaf from the salad.

"Aren't they supposed to be here now?" Laurel asked.

Madison turned to her and to the camera crew that had set up in the corner of the room. She had gotten so good at ignoring them she'd almost believed that she was alone in her apartment. "Yes, but you know my sister. She likes to be fashionably late." She held up her phone. "I'll text her," she said.

Laurel looked surprised; she wasn't used to Friendly, Helpful Madison.

WHERE THE HELL R U? GET YR HIPPIE ASS OVER HERE, Madison typed. (She couldn't be 100 percent friendly, after all.)

And then, almost as if the text had magically summoned her guests, Madison's security phone sounded. After she saw them in the little screen and buzzed them in, she glided over to the door and waited a full minute, aware that the cameras were now rolling. She opened the door with a big smile on her face.

"Namaste," Sophie greeted her, leaning in to give Madison a kiss. She was wearing a lavender tunic over black leggings; a large crystal hung from a gold chain around her neck. "The divine in me salutes the divine in you."

"Yeah, hi," Madison said.

Behind Sophie, Charlie shifted from foot to foot nervously. He took a step forward and then paused; it was obvious that he couldn't decide whether to hug Madison or kiss her or what. Madison reached for his arm and led him into the apartment. "Come on in," she said.

"Wow," Sophie said, taking in the lunch spread. "Nice."

"Organic," Madison announced. "You guys want to eat now or hang out for a few minutes first?"

"Let's eat now." Sophie sniffed at the soup. "This isn't made with chicken stock, is it? You know I'm a vegetarian."

"Oh really," Madison said skeptically. "How enlightened of you. Well, it's vegetarian, don't worry." She turned to her father. "Here, take a plate. You look hungry."

Charlie took the proffered plate and stood over the table. He pointed to a stuffed grape leaf. "What's that?" he asked.

"Dolmas," she told him. "It's rice and herbs and spices wrapped inside a grape leaf."

"Oh." Charlie still sounded confused. He hovered for a while and put a few dollops of things on his plate. Madison ladled some soup into a bowl for him and gestured for him to sit down at the far end of the table, next to Sophie, who already had a heaping plate of food.

She herself was too wired to feel hungry—plus she didn't like to eat on-camera. Chewing was so . . . *unbecoming*.

"So, how are you liking your new house?" she asked her dad, taking a sip of hibiscus tea.

Charlie smiled. "It's wonderful, Sweetpea. I wake up in the morning in that comfortable bed and feel like the luckiest man in the world."

"Good," Madison said. "It's about time you felt lucky."

"When are you going to rent me a house, sis?" Sophie asked. "My apartment is too small. There's no space to do yoga."

Madison gave a ladylike little snort. "Um, right after I finish paying off your rehab." *Oops*, she thought, *must remember to play nice.*

Sophie looked hurt. She was so pretty and so pitiful, all at the same time—the cameras were going to love that.

"Just kidding!" Madison said brightly. "I'm sure we can find you a better place soon!"

She glanced over to her father, who was only picking at his food. "What's the matter?" she asked. "Don't you like it?"

Charlie met her eyes sheepishly. "Honestly, Sweetpea, I don't know what any of this stuff is. You're looking at a guy who lives on burgers and microwave popcorn."

She reached over and patted his hand. "Just try it. It's all good, and it's all good for you. You've got to get used to taking better care of yourself."

"Mmmhmm," Sophie said, her mouth full. "You should try yoga too. It's so rejuvenating."

Madison's BlackBerry buzzed and she glanced down at the screen. FAMILY MEMORIES!! Laurel had written.

Right. Okay. Madison quickly racked her brain for some happy childhood memory, one that wouldn't feel like a complete non sequitur. The problem was, there weren't that many to choose from. There was the time they got that puppy—but then their mom made them give it away because it peed on the floor. Or what about that Christmas when they got canned food from the local food bank in their stockings?

She was striking out on the nostalgia front—she should have given this more thought beforehand. Then suddenly she recalled a tumbling class that she and Sophie had taken when they were little. Yoga—gymnastics. Perfect transition.

"Remember how we took that gymnastics class at the Y?" Madison said. "How it took you, like, two months to learn how to somersault?"

Charlie laughed. "Oh, and then once she did? She wouldn't stop with the somersaults. She did them up and down the hallway."

Instead of getting defensive, Sophie smiled, too. "Oh my God, I did them until I was practically sick to my stomach. I got so dizzy!" Then she paused, as if something had just occurred to her. "You know, I bet I have pictures of that," she said.

"Really?" Madison asked. Sophie had picked up the cue perfectly; as much as Madison hated to admit it, the girl was a natural. "Where?"

"Actually," Sophie said, pretending to be self-conscious, "I have an old photo album. I brought it because I thought it might be fun . . . you know, all of us together again?"

"Oh, bring it out!" Madison said.

Thankfully Charlie had left when Madison was still young enough to be naturally darling: before her blond hair darkened, before she gained weight, before her adult teeth came in completely crooked. It was a good thing Trevor hadn't asked to show an album from Madison's junior high or high school years; she would have died before allowing such a thing.

Sophie extracted a battered-looking album from her giant hemp-fiber bag and the three of them went into the living room to gather on the couch. Charlie brought his plate in and continued to pick at his food. Madison hoped he wouldn't spill any tabouli on the carpet.

The camera came in close, focusing on the photographs. They were beginning to fade and turn yellowish, which gave the scenes a sort of golden glow.

"Oh, look," said Madison, pointing to a picture of the

two of them all bundled up in snowsuits. "Remember that storm? When school was canceled for, like, a week?"

"Totally." Sophie nodded. "That was awesome."

Charlie laughed. "Awesome for you two. I seem to remember having to dig the truck out from under six feet of snow. And then, after I dug it out, I got stuck on the turnout to the highway. Had to leave it there for two days." He shook his head. "I guess looking back now it's kind of funny."

"What's that saying? 'Tragedy plus time equals comedy'?" Madison asked.

Sophie shrugged. "Who knows? But you sure knew how to rock snow pants, Mad. Too bad you live where you'll never need them again."

"We all live where we'll never need them again." Madison squeezed her dad's arm.

Charlie stood. "Sweetpea, where's your bathroom?"

"Go down that hall, and it's the third door on your left."

She watched her father walk away and was pleased to see that he'd bought a new pair of jeans. Those khakis of his had gotten seriously tired.

Sophie turned the page and came to a picture of their mother in a flowered dress. "She sure was pretty back then," she said.

Madison nodded. Her mother had been the Rensselaer County Fair Queen three years in a row when she was young. It was sad, thinking about the way she'd let herself go. Madison would never, *ever* let that happen to her.

"Is that Licorice?" Sophie asked.

Madison peered at a dark blur in the corner of the picture. It could have been her old cat or it could have been a shadow. "Not sure," she said.

"This is kind of fun, isn't it?" Sophie asked.

Madison nodded. "Yes," she said. "It actually is."

Charlie came back into the room then, looking slightly embarrassed. "I opened the wrong door," he said. "Ended up in your roommate's room."

"Oh, Gaby, right! Well, she doesn't bite," Madison laughed.

"Should we take her a plate of food?" Charlie asked.

Madison shook her head. "No, she's on a juice cleanse."

Charlie ran his hands through his hair. "I tell you, it's a different world you girls live in out here."

"Maybe it is," Madison said. "But I'm glad you're in it. So start liking it, all right?"

27

GOOD TIMES, GOOD TIMES

"How come your furniture is so much softer than mine?" Kate asked as she settled into an overstuffed chair at Madison and Gaby's. "I swear, it's like sitting on rocks over at my place."

Madison handed her a glass of Champagne. "We needed extra cushioning for Gaby's bony butt."

Gaby poked her head into the room. "Really? You think my butt is bony? Thanks!"

Madison rolled her eyes. "That wasn't supposed to be a compliment," she said to Kate. "But whatever."

The three of them had gathered to watch Gaby's interview with Carmen from last week. Naturally the PopTV cameras were there to film their reactions. But Carmen wasn't, even though the shooting schedule had said she would be. It was kind of weird, Kate thought. Shouldn't Carmen see the airing of her interview on-camera, too? Wasn't her reaction more important than Kate's, for example, considering that she had had nothing to do with the segment? Well, she had to assume that Trevor had some reason for Carmen's absence, and that she'd either never know what it was or she'd find out in a couple months when the episode aired. (Or she could just ask Carmen later, she guessed.)

The other weird thing about today was that the *Gossip* magazine piece had come out. It was the first public announcement of Kate's involvement with *The Fame Game*, and now her email inbox and Facebook profile were crowded with messages—some from friends and family, and some from people whose faces she could hardly even remember. (Darcy Krapke? Hadn't Kate last laid eyes on her back in the fifth grade?) It was exciting, having so many notes of congratulations and best wishes, but it was also sort of unsettling. Pretty soon everyone she'd ever known (and a lot of people she'd never met) would be watching her in their living rooms at night. What would they think of her? She shuddered. It was too much—she needed to pretend, for as long as possible, that it wasn't happening. That was the only way not to freak out entirely.

And then there was Madison's reaction after she read the article. She'd called Kate—which she *never* did—and said, "Welcome to the world of *Gossip* magazine! Hey, whatever happened with that guy you met at Whisper? What was his name?"

Kate had been so caught off guard that she didn't answer for what felt like a full minute. Madison had asked the question so innocently, but the timing and the fact that she was asking it at all made Kate think there was nothing innocent about it. "Oh, um, yeah, it kind of fizzled out," she finally managed, certain that Madison knew she was lying.

"It's coming on, it's coming on," Gaby squealed, as the *Buzz! News* logo revolved in a glittering ball on the giant flat screen.

Madison settled in on an ottoman, but Gaby seemed too nervous to sit.

"Calm down," Madison said. "The interview is always in the second half of the show. And we're watching in real time so we can't skip commercials."

"Oh," Gaby said. "In that case I'm going to go grab some water. Anyone want anything?"

"No thanks," Kate and Madison said at the same time.

Madison turned to Kate. "So, how are the songs coming?" Her smile was bright and eager.

Kate couldn't tell how sincere her interest actually was, but as long as she wasn't asking about Luke, she decided to pretend it was 100 percent genuine. Madison had seemed so much mellower these days, and Kate was settling into kind of, sort of, actually . . . liking her. "Good," she said. "I've got a bunch of new ones that I'm hoping to perform pretty soon. Maybe another open mic at Grant's or something."

Madison nodded. "You should get a real gig sometime. You know, where you don't have to share the stage with a bunch of folk-song freaks."

"Uh, yeah," Kate said. "Maybe someday." It would be nice, she had to admit; there was always a high percentage of weirdos at an open mic. It just came with the territory. "Once there was this guy who was working on a whole song cycle about bumblebees. . . ."

Gaby reappeared with a giant bottle of water. "Hey, where's Carmen, anyway? Is she out with her new man?"

Kate glanced down at the coffee table, where the latest issue of *Gossip* was prominently displayed. She was sure Trevor had told Gaby to ask that question. She shrugged. "I haven't heard from her," she said. "I talked to her yesterday, but . . ." She didn't finish the sentence.

Though Kate wanted to push the thought from her mind, she couldn't help but remember yesterday afternoon, when Carmen and Luke had stopped by Stecco for lunch while she was working. Although "stopping by" wasn't exactly accurate. It was all worked out in advance, of course—Luke's agent had to give him the go-ahead to appear on the show (just once! just to talk about *The End of Love!*); the Stecco manager had once again okayed the filming as long as the entrance and sign were prominently displayed on air; the customers and employees who might be in the shot had all signed releases—but Kate had been unprepared for how uncomfortable she'd feel.

Carmen and Luke were seated at a table near the bar, so that Kate would be in the background in most of the intimate shots. Luke looked happy and handsome in a cream polo, and Carmen was stylish in a vaguely Indian-looking print blouse and skinny jeans. Kate, of course, was wearing unflattering black pants, a white oxford shirt, and a green-and-brown-striped tie. This fact alone made her want to crawl under the counter and curl up in a little ball.

But of course she couldn't do that, could she? No, she'd had to serve them their water (no ice for Carmen, extra lemon for Luke) and smile while doing so.

"Hey, you guys," she'd said brightly. "How awesome you could drop by! Your server will be by in a few minutes to take your order, but I'll come back and check on you."

Carmen had been her typical nice self, but Luke seemed slightly uncomfortable. *Good,* she'd thought. *He ought to be.*

Their directions were to discuss their upcoming movie: who else would be cast, how long the shooting would take, what it might be like to work with Colum McEntire, who had a legendary hair-trigger temper, blah, blah, blah.

Kate watched them and eavesdropped as much as her duties would let her. Their interaction was all totally harmless. They were laughing a lot, but just the way old friends do. Of course, she thought, Trevor could take the footage and turn it into whatever he wanted. *L.A. Candy* had been full of "meaningful" looks and pauses and she now knew why: That moment when Carmen looked longingly at a piece of cake at the table behind them? The time when Luke accidentally brushed Carmen's hand when they both reached for a breadstick? No doubt by the time the reels were cut and the scene edited, it'd look like the two of them were more in love than Romeo and Juliet had ever been.

Kate might have considered telling Laurel how having the two of them in her face made the whole situation even more unpleasant for her, but Laurel was off filming Madison at some fund-raiser or something, so she had not a single ally on the other side of the camera. There was also a small—very small—part of Kate that wondered at the timing of this lunch at *her* restaurant. Had Laurel said something to Trevor? Had Madison? Was Trevor actively throwing Carmen and Luke in her face because he knew it would be torture for her and wanted more drama or simply because he knew he could secure the location? Maybe he was even getting a little deep, showing the haves and the have-nots in one all-encompassing exchange.

Ugh.

Thankfully, it was over in an hour, and Kate could stop analyzing it as it was happening. When everyone was going their separate ways, Luke had mouthed, "I'll call you tonight." And, when no one was looking, he'd blown her a kiss. But it hadn't really made her feel better.

"Hey," Madison said now, jabbing Kate with a bare, pedicured foot. "Gaby's about to be on TV! Get excited."

Kate shook off the memory as best she could. "Sorry," she said. "I was just wondering if I should text Carmen to see where she is."

"Don't bother," said Madison, sinking into the couch. "Like Gab said, she's off with her man of the moment."

"What do you mean, of the moment?" Kate asked. Carmen didn't seem like the serial dating type.

Madison shrugged. "I mean, come on, Luke Kelly is a total flirt. I give their relationship two months, tops."

Kate frowned. Luke was a flirt? Where was Madison getting this information exactly?

She knows, Kate thought. *And she's just trying to get a rise out of me. Maybe she and Laurel worked this out together.* And then Kate realized the ridiculousness of Madison and Laurel teaming up to do anything and decided that if Madison knew anything it's that Kate was dating an unknown actor named Luke, and now Carmen was dating Luke Kelly. . . . The rest was just a fishing expedition for her.

"By the time filming on the movie starts, they'll be done," Madison went on. "But they'll probably pretend to still be together for the tabloids. Seriously, this has nothing to do with passion and everything to do with publicity. It's so transparent."

Kate downed her entire glass of Champagne in two swallows. Madison might not know the true story of Carmen and Luke, but she sure had sussed out the gist of it, she thought. Well, Madison was a pro.

A commercial came on and suddenly all three girls were staring at the TV. It was *their* commercial. Kate was transfixed as quick cuts of images of herself flew by (meeting Madison and Gaby at the pool! Carrying her guitar into Grant's!). The trailer had a lot of her in it, but they'd packed in a lot of unfriendly glances between Madison and Carmen, too. It all happened so fast that Kate could barely remember what the text that flashed on the screen throughout had said. Something about "from the creator of *L.A. Candy*" and "a peek behind the scenes of what it takes to make it in Hollywood." And then something about fame and those who are born with it (cut to Carmen on the red carpet) and those who are chasing it (Madison and Kate out shopping; Gaby walking out of her dressing room), and how staying in the game is only the beginning. Or something. Gaby was barely in the commercial, but she didn't seem to mind because the second it ended, her show came back on.

"Look, oh my God, there I am!" Gaby squealed.

And sure enough, there she was on-screen, looking overly made-up and highly self-conscious. Beside her on the set, in a matching armchair, sat Carmen, smiling and obviously much more at ease.

"So, you've just been given the role of Julia in *The End of Love*. It's your first picture with a major studio. How are you feeling about it?" asked the on-screen Gaby.

"Good solid opening," said Madison supportively.

"Oh, I didn't write the questions," Gaby said. She was chewing on her nails.

No, of course you didn't, thought Kate. She watched the interview, but she wasn't really listening. It was all so fake; she didn't have the energy for it. She'd just seen herself on national TV for chrissakes and even that looked fake. What she did have the energy for, she thought, was another glass of Champagne. She reached over to the bottle that was open on the coffee table and poured herself a flute full of the sparkling liquid.

"Cheers," Madison said, clinking her glass with Kate's. "To—" She stopped, blinked, and then laughed. "To what? I have absolutely no idea."

"To more Champagne!" Kate said, suddenly feeling a little better, as if the glass she'd just finished had gone straight to her head.

"You guys," Gaby whined, "you're not paying attention."

"Sorry!" they said in unison and turned their attention to the screen, where they were treated to the sight of Gaby mispronouncing the word "relevance."

When it was over, they clapped enthusiastically and Gaby took a modest bow. "I wasn't horrible, was I?"

"Not at all," Kate said, meaning it. "You were cute."

"Oh, good," Gaby said. Suddenly she frowned. "Did you see those earrings I was wearing?"

Kate shook her head. She'd barely paid attention to the interview at all; how could she be expected to notice Gaby's accessories?

"Nope," said Madison, pouring herself and Kate another glass of Champagne.

Wow, Kate thought. *Did I really finish that second glass that fast?*

"Well, they were diamond solitaires. Big ones. And I can't find them anywhere."

Kate leaned back in her chair and crossed her feet at her ankles. She was getting happier and more comfortable by the minute. She should *always* have Champagne! "Oh,

Gaby," she said lightly. "I'm sure they're just in your room somewhere. Remember when you bought that pair of earrings twice because you thought you'd lost them?" Kate pointed to her own earlobes, from which the earrings in question dangled prettily. "I'm sure that's what happened to them. Thanks again, by the way, for these. They're my favorites."

Madison laughed. "You *are* always losing things, Gab."

"But I've looked all over the place for them," she said. "And I can't find them. And they were really, really expensive."

"Well, when did you last see them?" Kate asked.

Gaby thought about this for a moment. "Yesterday morning," she said. She seemed to think a little bit more, and then she started to say something. "I—" But she stopped and gave Madison a strange look.

Madison didn't see it, though; she was gazing at the picture of herself in the *Gossip* spread. "I'm sure they'll turn up," she said, running her finger along the edge of the magazine. "Really."

"All right, guys, I think we've got it." The director of the day motioned for the camera guys to stop rolling and start packing up.

The PopTV crew began breaking down and carting all their heavy equipment back to the extra bedroom. One of the camera guys called, "Save some of that Champagne for me."

"There's a whole other bottle in the fridge," Gaby said,

momentarily forgetting about her earrings, thanks to the sight of a man with well-defined biceps.

Madison snorted. "Cast can't date crew, remember?"

"Who said anything about dating?" Gaby asked.

But it turned out that the camera guy was only kidding around and being friendly; he actually had to go home to his wife and new baby.

When the crew left and the three girls were alone, Gaby turned to Madison. "I didn't say this on-camera because I didn't want to embarrass you. But Mad, the last time I saw those earrings was yesterday morning before your dad came over."

Madison sat up. "Excuse me?" Her voice sounded like a steel blade.

Gaby paled slightly but held her ground. "I'm just saying. Those earrings were sitting on top of my dresser. And now they aren't."

"So you're accusing my father of taking them?"

"I don't know," Gaby squeaked, clearly a little afraid of her roommate.

Maybe it was the Champagne that made Kate bold, or maybe it was the fact that Madison's father was a convicted criminal, but she leaned forward and said, as gently as she could, "You know, Madison, you haven't seen your father in over a decade. You might not know him as well as you think you do. Who knows what—"

Madison stood up, her cheeks flushed with anger. "Who

the hell are you two to judge my father? An idiot and a nobody. How dare you accuse my father of stealing?" She turned to Gaby. "You with your apparent eating disorder and your inability to pronounce even the simplest words! Your room looks like a bomb went off in it. You're an absolute mess. How do you expect to find anything?" Then she turned to Kate. "And you, Little Miss Wholesome, with your nice little Ohio family and their nice little minivan and their nice boring little lives! Only you're not really so wholesome, are you? What do you know about *anything*?"

Kate's heart began to pound in her chest. She didn't know what to say. Madison didn't know anything about Kate's life in Ohio, but she certainly seemed to know something about it here.

"I'm just saying," Gaby whispered. "I've looked everywhere."

"Have you looked up your ass?" Madison hissed. "Maybe it's up there, right next to your fat head." Then she grabbed her purse and stormed out the door.

Gaby turned to Kate. "Ouch," she said.

"No kidding," Kate said. Then she set down her Champagne glass on the floor, gave Gaby a heartfelt hug, and slunk back to her apartment.

In her bedroom—which also looked like a bomb had gone off in it—she turned on her computer and checked her email. There was a message from Ethan.

No funny videos tonight. Just writing because it was the annual art fair and costume parade in the Short North. Remember when we dressed up like Jack White and Meg White? Good times, good times.

She was about to type a reply, but she noticed that her contacts list said that he was still online, even though it was past midnight in Ohio. She IM'd him. *You up? Want to Skype?*

A moment later, her computer rang.

"Hey," she said as she turned on the video. "What are you still doing up?"

Ethan's face appeared on her screen, slightly pixilated but still familiar, still handsome. "Waiting to talk to you," he said, smiling.

"Liar," she said. She giggled. She was still feeling the wine.

He shrugged. "Maybe, maybe not. But check you out—you got a new 'do."

Kate self-consciously touched the haircut Madison had taken her to get. "I thought guys didn't notice that sort of thing."

"Most guys wouldn't," Ethan said. "But I'm not most guys, am I?"

"Uh, no?" Kate said.

"It looks good on you. But different, too. You've gone all Hollywood on me already."

She looked at the little video screen that showed her

face. "Oh, come on, I look the same, don't I?"

Ethan shook his head. "Nope. But who cares? You're beautiful no matter what you do."

She ducked her head, hiding the blush in her cheeks. It was so good to see him, so good to hear his voice. She wished he were here in L.A. so they could sit at her kitchen table and make up fake band names (the Dangles; Manly Panda) and silly song titles ("Mom Jeans Genie"; "What's That Funny Smell?"). And then, after a little while, she could tell him all about the absurd Luke situation.

But even though they'd been broken up for almost a year now, they'd never talked about seeing other people. And it didn't feel right to start doing it now, as much as she might want to.

She looked up again, and there was Ethan, smiling, waiting for her to say something. "I miss you," she said suddenly.

"I miss you, too," he said.

He put his hand up to the screen, and she put her hand up to meet his. They stayed like that for a moment, holding hands from two thousand miles away.

28

PART OF A LARGER PLAN

"Well, look what the cat dragged in," Philip Curtis said, smiling at Carmen as she came into the kitchen, a bunch of tulips in her hand. "Long time no see."

She gave him a kiss and a little poke in his ample gut for the cat comment, then began opening cupboard doors, looking for a vase. It was her first Friday night family dinner in weeks, and she hadn't wanted to show up empty-handed.

"Things have been busy," she said. "I just got off a shoot, as a matter of fact." They'd filmed her shopping with Fawn on Robertson, which had been fun; she hadn't hung out with Fawn much lately. But the real reason for the scene wasn't their little spree. It was actually just an excuse to film Carmen saying, after an hour or two, "Well, I've got to get home to Casa Curtis. Mom just got back from her ten-city tour, and Dad says he's about to sign the next Adele." It was pretty crafty of Trevor, Carmen thought; even though her parents didn't want to be on *The Fame Game*, he frequently found ways to make them a presence.

She opened yet another cupboard, certain she'd find a vase. But instead she found a new blender, still unopened in its box. "Did Mom move things around in here?"

"Your mother, as you may recall, has been gone on tour for weeks. So I put things wherever I felt like it."

"Oh, so that must be why the wine is next to the Cheerios."

Philip shrugged. "Sometimes you need a little pick-me-up with breakfast."

"Very funny," Carmen said. She finally located a crystal vase in a cupboard that normally held baking supplies. "Aha," she said, holding it up. "Victory." She quickly trimmed off the ends of the tulips and arranged the flowers in the vase.

"Oh, those are just gorgeous, Carm," said her mother, gliding into the room. "You're so sweet and I've missed you like crazy." She gave her daughter a squeeze with a tan, slender arm and then a kiss on the cheek.

"I've missed you, too," Carmen said. "Both of you." She climbed onto one of the stools by the kitchen island and reached for a plate of olives and crostini. "I know you're probably jet-lagged still and everything, but please tell me you made dinner, Mom. I'm totally not in the mood for Hamburger Helper."

Philip looked affronted. "As if that's the only thing I can cook!"

"Oh yeah, right," Carmen said, laughing. "There's also Tuna Helper and frozen pizzas."

"Exactly," Philip said. "I'm a whiz in the kitchen."

Cassandra held up a hand. "Don't worry, I cooked. We're having roast chicken with lemongrass and ginger." She twisted her long dark hair into a bun and sat next to Carmen on a kitchen stool.

"Sounds great," Carmen said. "Too bad Drew couldn't come."

Philip nodded. "Yes, but he's got to earn his keep. There's a show at the Bootleg I wanted him to check out."

"Let's just eat in here, then," Cassandra said. "No Drew, no dining room."

"I had no idea it was Drew who was keeping us so civilized all this time, but fine by me," Carmen said. "Is it going to be ready soon? I'm starving."

"Shopping works up an appetite, doesn't it?" Philip asked.

Carmen looked at him in surprise. "How'd you know?"

"That gleam in your eye. It's just like your mother's. It's the gleam of material conquest. You must have found a four-hundred-dollar pair of cashmere socks or something."

Carmen laughed. "It's summertime, Dad. In *L.A.* What would I need cashmere socks for?"

"Who knows? I don't follow the whims of fashion. Maybe they're all the rage because Gwyneth Paltrow likes them," he said. But he smiled, and Carmen knew that he was pleased to make the sort of money that would allow his daughter to buy a pair of four-hundred-dollar socks, should she in fact want them.

The timer on the oven beeped, and Cassandra extracted a beautifully roasted bird. "Voilà," she said. "There's roasted veggies in there, too. Because God knows Philip didn't touch a vegetable the whole time I was gone."

"Isn't scotch a vegetable?" he asked, winking at her.

She rolled her eyes and proceeded to serve them their dinner on white bone china plates.

"So," Philip said as he sliced into his chicken, "I read something interesting about you the other day."

Carmen hoped it was something besides the Luke business. "What?"

"That you're dating that Australian actor—what's his name?"

"Luke Kelly," Cassandra said. "He's her costar in *The End of Love*. Oh, honey, it's just so exciting about the movie! Did you get the bouquet I sent?"

"Yeah, thanks, Mom; it's on my dresser. And yeah, it's amazing about the movie. But that Luke thing? Untrue. I'm not dating him. Didn't you tell him, Mom?"

"Tell me what?" Philip asked. "You didn't break up already, did you?"

Carmen laughed. "No, Dad! I haven't had a boyfriend in forever—you think I'd get rid of one so quickly now? The truth is that we were never dating in the first place. We're just friends."

As she proceeded to explain the story to them (leaving out the part about their casual hookup, of course—she didn't tell her parents *everything*), she saw the expression on her father's face change from surprise, to bafflement, to distaste.

"So it's a lie then," he said when she had finished. "Is this your musician friend Drew told me about?"

Carmen nodded, happy that Drew was talking up Kate at work.

"You're participating in a lie that very likely is causing your friend Kate stress, if not downright pain. How is that a good idea?"

Carmen sighed. "Oh, Dad, she understands! It's all part of a larger plan." *I hope* she understands, *she thought but didn't add.* I mean, I think she does.

But her dad shook his head. "I don't like it," he said. "I don't like dishonesty, and I don't like the fact that this TV show hasn't even aired yet and it's already turning your life around." He pointed a chicken leg at her—a gesture that was maybe meant to look intimidating but which merely looked comical. "This isn't how things are supposed to work."

Carmen bristled. "Yes, the show has turned my life around, Dad. For the *better*. You know that Colum McEntire wasn't even going to let me audition? And then Trevor Lord convinced him to give me a chance, and then I was so good that *he gave me the lead*. The lead, Dad! In a movie I otherwise would have been lucky to be an extra in." She realized that she was gripping her fork so hard that her knuckles were white.

"I'm sure you both have a point—" Cassandra began.

"What I'm seeing, Carmen," Philip interrupted, "is a pattern of you pretending to do something, or be something, for the benefit of other people. You took the fall for Fawn when she shoplifted, and now you're letting Luke pretend like he's your boyfriend because he and his slimeball agent think that's better for his image. What else will you agree to do?"

Carmen blinked at her father. She hadn't seen him this upset in a long time, and she was torn between comforting him and yelling at him. She understood that he had a point, but he was blowing the whole thing way out of proportion.

"Well?" Philip asked.

Carmen shook her head. She decided not to fight him. The premiere was in a week, and she couldn't risk a blowup that would prevent him from coming. "Seriously, Dad," she said, reaching across the counter to touch his hand. "You have to trust me on this one. Everything is going to work out in the end, and I'm only going to be better and stronger after this experience. Okay?"

Philip looked toward Cassandra, who nodded slightly. She had always been more understanding of Carmen's strange half-famous life, perhaps because she herself was so used to the spotlight.

"You think she knows what she's doing?" he asked his wife.

"I do," Cassandra said. "We raised a smart girl, Philip. Let's trust her. Let's see what amazing things she does with the opportunities she's been given."

Philip gazed into his scotch, swirling the ice cubes around in his glass. After a moment he looked up. "Okay," he said finally. "Consider my objections raised and withdrawn. For now." He shot Carmen a look. "I just want you to be careful."

She smiled at him. "Daddy, I will be. Thank you for understanding. Does this mean you guys will be at the premiere then?"

"I wouldn't miss it for the world," Cassandra said.

"Me either," said Philip.

Carmen beamed at both of them. "Thanks, you guys."

Her mother patted her arm and then suddenly looked very serious. "You know what this means, Carmen," she said.

Carmen was puzzled. "No . . ."

"Barneys," Cassandra said. "You, me, and a gold AmEx."

Philip rolled his eyes. "I could have predicted *that*."

Carmen laughed. "Well, just like Friday night dinners, shopping is a family tradition," she said. "Right, Dad?"

And of course Philip Curtis had to agree.

29

LUCKY GIRL

Madison was curled on the couch in her dad's house, the Pendleton wool throw she'd bought for him wrapped around her bare legs. Charlie kept the air-conditioning on twenty-four hours a day, so the house felt like a giant, well-decorated walk-in freezer.

"Oh, come on," she muttered into her phone. She was on hold for Trevor, who—she was quite sure—was making her wait just for the fun of it. She tapped her fingers on the arm of the sofa and made a mental note to book an appointment with her manicurist. The premiere for *The Fame Game* was only three days away, and red-carpet preparations were already underway: Madison had stepped up her routines with her trainer, made appointments for an oxygen facial, a wax, and a spray tan, and had avoided so much as being in the same room as a carb. The extra bedroom in Charlie's house was overflowing with dresses that various designers had sent her, each of them hoping that she'd pick theirs to don on the red carpet.

"Madison," Trevor crowed into her ear. "So sorry to keep you waiting."

Sure you are, she thought. But she said, "No problem, Trevor, I know you're a busy man." (She wanted to start off the conversation on a friendly note.)

"What's up?" Trevor asked, immediately sounding suspicious.

Whoops, maybe she shouldn't have been so nice. "I have a problem," she said.

Of course you do, she could practically hear him thinking. Trevor cleared his throat. "If you're talking about that PA who made a pass at Gaby, it's been taken care of and won't happen again," he said.

"What?" Madison said. She didn't know anything about that—but on the other hand, she didn't care at all. "Oh, never mind, I have no interest in whatever the PA did. What I called to talk to you about is my living situation."

"It's a little late to be complaining about your apartment," he said. "If you wanted the extra square footage you'd have had to give up the balcony. We discussed that back in June."

"Will you just let me talk, please?" Madison said. "It's not the apartment. It's Gaby. I can't live with her anymore."

"I can ask her not to bring guys home—"

"I said *let me talk*," she said fiercely. "What I'm trying to tell you is that Gaby accused my father of stealing a pair of her earrings. And I can't live with someone who says

266

that kind of thing about him. He did his time already—three years. He paid his debt to society. And for the record, he was not even *aware* of the robbery that his friends perpetrated that night, not until later. Don't you think he's suffered enough?" She took a deep breath and waited for Trevor to respond. It took him a little while.

Eventually he said, "Well, Madison, you know I want to keep you happy. But I can't have all you girls living in separate places. You're already doing such different things during the day—if three of you didn't live in the same building we'd lose all sense of cohesion."

"So put me in another apartment in the building if you have to."

Trevor sighed. "There's nothing open. Besides, having you and Gaby in the same place gives the show a home base. That's where you girls will have your dinner parties, your movie nights, your late-night girl talks. Do you think I want to film a party in Kate's little place? No! Your apartment is the heart of the show because you're living in it."

"Because *I'm* the heart of the show," Madison said. "The star."

"Ex*act*ly."

The air-conditioning kicked on again, and Madison pulled the blanket tighter around her. She was holding on to some serious currency—clearly there was more to the story about Carmen and Luke dating and all she had to do was hint about it to Trevor—but she wasn't sure if now was the right time to use it. She knew that Trevor was right; future impromptu dinner parties should take place at that lovely long table in their airy, nearly spotless apartment (naturally, maid service was part of her contract)—not in Kate's little hovel, and certainly not in Carmen's house. Wherever it was that Carmen lived, Madison hoped never to go there; it was enemy territory.

"You can't make me spend the night there," she said. "I can pretend to live there, and I can go there for scenes. But I'm going to sleep somewhere else."

"Fine by me," Trevor said. "Do whatever makes you happy. Just make sure that it looks like you live there."

"Fine. Whatever," she said and hung up. She hated being refused, but she couldn't argue with Trevor's reasoning. And, really, she needed to get to the bottom of the Kate/Luke/Carmen thing before she tried to benefit from it. Like Nick had said, she had to be better at keeping tabs on her costars.

To make herself feel better, she padded into the spare bedroom and surveyed the bounty of dresses she had to choose from. There was the rose-colored Rodarte, the midnight-blue Talbot Runhof, the red Max Azria, the shimmery gold L'Wren Scott. On the floor were boxes of heels: suede wedges, peep-toe pumps, strappy sandals, sexy slingbacks. She had her pick of it all. Not to keep, necessarily—but to wear and love and be photographed in. She didn't mind having to return them. She never wore the same thing twice anyway.

What a long way she'd come from Armpit Falls, where the best dress she could hope for was a hand-me-down from a neighbor or some sad reject from the Salvation Army. Where she had to wear the same pair of shoes for years: when they were too big (cotton balls in the toes), when they fit (briefly), and when they were too small (thin socks and blisters).

Normally Madison did an excellent job of pretending to everyone, herself included, that her impoverished past had never existed—but being around Charlie often reminded her. It was good not to forget where you came from, she thought. Good to appreciate how much better things were now. PopTV was going to film her getting ready for the big night, and she got to go to the premiere on the arm of her dad. She couldn't believe her luck.

She touched the shimmering blue fabric of the Talbot Runhof gown and considered slipping it on. It had a slightly asymmetrical neckline and a long, columnar body that made her look even thinner and taller than she was. Its dark color would contrast beautifully with the diamond necklace she'd picked out from Luxe Paris, a boutique French jeweler that had just opened its first American store on Rodeo Drive.

Last week, the jeweler's publicist had called to offer to loan her the piece of her choice. He had, in fact, practically *begged* her to wear a Luxe Paris design on the red carpet. She'd been charmed by his enthusiasm (he was a huge *Madison's Makeovers* fan), so she'd agreed. She'd taken

Charlie with her to pick out the jewelry. This was partly because she wanted to spend more time with him, and partly because she wanted to impress him further with the life she'd built for herself—a life where she could walk out of a store with a necklace worth six figures, just because she was Madison Parker.

In the Luxe Paris shop, a pale pink room full of roses, a petite redhead had brought out sapphire bangles, diamond collars, emerald teardrop earrings, and ropes of black pearls.

"Wow," Charlie had whispered. "Just look at all this stuff."

Madison had delicately sifted through shimmering piles, holding up one glittering piece after another. Should she go with rubies? Sapphires? *No*, she thought, *definitely diamonds*. She could have spent hours there, just admiring herself in the mirror as she modeled a fortune in jewelry. In the end it was Charlie who found the perfect piece: a drop necklace with pear-shaped and marquise diamonds. He showed her earrings, too—beautiful triple teardrops—but the redhead said she was only authorized to loan Madison one piece.

"One?" Madison had said, raising her eyebrows.

The redhead had flushed. "I could call my supervisor. . . ."

Madison briefly considered making her do it, just to throw her weight around. But she was planning to wear her hair down for the premiere, which meant that no one would see her earlobes anyway.

"The necklace is enough, Dad," she said. "Really."

And all she'd had to do to get it was sign her name on a dotted line, declaring herself responsible for its safe return. It was just like a library book, except that it cost two hundred thousand dollars. If she didn't return it, she'd have to give over her car, her bank accounts, and her first-born child (if she ever had one of those sniveling brats, which was doubtful). And even that wouldn't be enough to cover it. But who cared about that? She wanted to sparkle—no, she wanted to shine like a damn klieg light. And so she would.

Now, in the spare bedroom of the West Hollywood bungalow, she slipped the circle of diamonds around her neck. It was heavy and cold. She shivered—a mix of chill and pleasure—but soon the necklace warmed against her skin.

Lucky girl, she thought to herself. *Lucky, lucky girl.*

"Madison?" Charlie called, knocking softly on her door. He'd been out when she woke up. *Out for a walk*, his note had said.

"Come in," she said. "Excuse the mess."

Charlie raised his eyebrows at the explosion of gowns on the bed. "Wow, you going to have costume changes or something?"

Madison laughed. "No, I'm only going to wear one. I laid them out so I could decide."

"Oh," he said. He took a few hesitant steps into her

room. "Listen, uh, Sweetpea." Then he stopped and ran his fingers through his hair. It was graying at the temples; she'd never noticed that before. "Um, you've done so much for me. And I wanted to say thank you."

"You don't have to thank me," Madison assured him. "I wanted to do all of it."

"Yes, I do have to thank you," Charlie insisted. He held out a small blue velvet bag. "Here, I got this for you. It's—well, you'll see."

Touched, Madison took the little bag and emptied its contents into her palm. "Oh my God," she whispered, looking up at her father in shock. "Where did you get these?"

Charlie ducked his head in embarrassment. "At that jewelry store we were at the other day."

Madison closed her palm around the diamond earrings. "These are the ones that match the necklace," she said. "But Dad, you can't afford this!"

Charlie looked offended. "They offer payment plans," he said. "I've got a job now. I *can* afford it."

"But—"

"But nothing, Sweetpea. You deserve them." He smiled at her, the corners of his blue eyes crinkling up. "You deserve all the diamonds in the world."

Madison flung her arms around his neck. "Oh, thank you, Daddy," she said. "I'm such a lucky girl."

30

HOW THIS HOLLYWOOD STUFF WORKS

"Do you want green or red sauce on your burrito, babe?" Luke asked, peering into the paper bag from Tacos Por Favor.

"Whatever," Kate said. She was sitting on his couch, looking at an old *Rolling Stone* review of Rihanna's *Talk That Talk*, which was apparently her "smuttiest record by far." And while Kate didn't consider herself a prude, exactly, she was a bit shocked by the quoted lyrics. All of her own songs seemed so G-rated in comparison.

"Oh, come on, red or green?" His voice was cajoling.

She flipped to the next page. "Don't they taste pretty much the same?"

"Well, one has tomatillos and the other has tomatoes," Luke said. "So, no, not really."

"Whatever. You pick," Kate said. She started to read an article about the demise of Sonic Youth.

Luke came into the living room with her burrito on a

plate and a little cup of both kinds of salsa. "What's up?" he asked. "You seem kind of off."

She looked up at him. He was so handsome; his brown hair was sun-lightened and his eyes were the prettiest green she'd ever seen. His face was open, expectant. He didn't want her to feel bad, she could tell.

But she *did* feel bad. She was mad at him for putting her in such an awkward position. Who hoped to be a star's secret girlfriend? It was fine when it was *their* secret and they were in it together, alone. But now there were agents and publicists and tabloids and Madison and somehow their sweet little secret had turned into Kate being Luke's dirty secret. She wanted to confront him about it, but she was afraid to—she wasn't a confrontation kind of person. Plus part of her was hoping that he'd take her in his arms and make everything better. That he'd somehow make everything bad go away.

She shrugged. "I'm just tired," she said. "Nervous about the premiere."

Was Luke planning to go? she wondered. Would he be Carmen's date? Because that would really add insult to injury.

He sat down on the ottoman near her, reaching out to circle her slender ankle with his hand. "It's the Carmen thing, isn't it?" he said.

She finally met his eyes. "Yes," she said. "It's . . . so much more unpleasant than I thought it would be."

Luke's hand on her leg was warm and gentle. "You're

not jealous, are you? Because there's nothing to be jealous about."

"No, I'm not *jealous*. I don't know what I am. But I know that it doesn't feel good that I can only be your girl-friend in the privacy of your house."

Luke sighed. "We've been through this," he said. "I'm just on the verge of really making it big. Maybe that makes me sound like a cocky bastard, but it's true. Everything I've worked for is right within reach, I can see it. I don't want to screw anything up." He ran his hand up her shin, and she shivered at his touch. "And since I don't know how this Hollywood stuff works myself, I listen to the people who do."

"It just sucks," Kate said.

"I'm sorry, Kate," he said. "I know it sucks. I mean, it sucks for me, too."

Kate plucked at a lifeless fern on Luke's windowsill, thinking that it couldn't possibly suck as much for him as it did for her. "Is it that I'm a nobody? Or that I'm about to be somebody, just not the kind of somebody that's good for your image?" she asked. Because she understood that—Facebook congratulations from old friends aside—she was still pretty much an unknown. But after the premiere on Wednesday, she'd be the girl from *The Fame Game*. The girl that every other girl growing up in the Midwest and dreaming of stardom hoped to be.

Life was going to change overnight; she realized that. Soon the PopTV cameras would be only a handful among hundreds: paparazzi taking stills; TMZ reporters documenting her movements on video; fans snapping shots on their iPhones. People would ask her for her autograph. They would want to touch her, to make sure she was real.

Luke sighed. "It's not about you," he said. "It's about what's good for the movie, and my career. I was on the verge of making it once before, and one misstep sent the whole house of cards crashing down. And I had no control over it. That was the lowest point of my career, in my life, even lower than when I was an out-of-work actor, because I'd been so close to finally making it. And then I wasn't. I can't be there again. You understand, don't you?"

Yes, Kate understood. All of a sudden she truly got it. She didn't want to, but she did. "Yeah, I do. A career is more important to you than your feelings for me. And that makes you different from the person I thought you were." She pushed aside her untouched lunch and stood.

"That's not true," Luke said, reaching for her hand.

She let him hold her lifeless fingers. "I came to L.A. because I wanted to follow my dreams. I didn't think about fame or money or any of it—I just thought about making music. Isn't that how you felt, too? About acting?"

"Of course," Luke said. "I still feel that way. I act because I love it, not because I want a nicer house or a bigger motorcycle."

"So do you love acting like Carmen's your girlfriend? Is that rewarding, too?" she said angrily.

"That's not fair," Luke said, standing now, too. "It's

a career move, Kate. I know you're not so naïve that you don't realize that." He moved to take her into his arms, and though Kate wanted more than anything to let him, she pushed him away.

"What's not fair is you treating me this way," she said softly. "You can either be with me publicly, or not at all."

She felt her breath catch in her throat. She hadn't meant to give an ultimatum like that. But she had, and she steeled herself for what he would say.

But he didn't say anything. He gazed into her eyes, and then he leaned close. His lips met hers in a shock of warmth and softness. "Oh, Kate," he whispered. "I like you. A lot. Why are you doing this?"

She sank into his kiss; she ached to be with him. "What's it going to be, Luke?" she asked, feeling the sting of tears in the corners of her eyes because she already knew his answer but still hoped she was wrong.

When he didn't speak, Kate knew she was right. She turned and walked out of his cottage, the tears already streaming down her face.

31

THE BEST OF FRIENDS

It was seriously cramped inside the limo, Carmen noted with some annoyance. The PopTV cameraman was probably six foot five, and Drew was almost that tall; plus there was Fawn with her weird long dress train and her own video camera, which she kept pointing in Carmen's face. And Luke, who had barely said a word since Drew not-so-subtly hinted that he was on Team Kate and he thought Luke was a douchebag (with the camera rolling—Carmen had accidentally-on-purpose kicked Drew for it). Carmen had hoped the limo ride to the premiere would calm her nerves, but so far it had done the opposite.

"Carmen Curtis, you look fantastic tonight. Tell me, who are you wearing?" Fawn said, pretending to be one of the dozens of reporters who'd be lining the red carpet.

"Give it a rest, Fawn," Carmen said. She turned to look out the window, hoping that would be enough to get Fawn to leave her alone for a minute. In fact, she was wearing Nina Ricci, and Fawn knew it. At least Fawn had stopped trying to get Luke to "say things in Australian."

Carmen watched the storefronts of Wilshire Boulevard slip by, their windows sparkling in the late afternoon sun. She knew what to expect from the coming hours—she'd been to more than her share of red-carpet events—but never one where she was a main attraction, and she didn't know how she'd feel about it. Would it seem wonderful? Or just weird? She looked at Luke, who seemed seriously out of sorts, and thought: *Just weird. For sure.*

"You want a mint?" Drew held out one of the candies that seemed to reside in every limo she'd ever taken.

She turned to him and smiled faintly. He was wearing a tux but no bow tie, and because his tattoos were covered up he looked as preppy and conventional as could be. "No thanks," she said, watching him unwrap it and then pop it into his own mouth.

"Suit yourself," he said. "Fawn? Doctor Rose?"

Luke shook his head, and so did Fawn. "Oh, I don't eat processed sugar. Ever. Or bread or dairy. And rarely salt or meat."

"She's following some diet Aja supposedly is on," Carmen explained.

"I hope she's here tonight," Fawn said eagerly. "You had your publicist call hers, right?"

"Sure," Carmen lied. "Of course." She'd been in a photo shoot with Aja several months ago and they'd had a nice conversation—but that was that. She hadn't called her.

"Almost there," Drew said, chewing another mint.

Their driver had slowed down in the inevitable traffic jam caused by all the limos ahead of them slowing, then stopping, their doors opening to reveal Hollywood stars and starlets, dressed in their glittering finest.

Carmen took a deep breath. It was all beginning now. This was her night. She wished she could enjoy it.

Her parents weren't coming until later, after the red carpet; her dad didn't want PopTV filming him, and her mom didn't want to run the risk of upstaging her. And in a way, she was relieved. This was her first real bid for independence, her best chance to come out from under their big, successful shadows. It would have been weird had they walked the press gauntlet with her. She had to do it on her own.

Or, not *entirely* on her own. As the driver opened her door, she saw her castmates already there at the start of the carpet, smiling and waving to the yelling crowd.

She made eye contact with Luke and he nodded once at her before opening the door and waiting to help her out of the car. "I'll see you guys inside," she said to Drew and Fawn, and then she took Luke's hand and stepped out onto the sidewalk. The plan was for them to hold hands as he walked her to where her costars would be waiting. The plan was now making her feel ill.

Kate greeted her with a hollow smile, and Carmen wanted to reach out to squeeze her hand. Kate had called the other night to tell her what had happened with Luke, and Carmen had immediately driven to her apartment to comfort her. She'd even broken her pre–red carpet diet to share a pint of Ben & Jerry's with Kate. Because appearances were important, but not as important as friends. But when Kate asked if Luke was going to be Carmen's date to the premiere, and Carmen said yes, it felt like everything changed between them. Carmen didn't think she'd done anything wrong, but it was starting to feel like she had.

And now they had to stand together on the red carpet and smile.

The camera flashes were like strobe lights at a disco. Carmen and Kate posed with their arms around each other as more and more cars pulled up, and more and more of the rich and famous climbed out. Even though her mind was elsewhere, Carmen was conscious of keeping herself turned partially sideways to the photographers, with her left foot planted in front of her right. She pointed her front toes to the cameras and placed her weight on her back foot. (All this to counteract the ten pounds the cameras added.)

She glanced over at Gaby, who was wearing a one-shoulder LBD that kind of looked like it was made out of a Hefty bag. But she was almost pulling it off, and she certainly looked happy with the attention. In a way, these were Gaby's best moments: when she was just smiling, looking pretty, and not being asked to think about anything.

In another few moments, Madison showed up—of course she'd be the last to arrive—and even Carmen had to admit that she looked stunning in a midnight-blue column dress. She was also wearing the most brilliant diamond necklace Carmen had ever seen. Behind her came Sophia, clad in what appeared to be a turquoise sari, and Charlie Wardell, looking for all the world like he'd rather be back in prison than take another step on the red carpet. Madison posed with them for a minute or two, then made an elaborate show of hugging them both before she came over to join the other three girls. She placed herself next to Kate, and together they stood smiling, united, as if they were all the best of friends.

"Where's your date, Carmen?" Madison said through her smile. "Is he double-booked?"

What the hell was that supposed to mean? Had Kate told Madison the truth about Luke?

After a while, Laurel appeared to usher them along toward the Hammer Museum at the far end of the red carpet, where the party was already underway. Carmen paused to speak to various reporters ("So, tell us about your new beau!"; "What's it like to work with Madison Parker?"), and her answers were gracious and vague ("He's a great guy and I'm so excited to be working with him."; "She's quite the character. You'll have to tune in to see . . ."). The camera shutters never stopped clicking.

Everything was going smoothly—but she couldn't shake the feeling that something was off. This was her life, but it didn't really feel like it. Reality TV, she realized, made everything just a little too unreal.

Above them the sky was darkening, and the lights of the museum glowed invitingly. The nervousness that

Carmen felt had vanished. So what if Kate was mad at her? So what if Madison knew about Luke. Carmen needed to stop worrying about everyone else and start worrying about Carmen. She was in control. Her eyes were wide open, just like her dad said all those weeks ago.

32

THE BIRTH OF A STAR

The garden of the Hammer Museum looked like something from a fairy tale, Kate thought, or like the most expensive prom she could ever have imagined. Paper lanterns hung like brilliant, multicolored moons over tables decorated with sprays of lilies and roses. Waiters glided along, carrying trays of Champagne and appetizers. Music was coming from somewhere, but already the sound of laughter and conversation was drowning it out.

She reached for a glass of Champagne and took a small sip (she'd learned, thanks to the night of watching Gaby's interview—or, more accurately, the morning after—that too much was not a good thing). She'd made it through the press gauntlet without tripping in her high heels or saying something stupid to an E! reporter, and now she had a little while to relax before the show really began.

Oh, who was she kidding—she had to play her song to the crowd! Relaxing was not an option tonight.

Gaby and her date—Trey? Jay? Kate couldn't

remember—were sticking close to her. They'd shared the limo to the museum, which had given Kate ample time to admire Trey's (or Jay's) new tattoo (a Chinese dragon on his calf, of all places) as well as learn about the various hair products that he used to keep his hair looking wet at all times. She forced herself to not think about Luke, and how if he'd been with her they would joke about this guy later, which of course was thinking about Luke. Luke who was coming with Carmen, which is why Kate was with Gaby. She knew she shouldn't be mad at Carmen—her friend hadn't really done anything wrong, but she couldn't help feeling strange around her now.

Gaby's contribution to the conversation was a long rave about Oscar Blandi's dry shampoo, as well as occasional musings about which celebrities would be in attendance at tonight's event. Gaby might not have a gift for words, but she had total recall for a celebrity guest list.

Kate had kind of wished she'd brought a book to read. Or had insisted that her mom and sister made the trip out. At least Natalie was around somewhere. Kate had given her invites to her, and no doubt Natalie was somewhere in this building wearing an amazing dress she'd made herself.

Now that Kate was here, she was feeling giddy. She hadn't known what to expect of the party, but as far as she could tell, PopTV had gone all out.

She had gone all out, too. She'd never been this done up before. Her dress was gray silk charmeuse, with a deep V-neck and a slit up the leg. It was so light and smooth that it felt like water against her skin. Her makeup had been professionally applied, and her hair was fashioned into a soft, braided updo.

Much of this was thanks to Madison, who'd helped her pick out her look after Kate finished rehearsing her song the day before. (She actually had a backup band this time—and who cared that Trevor had instructed the band to "pep up the song"? She had a professional band performing with her!) The PopTV cameras were there, of course, so they could capture Madison's advice for how to "slim the silhouette," "elongate the neck," and "accentuate what curves you have." Kate wasn't really listening to Madison's various monologues, but it occurred to her that Madison must miss having her own makeover show; she seemed like she was really good at it.

While Madison directed her to try on various dresses, Kate thought about the last time they'd seen each other, when Gaby had lost her earrings and Madison had called Kate a boring little nobody. She knew Madison had been defensive about her father—that was the reason she'd lashed out, but did that excuse it? Kate had to admit that it bothered her still. She felt too nervous to bring it up, though. She hoped that they could just forgive and forget without ever talking about it.

"Yes, this is the one," Madison had said when Kate tried on the Halston Heritage dress that she was now wearing as she gazed out over the glittering crowd. "It has a beautiful line and the color is great on your skin. It also makes you look at least four inches taller."

"Um, isn't that the heels?" Kate had asked, poking her patent-leather peep-toe pump out from below the gown's hem. They were the highest heels she'd ever worn, and she was seriously worried she might break an ankle.

Madison shook her head. "Heels add height, but so does the cut of a dress."

"So I look, like, eight inches taller total?" Kate had asked.

She was trying to be funny, but Madison didn't laugh.

After the camera crew had gotten what they needed, Madison had abruptly turned to go, and Kate realized she was going to have to say something to clear the air. She didn't want to make an enemy of Madison. That seemed like a bad idea for all sorts of reasons.

"Wait," Kate had called. "I can tell you're still mad about the other night. And I just wanted to say I'm sorry."

Madison had turned around and raised an eyebrow, waiting for Kate to continue.

"It wasn't fair of us to bring your dad into it. You know him, Madison, and we don't. You say you trust your dad, and I'm sure that you're right to. I'm really sorry if I ever suggested otherwise." She smiled shyly. "Friends?"

Madison had paused at the door and looked at her for a moment, as if deciding whether or not to just keep walking away. She didn't, though; she smiled. "Friends," she'd said.

Now, Madison was over by the stage, introducing her

father to one of the PopTV executives while Sophia hovered in the background (even though Madison had told Kate her sister's name was Sophie, Kate still thought of her as Sophia—after all, she didn't think of Madison as Madelyn, and that was *her* name), smiling and emanating love vibes. (Kate had to wonder how long that would last— she'd seen Sophia on *L.A. Candy,* and as far as she was concerned, people didn't change. Not *that* much, anyway.)

Kate felt someone tap her on the shoulder and turned to see Carmen's friend Fawn, who she'd met a couple times.

"Oh my God, you look amazing!" Fawn said while giving her an enthusiastic hug.

"Thanks," Kate said, a little taken aback. Fawn had previously said about ten words to her.

"It's cool that you were okay with the whole Carmen and Luke thing, considering," Fawn said.

What the hell was she talking about? "Considering what?"

"Y'know, that they'd hooked up before you guys met."

Weeks of having cameras in her face must have finally had an effect on Kate, because she barely flinched, even though what she was thinking was: *What. The. Fuck?!*

"Kate!" cried a voice, and Kate saw Laurel, dressed in a slinky red number, and for once not carrying a travel mug of coffee, hurrying toward her.

"Um, I've got to go," she said to Fawn. "But I'm sure I'll see you later!" Kate hoped to never see her again. She turned to Laurel.

"Kate, are you ready? You're on in five."

Kate felt her stomach practically explode with butterflies. "No?" she squeaked.

Laurel gripped her arm with long, cold fingers. "I'm nervous, too," she said. "But everything is going to be amazing. Okay? Now, the plan is that Trevor will introduce you, and then you'll play your song."

Kate's shock and anger dissipated as she had a moment of even greater panic—*where was Lucinda?*—but then she remembered that her guitar and all the backup instruments were waiting for her on the stage. (For the first time in her life she'd had a roadie to lug her guitar and amp around—in a way, that helped her feel like she'd made it already.)

It had been so crazy to get the phone call from Trevor the other day. For one thing, he'd never called her before, whereas Madison made it sound like he called her every night to tuck her in with a good bedtime story from her favorite gossip mag. For another thing, he'd said that Mike from Swing House had sent him the song, and he wanted to use it as the opening music for the series.

"Girls across the country are going to be singing 'Starstruck' on the way to school next week," Trevor had said after he told her he was sending a messenger with a contract for her to sign. "It's going to be your first hit. Did I mention you can buy the MP3 of it on iTunes starting tonight? Yeah, took care of that the other day."

Kate just hadn't known what to say. When she'd first heard the final version, she couldn't believe it was her song.

It was a far cry from what she'd recorded herself. Mike had layered in one of her ukulele tracks and added some drums, making the sound as lush as it did in Kate's head. Plus, he'd used one of her joke takes in the chorus, about being ready for the game. At first Kate was annoyed but then realized it did make the song more appropriate for the show's opening.

Laurel's grip tightened on her arm. "Don't worry, you're going to kill it. And then the other girls will come up on stage, and you'll stand there together and introduce each other and the episode. Got it?"

Kate nodded. She was staring at the stage, imagining herself already up there, singing and playing better than she ever had before. But she also couldn't help remembering all the YouTube videos that Ethan had sent her over the last six months: the guy auditioning for *American Idol* whose only talent was holding a note so long that all the judges kept checking their watches; the kid who tried to sing "Happy Birthday" on *Good Morning America* but instead hyperventilated and passed out. She *so* did not want to be like those people. But her fingers felt stiff and her throat was tight with worry. And her heart hurt a little too. More from Luke's betrayal or Carmen's? She wasn't sure.

"Seriously, you're going to be great," Laurel said, and Kate nodded, still staring at the stage.

A moment later, Trevor appeared on it, looking slick and intimidating in a pin-stripe power suit and a platinum Rolex that must have weighed at least a pound. He took the microphone and smiled, and the crowd immediately hushed.

"Good evening, ladies and gentlemen—and agents," he said, and the sound of polite laughter rose up from the room. "I'm thrilled to welcome you to the premiere of PopTV's next hit show, *The Fame Game*. Before we start the episode, I'm going to call up our newest star, Kate Hayes." He smiled in Kate's direction, and Kate felt the butterflies in her stomach doing cartwheels and somersaults. "You all have been in the room with her for half an hour now, and you probably didn't notice her."

Wow, thanks a lot, thought Kate.

"Maybe you said to yourself, Oh, there's a pretty little redhead. I wonder what cop show she's been an extra on. But ladies and gentlemen, tonight you get to witness the birth of a star. It starts tonight, and it continues all season long. Ladies and gentlemen, I give you . . . Kate Hayes!"

All eyes in the room turned toward Kate as she ascended the stairs to the stage. With each step, the hurt and confusion she felt hardened into something like determination—she would go onstage and kick ass. She was no longer Kate Hayes, that girl from that YouTube video. That girl was not good enough for Luke. Screw Luke. Once she was on her mark, the spotlights blinded her; the crowd was a dark blur. She reached for Lucinda and brought her into her arms as she sat on the stool at center stage. Behind her, the backup musicians quietly took their places.

She took a deep breath and willed the butterflies away. She could not afford to choke! She tried to imagine that she was in her room back in Columbus, and the only person watching her was Ethan with his video camera. Everything had been so much simpler back then, she thought.

Simpler, but also a lot less exciting.

She closed her eyes and felt her fingers touch the strings of her guitar. *Here goes nothing*, she thought.

33

EMPTY

Madison didn't normally sleep late—she had a regular 8 a.m. date with her trainer—but the morning after the premiere she didn't wake up until 9. And then she lay around in bed, feeling generally pleased with life, for another half an hour. Outside the window she could see the brilliant red rosebushes that she knew Charlie carefully watered every day. She was glad she'd gotten him this house instead of a fancy apartment in the Marina; he took so much pleasure in having a yard.

Madison stretched out luxuriously against the 600-count Donna Karan sheets. Last night had gone almost as well as she could have hoped. She'd looked amazing, and she knew that when she logged on to her computer there would be hundreds of pictures of herself on gossip blogs and entertainment sites (*Madison wows in midnight! Madison sparkles in Luxe Paris!*). Her face felt sore from smiling, and her right hand was still stiff from all the autographs she'd stayed to sign.

The reaction to the show had been unanimously positive, and afterward people had rushed up to congratulate her, including an executive from PopTV Films and an actor on one of HBO's series whom Madison had always thought was hot. He'd asked for her number and promised to call her next week when he got back from Cabo, where he and some friends were opening a restaurant.

Things had not been completely perfect, however. For instance, Carmen had gotten more lines during the introductions on the stage. Kate had flubbed the beginning of her song and had had to start over. (She really needed to get that stage fright under control if she ever wanted to make it in the music industry.) The whole evening Gaby had insisted on dragging around that moron, who kept telling Madison that she should date his best friend because he could tell she'd "totally love him." As if she'd ever be seen with some cologne-drenched ex–frat boy with a Camaro and a collection of Ed Hardy shirts!

And while Charlie had smiled happily all night, he also seemed overwhelmed by the cameras and the hubbub. He'd been shy with the reporters: When he couldn't avoid them completely, he had mumbled out answers to their questions. Madison had then had to translate: "He said it's a dream come true, being back with his daughters! Yes, this is the first time he's been to L.A., and yes, he absolutely loves it!"

Sophie, of course, had been the opposite of Charlie; she'd tried to elbow in front of Madison at every opportunity she had. Apparently the whole one-love, peace-on-earth, all-is-mellow business didn't translate to the press line. Although it hadn't mattered much, because Madison was the one that everyone had wanted to talk to. She had smiled and flirted and hinted at upcoming story lines like the pro she was, and everyone had eaten it right up.

The only really bad thing—the thing that she was trying not to think about—was that Trevor had chosen Kate's song for the opening of *The Fame Game*. How had he not run this by her first? It was beginning to feel like Jane Roberts all over again. But maybe Sophie's sweetness-and-light act had rubbed off on Madison a little bit, or maybe being back with her dad had reminded her that there were other things in life besides fame. Madison wasn't sure, but she didn't have the urge to call Trevor up right now and scream into his ear.

She snuggled down under the covers for one last moment. She'd probably change her mind later. But right now she'd just go drink some coffee in the kitchen and relax a little. Then she could read Trevor the riot act. But for now, he could enjoy his morning.

Slowly, lazily, she swung her legs out of bed. As she got dressed, she decided that she should take Charlie to breakfast. It would be a celebratory meal—she might even allow herself a pancake. She pulled her hair into a smooth ponytail and brushed a little mineral foundation over her face. On her way to Charlie's room she put on some lip gloss and reminded herself to tweet about the color later.

His door was closed, so she knocked. No answer. "Dad?" She turned the handle and peered inside. His room was perfectly neat, and his made bed was empty. She shrugged and turned toward the kitchen. Well, Charlie was an early riser, too. Probably he'd run out to get them bagels. Or even donuts. He knew she'd always loved donuts, even if she never ate them. Madison decided that when he returned with half a dozen crullers, she'd allow herself half of one.

There was a pot of coffee ready, and Madison poured herself a cup. She was beginning to feel the rumbling in her stomach (maybe she'd eat a *whole* donut) when her Black-Berry vibrated on the kitchen table. She glanced down at the screen: Luxe Paris. She sighed. She knew that she had to return the necklace, but she wanted to wear it for a little bit longer. It would make even her nightgown look Oscar-worthy. She let the call go to voice mail.

After she'd finished her first cup of coffee, she checked her voice mail and found that the jeweler had called three times already this morning. Wow—it wasn't even noon on the morning after the premiere, and Luxe Paris was lighting up her phone like she'd stolen the diamonds and fled to Rio. The nerve! They'd gotten great press out of her wearing that necklace, Madison knew that for a fact. (And the earrings, too, but of course those were hers.) Next time she'd go with a more established jeweler if they didn't stop harassing her.

She had a message from Trevor, too. No doubt he wanted

to work his magic on her and try to make her complaint disappear.

She showered, drank a second cup of coffee, and finally picked up her phone when Luxe Paris rang again.

"Seriously," she said, "you guys could let a girl sleep in."

"Madison Parker?" said a cool, French-sounding female voice on the other end.

"Speaking," Madison said. "Obviously."

"This is Adele Pinchot from Luxe Paris. I'm afraid we have a situation."

Madison sat up a little straighter; the woman's tone was not friendly. "What?"

"We are missing some jewelry," Adele said. "This was discovered in inventory late last night. The missing items were last seen when you and your father were—"

"Wait a second," Madison interrupted. "Are you trying to say that—"

But two could play the interrupting game, and Adele cut in. "I'm saying that we reviewed the security tape, and it shows a man in a blue shirt holding a pair of earrings, and then slipping them into his pocket."

Madison stood up so angrily that she knocked over her chair. "A man in a blue shirt? That could be fifty percent of the L.A. population."

"The earrings missing were the same pair you were photographed wearing last night," Adele continued.

"My father bought those earrings! He put them on a payment plan!"

"Ms. Parker, I can assure you—"

But Madison had already hung up the phone. She paced around the living room, still in her bathrobe. She wanted her dad to get back to the house right now so she could tell him about the insane people at Luxe Paris. How long did it take to get a dozen donuts? she wondered. She cursed the fact that she hadn't bought him a cell phone yet. It was next on her to-do list.

She should get dressed, she thought, so she hurried into her room for a pair of jeans and a cap-sleeved sweater. (Madison Parker would never be so casual as to wear a T-shirt.) There, on the nightstand, was the blue suede box from Luxe. She pulled it to her chest, almost hugging it—if she had the money she'd buy this necklace today, although she wouldn't want to give them the business after what had just happened. *Well*, she thought, setting the box down on the bed and lifting its lid, *someday soon I will have the money, and I will spend it on diamonds from Cartier.*

And then her heart seemed to stop: The earrings were lying there on the silk, but the necklace was gone.

Where were her diamonds—or, rather, where were Luxe Paris's diamonds? She remembered putting them in the box last night after she and Charlie got home, after they'd had a cup of tea in the kitchen. Madison *always* put beautiful things back where they belonged: Her Louboutins lay nestled in their boxes; her silk clutches were wrapped in tissue paper on a closet shelf; and her gowns were hung in perfect rows, inside labeled canvas garment bags.

Fear coursed through Madison's veins like ice. She walked into her bathroom and looked around the vanity. *Think, think, think!* She hadn't even been tipsy when she got home. She hadn't drunk anything at all, in fact, because Charlie didn't drink and she didn't want to make him uncomfortable.

She scoured the bathroom, her room, the kitchen, everything. "Dad!" Madison cried out. "Dad!" Her voice grew desperate. She knew he wasn't in the house, but she wanted him here, right now, to calm her down. To help her look. Where the hell was he? How long did it take to buy a box of fucking donuts?

She walked back into his room, and that was when she noticed what she should have seen before: The door to his closet was ajar, and the hangers were empty. There was no new suit, no chinos, no work boots, nothing.

She sank down on to the bed. She clutched at her heart, which was beating fast and hard in her chest. Gaby's accusation flashed in her mind. Almost unconsciously, she dialed her sister.

"Have you seen Dad?" Madison asked, without even saying hello.

Sophie cleared her throat. She was obviously just waking up. "Since last night? No. You're the one who lives with him."

"He's not here." Madison closed her eyes and gripped the phone harder. "I need to find him. Now."

"He probably just went out for a walk or something,"

Sophie said sleepily. "Call me later when he shows up."

"No. I'm coming over, so get dressed. I have to find him, and you're going to help." Her BlackBerry buzzed— Luxe Paris was on the other line. "Seriously, Sophie. Get your kombucha-loving ass out of bed. We don't have much time."

34

SO DAMN CATCHY

Trevor sat alone at a table for five on the Chateau Marmont patio, enjoying the sun, the September breeze, and a very large Bloody Mary. Normally he saved his cocktails until after 5 p.m., but today he had a reason to celebrate. The overnight ratings for *The Fame Game* had been fantastic—so great, in fact, that he'd called the girls this morning and told them to meet him for a congratulatory lunch. "Come break those pre-red-carpet diets in style," he'd said. "The eggs Benedict are the best in the city."

Everyone had jumped at the chance—everyone except Madison, who wasn't picking up her phone. Trevor found this somewhat strange, especially since he'd been half expecting an early-morning call from her, reaming him out over having chosen Kate's song for *The Fame Game* opening. Or for not devoting 75 percent of the first episode to her. Or for filming her from the left side too often. (She preferred the right.) Or for any number of other supposed slights, infractions, or missteps. Madison had always made sure to make her needs and preferences known. Calling her a squeaky wheel was putting it mildly. But she was a squeaky wheel who brought in an audience.

Trevor gazed contemplatively at a vaguely familiar starlet and her tattooed boyfriend, who were drinking coffee in the corner. He wondered if Madison was already on her way to the restaurant—if she was saving up her venom so she could dish it out in person. He wouldn't mind; he had grown accustomed to it.

Somehow, though, he doubted this. Having Charlie around had softened Madison a little. It made her a more complex character, one that the audience could really sympathize with. And that was fine with Trevor—to a degree. He couldn't have everyone being nice to each other all the time, though, or else he'd lose viewers faster than you could say *Jersey Shore*. No, he relied on Madison to be cutthroat. Or, at the very least, shamelessly self-serving. (He *loved* how she couldn't quite keep the scorn from her face at events she deemed beneath her; it looked so good on-screen. He'd have to send her to the ribbon cutting for a new strip mall or a pool party sponsored by Summer's Eve in the next few weeks. . . .)

He also thought about how to ratchet up the tension between her and Carmen. Considering Carmen's privileged, happy family and Madison's poor, crazy one, they seemed like natural antagonists. So it was surprising that Madison hadn't gone for Carmen's throat by now.

But then again, he reflected, there did appear to be some friction between Carmen and Kate. They'd seemed like buddies for weeks, but something was going on with them at the premiere, and his instincts told him it would be a story worth sharing. Kate, especially, was congenitally nice; why would she be angry at Carmen? He'd have to dig deeper on this one. That was one of Trevor's greatest strengths: He found a button, and then he pushed it. Hard, if he needed to. He located a psychological wound, and then he stuck a knife in it.

But wasn't it all ultimately in service of his girls? (And ratings, his reputation, and his year-end bonus, etc.?) When he won, they did, too. Ratings for him meant attention for them, and that's what they were after, wasn't it? In the end everyone benefited in their own way.

He fished a pickled lime out of his Bloody Mary and placed it on the table. Yes, he'd have to give more thought to Kate Hayes, too. Funny how she hadn't mentioned her pathological stage fright when she was auditioning. It had certainly been a surprise when she flubbed her song so badly at first, in front of all those people. He'd thought he might have to race up on stage and whisk her away to the bar—then, after three or four tequila shots, he'd send her up again. But she'd recovered her courage, and she'd ended up playing very well. And in a way, he thought, her mistake had made the crowd like her more; their applause had been wild. Yes, he could definitely make her stage fright work for the show. Maybe she could see a vocal coach. Or a hypnotherapist? He made a note in his Black-Berry to have Laurel investigate the possibilities. Hiring Laurel had definitely been a smart move. The girls liked her a lot more than they liked Dana. Laurel was like a peer, which meant they no doubt trusted her more. It was Laurel who'd helped get Kate's song to work for the show, directing Trevor to one of Kate's outtakes for better lyrics. It was even Laurel's suggestion to change the title from "Lovestruck" to "Starstruck."

He turned his thoughts toward Gaby next, who had been her usual ditzy self last night at the premiere, lean-ing on the arm of some Venice Beach caveman. She was on thin ice at *Buzz! News*, he'd been told; apparently she showed up late for work and then spent most of her time hanging around the green room, looking for celebrities. Judging from her on-camera interviews with Lacey Hop-kins and Carmen Curtis, Gaby didn't have much of a future in celebrity journalism.

When *Buzz! News* fired her, which they inevita-bly would (and which would be a good scene to film, of course), Trevor would have to find her another gig. A friend of a friend was looking for a cohost for a late-night nightlife guide show—someone who could go to clubs and restaurants and ask a few questions of the owners. Surely Gaby could handle that, right? The stakes were lower than they were for *Buzz! News*.

He was musing on this when he heard the volume of voices around him rise. Without looking up, he knew: His girls were entering, and not without being noticed.

"That's that singer from *The Fame Game*," Trevor heard the starlet tell her boyfriend. "I loved her song. *Lovestruck, starstruck, ready for the game*," she sang. "It's so damn catchy."

Trevor smiled to himself. He considered ordering another Bloody Mary—a little extra celebration. He was imagining the bigger office he'd be getting any day now. And maybe another car. A Maserati this time, perhaps?

When he finally looked up, he saw Kate, Gaby, and Carmen coming toward him, smiling as the others on the patio whispered and pointed.

Yes, Trevor thought, *The Fame Game* had begun. And he already felt like he was winning it.

35

NOBODY LOSES

Madison and Sophie drove to Mack's Auto Body Shop, where Charlie worked in the afternoons; to the gym Madison had bought him a membership to; to the Denny's on Wilshire where he liked to eat breakfast; and even to the disgusting Downtown L.A. motel he'd lived in before the bungalow. But Charlie Wardell was nowhere to be found.

Now Madison sat in the driver's seat of her Lexus, her knuckles white on the steering wheel. Sophie was silent beside her, clutching the crystal that hung from her neck. In the parking lot of the E-Z Inn, a guy wearing a Whitesnake shirt and a trucker's cap was leering at them, obviously unfamiliar with such clean, fresh-faced girls. He finished the cigarette he was smoking and then started walking toward Madison's car.

"Um, I think we should get out of here," Sophie said, watching the man out of the corner of her eye. "I'm not really in the mood to make a new friend."

Madison slammed the car into reverse, but she kept her foot on the brake. "What about your 'we are all God's people' crap?" she demanded. "Doesn't the divine in you salute the divine in him?"

"Um . . ."

The man got closer and instead of driving away, Madison rolled down her window. "Have you seen Charlie Wardell? The guy who was living in that room right over there?" she asked, pointing.

He stopped and scratched thoughtfully at his stomach. "Nope," he said after a time. "Not for a while now."

"Thanks," said Madison, and rolled up her window again, but not before she heard him ask her if she wanted to go to lunch. "They got two-dollar tacos just up the block," he called.

She pulled out of the parking lot, tires screeching, and made her way to the freeway. She was having trouble breathing, and her heart felt like it might explode.

"Where are you going?" Sophie asked, her brows furrowed. "Shouldn't we, like, retrace your steps? Maybe you lost it at the Hammer Museum and some waiter—"

Madison lifted a hand to silence her. "I did *not* lose it," she said fiercely. "Charlie stole it."

"You can't be sure of that," Sophie said. "Don't say such awful things about Daddy."

"Don't you ever call him Daddy again," Madison hissed. "That bastard stole my necklace. And he gave me stolen property as a gift. And he probably took Gaby's earrings, too. And now he's gone. He's split town. He didn't even write a note to say good-bye. Which is exactly like the last time he left us, Soph, but you were too young to remember."

"Really, Mad, you could be totally wrong. I'm sure you just put it—"

"Shut up," Madison said between clenched teeth.

Sophie stopped talking. Her hands twisted in her lap. "It's my fault," she eventually whispered. "I brought him to you."

Madison would have loved to blame her sister, she really would have. Sophie had been nothing but trouble since she showed up in L.A. But Madison knew now that Charlie would have found her himself. Sophie was simply the one he got to first. "It isn't your fault," she said. She banged her hand on the steering wheel and cursed. "I trusted him, too."

But even now, there was a tiny part of her that still believed in him. He wasn't gone forever; he'd just tried to take the necklace back to Luxe Paris for her, and he'd gotten lost along the way. . . . After all, he'd made her coffee. What criminal pauses in his escape to make his daughter a pot of coffee?

She drove them back to the bungalow, with its blossom-draped trellis and its green, well-tended yard. The sight of it made her heart beat even faster and more painfully. She'd found this place for him and then moved into it because she wanted to be a family. And she'd believed that he wanted that, too.

Her hope and her stupidity were almost too much for her to stand. What had she been thinking? She felt like screaming.

But she didn't. She just got out of the car and walked up the sidewalk. Her legs felt like they were made of stone. Sophie staggered after her, her Birkenstocks slapping against the concrete.

At the front porch, Madison turned around. "I would have given him anything," she cried. "But instead he had to take it and run away."

"Oh, Mad," Sophie said, holding out her arms.

Madison brushed them away. "Really—thanks for your help and all. But you should go."

Sophie gazed at her with wide blue eyes. "But I don't have a car," she said.

"I'll call you a cab," Madison said. "I just need to be alone."

Sophie nodded, and then went to wait on the bench near the front gate. Madison turned and went into the house. It was cool and dim inside, and she stood in the middle of the living room and felt the tears begin to run down her cheeks. She clenched and unclenched her fists. This couldn't be happening—and yet it was.

She sank down onto the couch, and that's when she saw the note. It sat on the end table, scribbled on the back of a Denny's receipt.

Sweetpea—I'm in trouble, but I didn't want to ask you for money. This is the best way. Just tell them you lost the necklace. They're insured. Nobody loses. I love you always.

—Charlie

She buried her face in her hands. The tiny part of her that wanted to believe he was innocent curled up and died.

What in the world was she supposed to do now?

She sat on the couch, unmoving, for an hour. She thought about taking Charlie to Luxe Paris, and how happy he had seemed to see her success. She thought about the day they went suit shopping, and she'd asked him to be her date for the premiere. She remembered the day they went to the Santa Monica Pier and he'd missed every shot with the air rifle. She thought about the unicorn he'd won for her when she was little, which was still sitting in the drawer back at her apartment. She thought about the earrings he stole for her. He wasn't innocent, and, Madison realized, he wasn't very smart. *I'm in trouble*, his note said. All the while, the tears streamed down her face. She loved him and she hated him, and she couldn't decide which feeling was stronger.

After another few minutes, she picked up the phone. She knew what she had to do.

"Hello, this is Madison Parker," she said, sniffling.

"Yes," said the cold voice of Adele Pinchot.

Madison steeled herself for what she had to say. "I have the earrings, and I'll return them to you today. But the necklace? I don't have it."

"What do you mean?"

She took a deep breath. "I don't have it because I had my father sell it for me. I've gotten into debt, and I just—"

"I'm having trouble understanding this," said Adele.

Madison squeezed her eyes shut tight. "It's all my fault. Everything was my idea. I'm responsible. You have to leave my father out of it." She was gripping the phone so hard that her fingers were going numb. She was doing possibly the stupidest thing she had ever done. She was terrified.

"We have your father on tape—"

"But I know that you haven't called the police yet, because you called me. And I'm telling you that every-thing was my idea. Do you hear me? *Everything was my idea.* So if you press charges, they're going to have to be against me." She wiped her cheeks; the tears had stopped.

"Ms. Parker, this is highly unorthodox."

You're telling me, she thought. She was in the middle of doing the dumbest thing of her life, for an even dumber reason: to protect her father, who, if he got caught, would surely get sent back to prison for a long time, and any chance she had at having a father would be over.

Madison nodded, as if Adele Pinchot could see her. "I know. But you've got to think like a Hollywood player. Look," she said, her voice sounding so much more certain than she felt. "You tell everyone that Madison Parker loved your jewelry so much she tried to steal it. You get a ton of free publicity. Luxe Paris, brand-new to L.A. and already making headlines! It'll be worth more than the cost of that necklace. I know the markup on jewelry—it's one hundred percent at least. You just leave my father out of it and I'll take the fall. And you'll come out looking like a million bucks." *And me?* thought Madison. *My career is over. Nobody loses? That's what you think, Charlie.*

Adele Pinchot cleared her throat. "Ms. Parker, I don't know what to say."

"Say yes," Madison urged. She stood and walked into her bedroom, where the earrings were twinkling against the white satin of their box. She touched them lightly with a fingertip. "If you don't say yes, then I will tell anyone who listens that you gave me the necklace and then tried to take it back. I'll sue you for breach of contract."

"*Pardonnez-moi?*" gasped Adele, slipping into her native French.

Madison barreled on. "It's been done before, you know. Harry Winston—your *competition* as jeweler to the stars—got sued for that very thing. And they had to pay a very large settlement to a certain Hollywood actress. Plus legal fees, which, as I'm sure you know, can really start to add up."

Adele was silent, and Madison knew she was thinking it over. Just like she knew that Luxe Paris would eventually agree to her terms.

And she, Madison Parker, would be accused of theft. The tabloids would have a field day, and Trevor would fire her (or worse, film her in an orange jumpsuit), and she would be kicked out of her apartment, and her friends— the few she had—would turn their backs on her.

And she'd be back where she started. With nothing.

She stared out the window, through the pink bougain-villea that framed the view, and saw that Sophie was still on the bench outside. She must have sent her cab away. The sunlight was shining on her hair, and it looked like spun gold.

Madison shook her head in disbelief. She could walk outside right now and she wouldn't be alone. She wouldn't have nothing after all. She'd have a sister.

While Adele was still thinking things over on the other end of the line, Madison headed out into the sunshine. She lifted her hand to wave to Sophie, and her sister turned and sadly smiled.

Madison returned the smile. She was screwed. Royally, profoundly screwed. But she'd crawled up from the gutter once before. She was pretty sure she could do it again.

Acknowledgments

A special thanks to the amazing people who made this book possible . . . (And because I've thanked them so many times now, here are some things I haven't thanked them for yet.)

To FARRIN JACOBS for sacrificing her time, health, personal life, and sanity in order to complete this book with me. And for wearing a party hat all day when I had to work on my birthday and for eating cake for all three meals.

To MAX STUBBLEFIELD for ending my Christmas card each year with "next year is going to be our year." Feel like "our year" was like two years ago, but you know . . . Merry Christmas anyway.

To NICOLE PEREZ-KRUGER for always being there with sound advice . . . Like "if you are going to take scandalous photos of yourself just be sure to crop your face out . . . or that you look really hot."

To KRISTIN PUTTKAMER for being the best auntie Kristin that my puppy, Chloe, could ask for. And for the million and one other things you do for me.

To PJ SHAPIRO for handling my most crucial legal matters . . . Like sending an aggressively worded letter to my crazy neighbor who keeps sneaking into my yard.

To DAVE DEL SESTO for hiding my money from me so I don't spend it all on shoes.

To EMILY CHENOWETH whose contribution to this novel was invaluable. I couldn't have done it without you.

To MATTHEW ELBLONK who I'd really like to thank, but I haven't slept for two weeks trying to make this deadline and you are the one who got me into this deal. I'll send you a nice thank-you card after it's been published.

A special thanks to MAGGIE MARR, SASHA ILLINGWORTH, and HOWARD HUANG as well as the team at HarperCollins: MELINDA WEIGEL, CATHERINE WALLACE, CHRISTINA COLANGELO, SANDEE ROSTON, GWEN MORTON, JOSH WEISS, TOM FORGET, SARAH NICHOLE KAUFMAN, LAUREN FLOWER, and MEGAN SUGRUE.

And, as always, a big thank-you to my friends and family. Your support (and frankly the fact that you put up with me) means so much to me, and I don't know where I would be without you.

2/16   NOVEL